REVIVED

REVIVED

REVIVED

cat patrick

LITTLE, BROWN AND COMPANY
NEW YORK   BOSTON

Also by Cat Patrick

Forgotten
The Originals

Little, Brown and Company

Hachette Book Group
237 Park Avenue, New York, NY 10017
Visit our website at www.lb-teens.com

Little, Brown and Company is a division of Hachette Book Group, Inc.
The Little, Brown name and logo are trademarks of Hachette Book Group, Inc.

The publisher is not responsible for websites (or their content) that are not owned by the publisher.

First Paperback Edition: April 2013
First published in hardcover in May 2012 by Little, Brown and Company

Library of Congress Cataloging-in-Publication Data
Patrick, Cat.
Revived / by Cat Patrick. — 1st ed.
p. cm.
Summary: Having been brought back from the dead repeatedly by a top-secret government super drug called Revive, and forced to move so the public does not learn the truth, fifteen-year-old Daisy meets people worth living for and begins to question the heavy-handed government controls she has dealt with for eleven years.
ISBN 978-0-316-09462-7 (hc) / ISBN 978-0-316-09463-4 (pb)
[1. Death—Fiction. 2. Moving, Household—Fiction. 3. High schools—Fiction. 4. Schools—Fiction. 5. Drugs—Fiction.] I. Title.
PZ7.P2746Rev 2012
[Fic]—dc23
2011026950

10 9 8 7 6 5 4 3 2 1

RRD-C

Printed in the United States of America

For Noah . . .
You're always standing beside me,
holding my hand.

I have seen a medicine

That's able to breathe life into a stone,

Quicken a rock, and make you dance canary

With spritely fire and motion; whose simple touch,

Is powerful to araise King Pepin, nay,

To give great Charlemain a pen in's hand,

And write to her a love-line.

—William Shakespeare, *All's Well That Ends Well*

one

one

one

I'm flattened and thrashing on the sun-warmed track next to the football field, lying on what looks like asphalt but what I realize now that I'm down here is actually that fake spongy stuff. It reeks like it was just installed. There's a woman kneeling beside my right shoulder, shouting into a cell phone.

"Her name is Daisy . . . uh . . ." Sharply, she sucks in her breath. "I don't know her last name!" she cries.

For a split second, I don't know, either.

"Appleby," another teacher shouts.

"Appleby," the first repeats to the 911 dispatcher. "It looks like she's having an allergic reaction to something."

Bee, I try to say, but there's no air. No word.

My jerking limbs are like venomous snakes to the students forming a circle around me: The kids jump back in fear. I gasp with my entire body but only one rationed breath comes through. I know it's one of my last.

When my P.E. teacher told us to jog the outdoor track to warm up for volleyball, I was excited about the fresh air. Maybe I'd get a little color on my cheeks. But then a fuzzy yellow and black menace wanted to join me, and decided that maybe he'd invite a few friends, too. I hit number one on my speed dial the second I felt the familiar pinch of the first bee sting; I only hope Mason makes it in time.

A wave of calm begins to creep through my body: I know it won't be long now. Everything, forehead to toenails, relaxes. When the threat of getting kicked disappears, the crowd tightens around me. My eyes bounce off face after face hovering above me. They're all strangers; high school just started yesterday, and no one I know from junior high is in my P.E. class.

Most of them look terrified. A few girls are crying. The principal shows up and tries to contain the crowd, but they're like magnets, drawn in by the thrill of someone else's misfortune.

"Move back," he shouts. "Move back so the paramedics will be able to get through!" But no one listens. No one moves back. Instead, without knowing it, they form a blockade between me and help.

I lock eyes with a pretty, dark-skinned girl whose

locker is near mine. She seems friendly enough to be the last person I see. She's not crying, but the look on her face is pure distress. Maybe we would've been friends.

I stare at the girl and she stares at me until my eyelids fall.

The crowd gasps.

"Oh my god!"

"Do something!"

"Help her!" a guy's voice pleads.

I hear sirens approaching. Tennis shoe–clad feet thunder away from me, presumably to wave in the paramedics. I wonder whether it's Mason and Cassie or the real ones.

My arms go completely limp.

"Daisy, hold on!" shouts a girl. I like to think it was my almost friend, but I don't open my eyes to see for sure. Instead, my mind goes blank. None of the sounds are clear enough to hear anymore. The world fades to nothing, and before I have the chance to think another thought,

I'm dead.

two

two

two

"Do you have everything you need?" Mason whispers through the darkness as we walk briskly to the waiting SUV. It's the middle of the night in Frozen Hills, Michigan, and we're minutes from our next move.

"Yes," I say, confident that I've left nothing behind but furniture and off-season clothing. I've been through this before: I know the drill.

"Let me take that," Mason says, pointing to the suitcase I'm dragging behind me on the cobblestone walkway. I let him because I feel a little wonky from the procedure. Not quite myself yet. Mason grabs the bag and what was bricks to me is feathers to him: He tosses it on top of the other suitcases in the back and soundlessly shuts the vehicle doors.

I climb into the backseat. From the front, Cassie turns to acknowledge me momentarily before going back to her work. She's still sporting a fake paramedic outfit, but she's thrown a faded gray sweatshirt over the top. Her strawberry-blond hair is pulled back in a taut, efficient ponytail. She pushes her rimless glasses, which make her look older, up higher on her nose as she reads something from her government-issue supercomputer disguised as a smart phone.

I watch Mason head back inside for the final sweep, then admire the outside of the house I've gotten used to over the past three years. It's a two-story redbrick house with black shutters that was built when people still used the telegraph; it has its own creaks and character and I'm going to miss it. Moments from goodbye for good, I realize that this house was probably my favorite. Then again, maybe the next one will be even better.

I think about how I'll design my new bedroom until I see low headlights approaching. I get a charge when the black sedan pulls up and two men in dark outfits get out; it's always sort of thrilling to see the cleanup crew arrive. Though they've probably never been here before, they walk through the low black iron gate and up the porch steps without hesitation. Mason comes out just as one of the agents reaches for the front door handle. The men pass without speaking, giving one another nothing but quick chin dips.

I watch the door close behind the agents. Like an owl in the night, I search wide-eyed for movement inside the house, but the windows stay dark; the night stays still.

Unless you catch them going in, you can't tell they're there. Ninja stealth in black chinos and fleece jackets, they'll erase traces of me and my faux family and leave the house so authentically bare that the real estate agent who comes to sell it will never for a minute think it was inhabited by anyone other than a nice young couple and their ill-fated teen.

After they fix the house, the team will infiltrate the neighborhood long enough to put minds at rest, seeding gossip about the sad family returning to Arizona or Georgia or Maine to deal with the loss. The rumors are always started by the unrecognizable guy at the gas station or the mousy girl using the computer at the library.

The agents—the *Disciples*—are trained as doctors, scientists, watchers, and bodyguards, but I've always thought most of them could make it in Hollywood, too.

Mason, in his recurring role as Loving Father, finally climbs into the driver's seat. In worn jeans, loafers, and a cozy brown sweater, with his tired green eyes and messy dark (but prematurely graying) hair, he fits the role he's played for eleven years now.

"Where are we going?" Mason asks Cassie. Cassie doesn't look up from her tiny computer when she replies in her Southern-accented voice.

"Nebraska," she says. "Omaha."

Mason nods once and puts the SUV in reverse. I check my former home once more for signs that there are government agents inside: no luck. Then I exhale the day and the town away and stuff a pillow between my head and the cool window, and by the time we're down the driveway and turning off of our street, I'm asleep.

When I open my eyes, it's light outside. Bright light. The kind that makes me want to throw a rock at the sun. I have a crook in my neck and my mouth feels like I ate salty cotton balls. I look at Mason in the rearview mirror; he feels my stare and speaks.

"Hi there," he says. I can't tell whether he's looking at me or the road because he's wearing dark sunglasses.

"Hi," I grumble.

"How do you feel?" he asks.

"Headache," I answer.

"That's normal," he says.

"I know."

"Water," Cassie says, offering me a bottle without looking my way. I take it and gulp down half in two seconds, then look out the window to the unidentifiable landscape zooming by at seventy-five miles per hour.

"Where are we?" I ask.

"Illinois," Mason says.

"ILLINOIS?!"

Cassie jumps a little but still doesn't look back at me. I take a deep breath, which for some reason makes me yawn loudly. I rub the sleep from my eyes and in a more measured tone ask, "How long was I out?" Mason glances at Cassie and then checks the clock.

"I'd say you were probably out about eight hours," Mason says as plainly as if he's giving me a weather report.

"Eight hours? How is that possible?"

"They added a calming agent to it...to smooth the rough edges," Mason says.

I nod, still feeling woozy.

"Maybe they need to tone it down," I say. "Unless they're going for TKO."

"I'll make a note," Cassie says, her eyes still glued to her tiny phone screen. In private, Cassie is free to be her workaholic robot self.

"What's our new last name going to be?" I ask. With every new town comes a new last name; first names stay the same for the sake of consistency.

"West," Mason says.

"Huh," I answer, rolling it around in my brain. Daisy West. Definitely more interesting than Daisy Johnson from Palmdale, but maybe a little too cute. Though not nearly as bad as Daisy Diamond from Ridgeland.

"I think I liked Appleby best," I conclude aloud.

"You were more used to it," Mason replies. "West is fine."

Shrugging, I consider my options for passing the time.

"I wish we could fly," I murmur to myself, but Mason hears me.

"That would be nice," he agrees. Unfortunately, our fourth passenger, Revive — the top secret drug that brings people back from the dead — makes that impossible. The drug is too precious to check and too secret to carry on. So every time we move, we have to drive; every time we drive, I'm at a loss about what to do. I wish I could read, but it makes me carsick, and since we left so suddenly, my iPod isn't charged. Eventually I settle on counting mile markers until I think I might pee my pants. I ask Mason to pull over at a diner, then, considering it's almost noon and all, we decide to eat, too.

After visiting the surprisingly inoffensive bathroom, I join Mason and Cassie at a booth in the back. They're sitting across from each other but aren't speaking; they look like a typical married couple. I make a split-second decision and scoot in next to Cassie, opting to pretend to be a mama's girl. Cassie looks up at me and smiles warmly.

We're in public now, so she's human.

"You're the spitting image of your mom," the waitress says to me when she comes to take our order. We've heard it before, but it's a false comparison. Cassie's brand of blond is straight with reddish tones, while mine is wavy and so dirty it's essentially light brown. Cassie's eyes are round and dark blue like the ocean, whereas mine are lighter than the sky at noon, wide set and almond shaped. She's nearly six feet tall, and I'm five foot six; she's curvy, and I can wear jeans from the boys' department.

But what makes the "look-alike" comment even more absurd is the fact that Cassie's only thirteen years older than me.

And yet, we play the part.

"Thank you!" Cassie says, hand to chest like she's beyond flattered.

"Uh, yeah, thanks," I mutter, hoping that I'm coming off as a typical teen who doesn't care to look like her mother. In truth, despite the fact that she barely has a personality, Cassie's pretty. I'm fine with people saying I look like her.

"You're most welcome," HELLO, MY NAME IS BESS replies. "Now, what can I bring you?"

I order a veggie burger and a chocolate shake; Mason orders coffee and a Spanish omelet; and Cassie orders a hard-boiled egg, dry wheat toast, and sliced melon on the side.

Bess writes in her notepad and leaves. Then, almost too soon for it to be made to order, the food rides in on Bess's wide arms. Quickly, she sets down plates, fills coffee cups, and pulls ketchup out of her apron pocket.

"Need anything else?" she asks. Three head shakes and she's gone.

We eat in silence, me downing my lunch as if I've never tasted food before, then wondering if the scientists at the big lab added a metabolism booster to Revive in addition to the calming agent. Knowing it's silly, I don't ask Mason about it. But I can't help but notice that Mason's and Cassie's plates are still half full when mine is all but licked clean.

"So, why Omaha?" I ask as Mason takes a bite of his

omelet. I watch his jaw muscles flex as he chews slowly, deliberately. After he swallows, he speaks.

"It's one of his favorite cities," he says.

Mason means the Revive project mastermind. Basically invisible and in control of a program that brings people back from the dead, he's earned the nickname God.

"Why?" I ask.

"Because it's moderate, I suppose. Not too small or too big. Rarely in the news. Friendly. Reasonably gentrified. You know what that means, right?"

I roll my eyes at him.

"So, all in all, it should be a good cover. Assuming..."

"Assuming what?" I ask.

Mason checks the tables around us, then answers in a low tone. "Assuming nothing *else* happens."

"I didn't mean to do it, you know," I say quietly.

"You never do," Mason says, holding my gaze. "But you didn't have your EpiPen, either."

"I forgot it," I say quickly.

It's a lie.

In truth, I spent way too long deciding what to wear, leaving only five minutes to arrange my hair into something resembling a style. I left for school in a rush, remembering the EpiPen, which probably would have saved my life, halfway down the block. I wasn't so late that I couldn't have gone back, but for some reason I didn't.

Having been trained to know when people are lying, Mason narrows his eyes at me. I assume Cassie's doing the same, but I don't look at her to find out. For a moment, I think Mason's going to call me on it, but thankfully, he moves on.

"Daisy, I think you should know that we nearly couldn't bring you back this time," he says so quietly it's almost like he's breathing the words. His bluntness, I'm used to—Mason treats me like a partner, not a daughter—but I'm surprised by the idea of permanent death.

"Was it a bad vial?" I ask.

"No, it was fine," Mason says. "It was . . . you."

"He almost called time of death," Cassie interjects. Stunned, I look at her, then back at Mason.

"Seriously?" I ask.

"It was very stressful," Mason says. There's a flicker of something like worry in his green eyes, and then it's gone.

I think for a moment before coming to what I consider to be a pretty rational conclusion: "But it did work, so everything's fine."

"But it might not be next time," he says. "I'm merely advising you to take precautions. Don't you remember Chase?"

My stomach sinks as an old memory sets in: Seven years after the bus crash that started it all, Chase Rogers died again, for seemingly no reason. He was Revived repeatedly, but—Mason told me—he seemed to have developed an immunity to the drug. Then he died for good.

"I'm not like him," I say quietly. Bess comes and sets down the check, which silences us for a few minutes.

"I'm not like him," I say again when the coast is clear.

Mason looks deep into my eyes. "I hope not. Just be more careful, all right?"

"All right," I agree.

Another family is seated at the booth directly behind us, so the conversation is over for now, at least.

"Are my gorgeous ladies finished eating?" Mason asks loudly enough for others to hear. The mom at the table behind us sighs. Mason can be charming when he wants to.

I look down at my plate, which has discarded raw onions, wilted lettuce, and a quarter of a pickle left on it.

"Uh...yeah," I say in my best disinterested-teenager voice.

"I sure am," Cassie says, patting her flat stomach. "I'm stuffed to the gills."

"Great," Mason says. "Then let's clear out."

We walk up to the front counter. As we wait for Mason to pay, Cassie fixes a stray piece of my long hair in that absentmindedly automatic mom-ish way. She looks at me with love; I roll my eyes and brush her hand away.

After Mason leaves a five on the table for Bess, he opens the OUT door, causing the bells on top to jingle, and holds it for his wife and daughter. In the parking lot, when we're still visible to the other diners, I stare at the ground and walk three steps behind my parents while they hold hands and Cassie laughs at nothing.

Then we get in the SUV and drive away.

three

three

three

Maybe it's growing up as part of an elaborate science experiment, but I can't leave a place without conducting a postmortem. So I spend the next few hours of the drive rehashing the past three years in Frozen Hills: a mental autopsy on Daisy Appleby by newly anointed Daisy West.

We moved to Frozen Hills the summer before seventh grade, after I died from asphyxia in Ridgeland, Mississippi. Well, outside of Ridgeland, if we're getting technical: I was swimming near some houseboats at the reservoir and got carbon-monoxide poisoning from an idling boat.

If I was going to die again, I consider myself lucky that it happened in the summer before school started. Even luckier: Junior high in Frozen Hills was grades seven

14

through nine, so I started with all the other brace-faced, zit-covered seventh graders. Days after I finished decorating my Juno-inspired bedroom, the school year began.

"Thinking about the past few years?" Mason interrupts my thoughts, smiling at me in the rearview mirror. He's familiar with my system.

"Yes," I admit. "I'm thinking about a birthday party."

"Ah," he says, nodding. "For Nora..."

"Fitzgerald," Cassie and I say in unison.

"Yep," I say before retreating into my brain.

Nora Fitzgerald.

She lived down the street from us, in a sunny yellow house with dark green shutters and a WELCOME sign on the front door. Her mom was one of those overly cheerful types who showed up with freshly baked cookies the second your moving truck appeared. Mrs. Fitzgerald's desire to worm into our world always unnerved Cassie. Paranoid, Cassie wondered aloud on several occasions if Mrs. Fitzgerald was actually a spy for a foreign government trying to steal the formula for Revive. She said that "suburban housewife" would be the perfect cover.

Two weeks after we arrived, Nora showed up on our front porch, undoubtedly shoved out the door by her mother, birthday party invitation in hand.

"Hi," she said. "I'm Nora."

"I remember from when you guys brought the cookies," I said. "I'm Daisy."

"Yeah."

We stared at each other in silence, me thinking that she looked like a Skipper doll and wondering if she owned any outfits that didn't match from her hair clips to her sandals, and her looking at me in my cutoff jean shorts and red-and-white-striped T-shirt like I was from an alien planet.

"Here," she said finally, offering me the tiny purple envelope. "It's an invitation to my birthday party next weekend."

"Oh," I said. "Thanks."

"Sure," Nora said. "See ya."

The next weekend, I faked being sick and watched the partygoers arrive at Nora's from the comfort of the window seat in my poster-filled bedroom. Looking back, that was probably the moment that defined Daisy Appleby. Those first weeks of school, Nora's birthday was all anyone talked about: It was a boy/girl party, and if you weren't there, you weren't anybody. For the rest of the year, Nora was polite to me at block parties and in the halls at school. But by eighth grade, she was braces-less, in a B-cup, and on track to be queen of the school, and I was nothing but the weird neighbor who kept to herself. Unknowingly, I had dissed the most popular girl in school.

It made me invisible.

Not that I minded.

The Revive program is built on secrecy, and being invisible at school is never a bad thing. Even if I make friends, it's not like I can get close to them. My family life is a facade, and we could move at any time.

Anyway, it's not like I was lonely in Frozen Hills. I had an after-school study group and I hung out solo with one of the other members every once in a while. And I'm not one of those people who get all self-conscious about going to the movies or to see bands alone. I'm not sure when normal kids learn to be embarrassed about things like that, but thankfully, it never happened to me.

I carefully catalog three years of memories and by nine o'clock, when we pull into our new hometown of Omaha, Nebraska, I have concluded that my time in Frozen Hills was a success. I navigated junior high without any major issues. I maintained cover and managed not to raise suspicions or get too close to anyone or anything that I had to leave.

Ready to focus on the future, I tune in to the city outside the car windows.

"It's bigger than I thought it would be," I say.

"It's the most populated city in Nebraska," Mason answers.

"How many people live here?" I ask, because I know he'll know. Mason's a walking Wiki.

"Almost half a million," he says. "There are actually several large corporations here...." he begins. That's the danger of pressing Mason's Search button: If he's in the right mood, he'll barf information.

I can't help but tune out, but I'm surprised when I find my thoughts floating back to Frozen Hills. Usually, I assess and move on. This time, something is bugging me.

Was there a missed opportunity there?

"Everything okay?" Mason asks, sensing my distraction.

"Everything's fine," I say. "I just think that maybe—if I get any party invitations in Omaha—I might actually accept."

four

four

four

I take a break from decorating my new room when a text alert chimes on my phone. It's Megan, one of the kids who died with me in Iowa eleven years ago; another of fourteen living "bus kids" that make up the Revive program test group. Megan lives in Seattle, but we keep in touch. Initially, we bonded over the program. Then we grew closer, like sisters who realize they're actually friends, too.

I tap my finger on the screen to read her message.

Megan: You didn't post.... Everything okay?

Under the pseudonyms Flower Girl and Fabulous, Megan and I coauthor a blog called *Anything Autopsy*, where we dissect music, books, fashion, food, and whatever else we feel like. The format is she said/she said style—or she said/he-she said, since Megan is transgender—and if one of us doesn't post, it's not as cool.

I type back:

Daisy: Sorry, we had to move.

There's a pause, and I imagine Megan's black-lined eyes bugging out of her head. The thought makes me laugh out loud.

Megan: Again???!!!???

"Unfortunately," I say aloud, even though she can't hear me. Then I type:

Daisy: Again. Bees.

Megan: I'm going to start calling you Honey.

Daisy: Please don't.

Megan: I guess daisies attract bees, too, don't they?

Daisy: I promise to post twice this week. Setting up my new room. Chat later?

Megan: Love you madly

Daisy: Love you more

I set aside the phone and pick up the paint roller.

People might say it's stupid to spend time decorating a space you'll likely soon abandon, but to me, putting my stamp on each new bedroom is a crucial part of any move. I mean, seriously: I live with science-obsessed secret agents; my bedroom is my retreat. And more than that, it's part of the cover. Assuming someday someone wants to see my room, it has to be in line with my personality. It has to look permanent.

For the first three days in Omaha, when Mason and Cassie are setting up the lab in the basement, I pretend I'm the designer on a home makeover show and create my perfect space. Since my sixteenth birthday's not for another month, I have to get Mason to drive me to Target, a crazy place called Nebraska Furniture Mart, and the paint store, but after that, it's all me and my vision.

In this house, I'm going for tranquil. I paint the walls a nice, mellow gray and cover as much of the wood floors, which are badly in need of refinishing, with a super-plush rug. On one full wall I install a new white open storage unit, then arrange my white nightstand and bed frame from Frozen Hills in the little nook part of the L-shaped room. I put the brown desk that I've had since I was ten under the largest window; when I find that it doesn't look right, I paint it lavender.

Then I add the little details that make all the difference. I sort my books by the color of their spines and stack them horizontally in the little storage-unit cubbies: a librarian's worst nightmare. I frame and hang only black-and-white prints and posters; I reroll all the others and store them under the bed. I thrift-shop on Etsy and craigslist to find an oversized D wall decal, a mirror to hang over my new black dresser from Target, sheer white window coverings, and a gray-and-white-striped beanbag chair.

"Where's the electric staple gun?" I ask Mason on the morning of the day before I'll start school at Omaha Victory High School. Mason's in the office waving motion commands at a massive computer screen tethered to one of the three tiny computers in the house.

"What do you need it for?" he asks.

"I'm re-covering my desk chair," I explain. I don't mention that I'm covering the seat with the fabric from my old comforter. Although, to be fair, I'm upcycling, so he should be proud.

"Garage," Mason says, rubbing his eye sockets. "Third drawer on the left. And be careful."

"I can't kill myself with a staple gun."

"Probably not, but how do you feel about blindness?"

"I'll wear goggles," I say.

Mason shakes his head at me and goes back to his work. I head downstairs in search of power tools.

When my room is finished, I sit and enjoy it for about five minutes; then I get antsy. I head down two flights of stairs to the lab in the basement to see how it's coming along.

"Holy, bright!" I say, squinting under the megawatt fluorescent bulbs covering every square inch of the ceiling.

"We need to see what we're doing," Cassie replies.

"Mission accomplished, and then some," I say.

Mason chuckles at me quietly.

I scan the large room, taking it all in. It's nothing compared to the main lab in Virginia, but it's impressive anyway. There are two workstations, both with the same mini computers and massive monitors as the one in the office upstairs. There's the PCR machine, used to amplify DNA, which looks like a fax machine crossed with a mini-fridge. There are spinners and shakers and rotators and the Homogenizer, aka the tissue blender. There's a hot plate, and dry ice; a water bath and a scale. And, of course, there are dozens of squeaking rats.

All of the Disciples have assignments, but not many of them need labs like ours in their homes. Duties range from monitoring other countries for breakthroughs similar to Revive to controlling the program's technology to managing relocation and surveillance. Agents in the big lab focus on advancing Revive—testing new iterations—

while agents like Mason and Cassie make sure those who got the original version are functioning normally. Inside the program, my guardians' job is to conduct ongoing testing and analysis on the bus kids; to the rest of the world, Mason is a psychologist and Cassie is a stay-at-home mom.

As always, I'm impressed by the pop-up, state-of-the-art lab in an otherwise pedestrian basement.

"You guys are making good progress," I say.

"Thanks," Mason says, smiling. "The space is larger than the one in Michigan, so that's helpful."

"Yeah," I say, giving it another look. Then my eyes fall back on Mason. "Well, my room's done," I say. "I feel like going out."

Mason raises his eyebrows, surprised. "What do you need?" he asks.

"Nothing," I say. "I want to get a library card. See if Omaha has any good shoe stores. Maybe catch a movie. I need to do *something* to get acclimated. I start school tomorrow, and I know nothing about this town."

Mason tilts his head slightly, considering it. "Okay," he says, standing and wiping his hands on his jeans. "I'll take you."

Cassie shoots him a look: Mason leaving means she'll have to finish setting up the lab alone.

"Let's all go," Mason says to her. "Daisy's right. It'll be good for us to get to know Omaha, too."

24

Cassie stares for a few seconds, then relents. Mason is, after all, her boss.

"At least let me change first," she says.

An hour later, I'm standing in the middle of the desert wondering how it would feel to be stranded without water.

"Think Revive would work if I died of dehydration?" I ask Cassie quietly, staring up at the shell of the Desert Dome at the Omaha Zoo.

"I think so, yes," Cassie says without taking her eyes off of a cactus. "We've done dehydration testing on the rats. Seventy-two percent success."

"That's better than asphyxiation," I say.

"And drowning," Mason adds.

Thinking of water reminds me of an exhibit I want to see.

"I'm going to the aquarium," I say.

"Meet us at the front gate at three," Mason says before turning and heading toward the bat exhibit. Cassie seems stuck to the cactus, so I walk toward the underwater experience alone.

"They're older than dinosaurs, you know."

I move my eyes from the sharks to the man, smile politely, and then look back at the tank. I can see in my peripheral vision that the man's eyes are back on the water, too.

"Amazing creatures," he adds with a hint of a disarming lisp. I feel free to answer back.

"I like the sea turtles better," I say, dreamlike, as I watch one swim by. My face is lit up by the shimmering sea.

"Hmm," the man murmurs. "You're right.... They're quite spectacular, too."

The man and I are two of maybe five people in a tunnel cutting through the aquarium itself. We are under the ocean, or at least a man-made version of it. It is sedative and beautiful: a claustrophobic's hell on earth. For a blink, I wonder what would happen if the glass overhead sprung a leak. I imagine drowning. Again.

"Is school out today?" the man asks evenly.

"No," I say. "We just moved here. I start school tomorrow."

"Moves can be difficult," says the man in a quiet, soothing voice.

"Mm-hmm," I say.

"What grade are you in?"

"Tenth."

"Ah, high school," the man says softly as another shark passes. "Well, good luck settling in."

I wait a beat, enjoying the patterns of the water reflecting across my face, then answer: "Thanks. Do you have any tips about the area?"

"Who are you talking to?" Cassie asks from my left side. Startled, I peel my eyes from the underwater world and glance at her. Then I look right, to where the man had been standing. There's no sign of him. Confused, I look back at Cassie.

"I was talking to some dude, and then he disappeared," I say.

"What did he look like?" Cassie asks automatically. It's a question I'm used to hearing. Mason and Cassie are always trying to teach me life lessons, like how to be a keen observer. Normally, I'm excellent at this game, but when I think of the man, only the word *average* comes to my mind. I try to remember his hair color or what his clothes looked like. I try to picture whether he wore a hat or distinctive shoes. Anything.

"I don't remember," I say honestly.

Cassie looks deep into my eyes for a moment, probably expecting the usual list of colors and textures and mannerisms. Finally, when she realizes that I'm not going to say more, she tugs at my arm.

"Mason's waiting. Let's go."

On the way to the car, I remember something about the man: his barely distinguishable lisp when saying certain things, like the word *creatures*. Excitedly, I look over at Cassie, wanting to tell her about it.

But like usual, she's on the phone.

five

five

five

Omaha Victory High School is brand-new and modern, sharp angles and manicured grounds, high-tech and functional. School starts at 7:45, but Mason, Cassie, and I arrive at 7:00 to check in and pick up my class schedule and locker assignment. We follow signs through the new-smelling and nearly empty corridors. A surprisingly young-looking, dark-haired woman in jeans and a blazer is waiting for us at the reception area.

"I'm Vice Principal Erin Waverly," the woman says, hand outstretched.

"Mason West," Mason says with a smile, shaking Ms. Waverly's hand.

"I'm Cassie West," Cassie says. "So nice to meet you." Her voice is sugary sweet like a doughnut this morning.

"And this must be Daisy," Ms. Waverly says, looking at me with a friendly smile. "Welcome to Victory."

"Thanks," I say.

We follow Ms. Waverly back to her office. Mason, Cassie, and I sit on a small couch across from Ms. Waverly's desk while she reviews my real but slightly altered birth certificate, government-manufactured school transcripts, forged yet accurate immunization records, and totally falsified proof of residence.

"You were in honors classes at your last school," Ms. Waverly observes before setting aside the transcript.

"Yes," I say.

"She's a little smarty-pants," Cassie teases as she smoothes back my hair.

"Mom!" I protest quietly, rolling my eyes at her and feigning embarrassment.

"I can see that Daisy's a good student," Ms. Waverly says to Cassie. "Unfortunately, we've got a larger than usual sophomore class this year due to some renovations at one of the magnet schools, and our honors classes are full."

Mason shifts in his seat. "But can't you make room for one more?" he asks.

Ms. Waverly holds up a hand. "Before you get too concerned, I think I have a solution."

"Oh?" Mason asks.

"Yes. I think based on Daisy's test scores, she'll keep up fine in junior math, science, and English."

I get a funny feeling in my stomach: a tinge of nervousness. Victory is grades nine through twelve, so I'm already starting high school a year after everyone else my age; now I'm about to be thrust into junior classes, too? But at the same time, it's better than the regular sophomore curriculum.

That's the equivalent of being held back.

Everyone agrees to the compromise, and soon enough, we leave the office, all smiles and optimism. I part ways with Mason and Cassie at the main doors. When they're gone, I set off for my assigned locker in the math wing, navigating multiplying students as I go. A professional new girl, I check out what kids are wearing and note that my hip-length red T-shirt and faded skinny jeans were the right choice this morning.

Like a chameleon, I blend in.

"Sweet TOMS," a voice says, presumably to me. I step back from my locker to investigate. A pretty girl a few doors down is pointing at my silver glitter slip-ons.

"Thanks," I say, wiggling my toes inside the canvas shoes. Thoughts of birthday party invitations fly into my brain, and I decide to try to keep the conversation going. "I like your hair."

The girl runs a hand through her two-toned tresses — golden blond on top and jet black underneath — and smiles with her whole face, from her Hollywood chin to her dark brown eyes. She's wearing a turquoise sundress and low cowboy boots, and I'm positive she has to be the most popular girl in school. Everything about her is cool.

"Thanks," she said. "My mom hates it."

"My mom hates these shoes," I say, shrugging, which is mostly true. Cassie doesn't like anything remotely flashy or attention-getting.

The girl laughs.

"I'm Audrey McKean," she says.

"Daisy West." I smile.

"You must be new; I know everyone."

Yep, she's popular.

"Today's my first day," I say. "We just moved here from Michigan." Another student approaches one of the lockers between mine and Audrey's, blocking our view of each other. Audrey peeks around him and makes a silly face at me, then slams her locker door and moves around the guy.

"So, what's your first class?" she asks.

"English," I say. "With Mr. Jefferson?"

"You're a junior?" she asks.

"Sophomore," I say.

"No way."

I raise my eyebrows in question.

"You look older," she explains. "You must be a huge nerd."

I look at her, surprised.

"I'm joking!" she says, hitting me lightly on the arm

31

like we've known each other for ages. "I'll walk you to your class. I've got Spanish in the next wing over."

"Wow, thanks," I say. "That's really nice of you."

"It's no big deal," Audrey says. "Come on: It's this way."

Audrey and I talk about our mutual love of casual footwear the entire way to first period. She raves about a new pair of laceless runners and I babble about pointed versus round-toed flats. It reminds me a little of the effortless way I chat with Megan, and honestly, I'm bummed when we arrive at my classroom.

"Hey, do you want to go off-campus for lunch?" Audrey asks.

"I..." I begin, confused by the attention from someone who *has* to have friends lining up to hang out with her. I channel a little of Cassie's paranoia and eye Audrey suspiciously. "Um..."

"Oh," Audrey says, her face falling so slightly I barely notice it. "That's okay if you have other plans. I just thought since you're new and all..."

"No," I say quickly, snapping out of it. "I don't have other plans. I'd love to go. Should we meet at the lockers?"

Audrey smiles brightly. "Perfect. See you then!"

Mr. Jefferson welcomes me to Victory, hands me a textbook that smells like soup and a syllabus printed on yellow paper, and directs me to an open desk on the side of the room farthest from the door. I smile at a girl who's watching me; it makes her look away. Happy that I get to sit by the window, I slide into my chair, which has been warmed by the morning sun. I grab a notebook and pen from my bag and start reading over the syllabus while the classroom fills up.

I can tell when the bell's about to ring because Mr. Jefferson stands up and walks to the podium, then clears his throat a couple times. I set aside the syllabus and scan the room, finding, happily, that no one looks too intimidating.

When the bell starts to ring, I jump a little: It's different from the ones in Frozen Hills. Here, the tone is like a longer version of the lowest beep in a hearing test. When it stops, I sit up in my seat a little straighter and pick up my pen, ready to take notes. Mr. Jefferson clears his throat once more, making me wonder if he has a cold or something, then opens his mouth to speak.

Just then, a guy darts into the room and slides into the open desk near the door. Curiously, I watch him until Mr. Jefferson clears his throat once more. Maybe it's a tic. I look at the teacher's podium and Mr. Jefferson is giving the late arrival a look, but he doesn't say anything.

Instead, he introduces me.

"Class, we have a new student joining us today," he says, gesturing my way. Like dominoes, each triggered by the one before, heads start to turn in my direction. Mr. Jefferson continues. "This is Daisy West, and she comes to us from Michigan. Let's all give her a warm Victory welcome."

A few people mutter "hi"; a handful smile or wave. I smile politely and wait for the spotlight to move off of me. After a few seconds, Mr. Jefferson clears his throat for what feels like the hundredth time and begins class. The dominoes reverse themselves and I quietly exhale.

Except that I have that prickly feeling, like someone is staring at me.

Warily, I search the classroom. Everyone in the row next to me and the next one over is paying attention to Mr. Jefferson. But when I get to the row by the door, I see that the late arrival is eyeing me. And that's when I realize what I hadn't before:

The guy is flat-out, undeniably, unbelievably hot.

He casually sweeps the front of his shaggy hair to the side with his thumb. The back of his hair flips out from behind his ears in that adorable way that makes it impossible to tell whether he needs a haircut or just got one. He's got dark eyebrows — the kind that sexy TV villains have — and almond-shaped brown eyes that make him look like he has a secret. He's slouching ever so slightly in his faded green T-shirt and worn jeans, and he smiles at me in a way that looks almost…familiar. Then he faces front and I feel like I've been dropped back to earth from the clouds.

I watch the guy for the rest of the period, but he never looks at me again. When the bell rings at the end of class,

I lean down long enough to put away my stuff and pick up my bag, and when I sit back up, he's gone. I'm disappointed until I realize that I'll see him again tomorrow, and every day for the rest of the year.

And for that, I silently thank Vice Principal Waverly.

At lunchtime, Audrey and I meet up at our lockers as planned.

"Hi!" I say as I approach.

"Hey, Daisy!" Audrey says back, matching my broad smile. "How's it going so far?"

"Pretty good, actually," I say. And then I look away, embarrassed.

"What?" she asks, reading me.

"Nothing," I say. "There's just a cute guy in my English class."

"Ooh, really?" she asks. "I want to hear all about him—but save it for the ride. We only have forty-five minutes."

We shut our lockers and turn to leave as two girls walk by. They look at me quizzically, then offer Audrey a pair of anemic waves, like they're being forced to say hello but aren't feeling it. Audrey shakes her head at them and refocuses on me.

"Hungry?" she asks.

"Always."

"Follow me."

*   *   *

Audrey expertly leads us through the crowded halls and shows me a few shortcuts on the way out to the student parking lot. Soon we're buckled into her bright yellow Mini Cooper.

"I love your car," I say.

"Thanks," she says. "I love it, too. I spent two summers' worth of babysitting money on the down payment, but it was worth it."

"You must have worked a lot," I say.

"My parents matched what I earned." Audrey looks a little embarrassed.

"Nice parents," I say.

"What do you drive?" Audrey asks as she pulls out of the student lot onto the main road.

"Nothing . . . yet," I say. "I won't be sixteen until next month."

"No way," Audrey says, shaking her head.

"Way," I say, and we laugh.

Audrey reaches over and turns on the radio. She pushes a couple of buttons and lands on an alterna-song. She puts her right hand back on the wheel and taps her thumbs in time with the beat.

"This okay?" she asks.

"Sure," I say, smiling. "Hey, have you ever had Mrs. Chang?"

"Geography or art?"

"Geography. There are two Mrs. Changs?"

"Yep," Audrey says, rolling down her window. The

breeze flits through the car; I scratch at a spot where a tiny hair is tickling my forehead. "No, wait, I think maybe art is Chung, not Chang," she says.

"Anyway," I say, "she seems tough."

Audrey shrugs. "I don't know. I've never had Chang or Chung." She gives me a funny smile and I can't help but laugh again.

Audrey cranks up the volume when a popular song comes on and we ride without talking, bobbing our heads and tapping our fingers to the music. We arrive at a pizza place and Audrey whips the Mini into a spot like she's racing someone for it. Inside, we both get the special: a slice of pizza and salad from the buffet. After we eat we have a little extra time to spare, so we play a quick round of lunchtime trivia and beat a trio of cocky businessmen wearing pleated Dockers that went out of style before I was born.

"I can't believe you know that Iowa is the hawk state," Audrey says as we walk to her car, full of pizza and giddiness.

"The Hawkeye State," I say.

"Oh, excuse me, Iowa expert!" Audrey jokes.

"You should talk! You know Eddie Vedder's full name!"

"Edward Louis Severson the third," we say in unison before breaking into giggles.

"Seriously, how did you know that?" I ask. "Are you a closet grunge head or something?"

"My mom has a crush on him," Audrey says, flipping

her hair off her shoulder. "She tells us about these amazing Pearl Jam shows she went to as a kid."

"Us?" I ask. "You have brothers and sisters?"

"Just one brother," Audrey says. "He's a junior at Victory. You'll meet him sometime."

"Oh, cool," I say, flattered by Audrey's assumption that I'll meet her family.

We climb into the car and the second she turns the key, we both lose it again: An acoustic version of Pearl Jam's "Jeremy" is playing on the radio. Audrey breaks into song and I can't help but join in; of course I know the lyrics. With the windows down, startling pedestrians walking by, we scream/shout/sing at the top of our lungs the whole way back to Victory like we're part of the Jamily.

Like we go way back.

Not until that night, after I've posted on the blog an analysis of Pearl Jam's record Ten—which is super old but still rocks—do I step back and consider the day.

I accepted the metaphorical birthday party invitation with Audrey: I went all in. And ultimately, I have to admit that it was fun. But being raised undercover, I can't help but question my own motives. Did I make a true friend today, or was Daisy West only pretending?

My text alert chimes: it's Megan.

Megan: What's with the post? I'm the one who lives in Grunge Capitol, USA.

Daisy: Our fans don't know that.

Megan: All 372 of them ☺

I smile and type:

Daisy: I assume you'll be refuting my claims in your post.

Even when she agrees with me, Megan strives to be contrarian.

Megan: Natch

Pause. Then she asks:

Megan: First day go okay?

Daisy: I think so. Do you ever wonder whether you're making real friends if you have to lie to them about your life?

Megan: No. You made a FRIEND?

Daisy: Maybe

Megan: Not some geek in a study group, right? A real, living, breathing friend?

Daisy: The geeks were friends

Megan: You know what I mean.

Daisy: I do.... No, she's cool. Her name is Audrey

Megan: Hey, D?

Daisy: Yeah?

Megan: Don't question this to death, okay?

Daisy: I'll try not to.

Megan: Okay good. Gotta go prove you wrong on the blog. Love you madly

Daisy: Love you more. Bye

six

six

six

"You don't have plans today, do you?" Mason asks when I creep into the kitchen after too little sleep. Last night, I made the mistake of picking up the latest book in a sci-fi series at eight thirty. By ten o'clock, I was way too absorbed to put it down. I finally went to bed at two AM.

"No plans," I grumble, easing into a chair. Mason flips over a pancake. "You're cooking," I observe. Mason's actually a really good cook, but he rarely does it.

"You need a solid breakfast," he replies. "We're doing your annual checkup today."

"Seriously?" I ask in protest. "No warning? And on Saturday?"

"Sorry, Daisy," Mason says sympathetically. "I think

it's better if you don't have warning; you don't have time to get worried about it this way."

"But why now?" I ask. "Testing doesn't usually happen until closer to the anniversary." The bus that went off the bridge into an icy lake and killed twenty-one people—seven for good—did so in early December. Testing usually happens at one-year intervals, as close to December 5 as possible.

Mason has a funny look on his face. "God asked for them early this year," he says.

"That's odd," I say. "I don't remember this ever happening before.... Has it?"

"No," Mason says.

"Bizarre."

"I think so, too, but I'm sure he has his reasons." Mason drops three pancakes onto my plate.

"Can we do it next weekend?" I whine before taking a bite. "I'm tired," I say, mouth full. After swallowing, I continue. "I mean, it doesn't make sense to do the test so early."

Mason looks at me, frying pan and spatula in his hands. "Whatever our opinions are, it's not optional," he says, surprising me with his abrasive tone. Mason's usually more chill. He turns toward the sink and, as he's walking away, he adds loudly, "We're doing the test today. End of discussion."

I read once about the extensive testing that astronauts go through before they get their ticket to space. In my humble opinion, the annual Revive exam is even more rigorous.

First, there's a physical, but it's not exactly "routine." Sure, they check my eyes, ears, reflexes, and heart, but then there's a complete neurological assessment and balance and coordination exam. They take tissue and hair samples to review in the lab; even when my throat is fine, they do a culture. There's a full-body skin scan, where all moles and other markings are carefully recorded. There's a review of my Health and Diet Diary, a body-fat assessment, and a challenging fitness test.

Not exactly what you'd get at your standard doctor's office.

Then comes the memory test. It's fun because it usually ends in a contest between Mason and me, and I always win. Last year, we argued for an hour about whether my school in Palmdale, Florida, was on Connecticut Avenue or Connecticut Street.

"Avenue," I said.

"You're wrong," he replied.

"I'm not."

"You were only five. You can't possibly remember."

"I can and I do. The bus picked up on the corner of Connecticut Avenue and First Street."

"How do you retain these things?"

"I just do."

I didn't want to tell him that I remembered because of him, that I used to stare up at that street sign wishing I was in the real Connecticut instead of on Connecticut Avenue—that's how badly I didn't want to ride the bus to school. Not until I broke down crying one morning did Mason realize that I had been totally traumatized by the whole bus incident.

He drove me to school after that.

The memory test is followed by the psych evaluation, which is slightly awkward because it's administered by my father figure, but so far it's been okay. Then there's an IQ test, followed by age-appropriate math, science, reading comprehension, and language exams.

While the testing is grueling, even brutal, I appreciate it for all that it gives the program, data-wise, about the bus kids. But there's one part I hate: the blood draw. Tissue samples are one thing—a quick pinch from numbed skin—but having fifteen vials of blood drawn at once is like having the life slowly sucked out of you. It starts with a poke and ends with wooziness.

It's the worst.

But even though I see the benefits of the Revive testing—including that dreaded blood draw—the process does drain me to the point of exhaustion. Since I live with two agents and am essentially their human lab rat, my test takes only one day, as opposed to four or sometimes five for the average Convert. There's no resting between sessions; for example, there's no recharging the brain between the psych eval and the IQ test.

After it's all over, overtired and blurry, I sign my name—my original name, Daisy McDaniel—at the bottom of an oath that binds me to a life of continued silence and make-believe. Then, instead of priming or primping for a party like everyone else my age at seven thirty on a Saturday night, I change into pj's and struggle to stay awake while I brush my teeth.

Because summer solstice is nothing compared to this; the longest day of my year is test day.

seven

seven

seven

Sunday, I wake up at noon, out of it and thirsty. I stretch, then drag myself out of bed. I'm not sure why, but I check my phone before doing anything else. There's a text waiting from Audrey:

Audrey: Want to come over and hang out?

I put on a bra and use the bathroom, then go downstairs to find Mason. He's not in the kitchen, so I check the basement.

Halfway down the stairs, I stop.

". . . just out of the blue," Mason is saying.

"But why would he contact Sydney?" Cassie asks. "She's not even active anymore."

I hold my breath at the mention of Sydney's name.

Cassie wasn't always Mason's partner. Sydney was with us for five years, until I was almost ten. I loved her like the mother I never had, but she fell in love with another Disciple and got pregnant. She left the program and her fake family for a real one, and I haven't spoken to her since.

According to the rules, when you're out, you're out.

Even knowing that, I skulked around the house for months after Sydney left, pretending to be okay with everything but crying into my pillow at night and begging Mason in private to bring her back. Even fully briefed on the rules, I felt discarded like an old pair of shoes.

Feeling icky for eavesdropping, I start down the stairs again, but this time I stomp loudly so they have a little warning. Mason shares most things with me about the program, but even so, the look on his face when I enter the lab tells me not to ask questions. At least not right now.

"Can I go to Audrey's house?" I ask instead.

Mason raises his eyebrows, and the usually emotionless Cassie looks my way, surprised.

"This is the girl you went to lunch with?" he asks.

"Yes."

"She invited you over?"

"No, I'm going to show up unannounced," I say sarcastically. "Of course she invited me!"

"Okay," Mason says, looking around at the explosion of papers and science stuff on his workspace. "What time?"

"Now-ish," I say.

"Give me twenty?"

"Okay."

I head back upstairs, where I text Audrey, then shower without washing my hair. I throw on shorts and a ratty T-shirt and flip-flops because apparently Omaha didn't get the memo that it's fall.

Mason makes me agree to eat something before we leave the house, so I inhale half of a sandwich and crunch a few baby carrots. On the way out, I grab a handful of red grapes. The grapes are sweet and delicious; I can't help but shovel them into my mouth as Mason chauffeurs me to Audrey's. I don't really feel like talking—not like I could, anyway—so I let my mind wander. Grapes in my cheeks, I end up remembering the third time I died.

I was five and a half years old, and I went to full-day kindergarten because Mason read some study that said it was better for kids. Anyway, there I was at kindergarten, and maybe I skipped breakfast, maybe I burned through my energy at recess, or maybe I was just a weird kid. All I know is that I was famished at lunch that day. I wolfed down my PB&J, then started in on my grapes, stuffing more than a handful in at once.

A monstrous red grape got lodged in my windpipe.

Since I was at a table alone—my one semi-friend was

home sick that day—no one noticed. Apparently, the sounds of a choking girl are no match for a rowdy elementary school cafeteria. I was on the floor by the time a fifth grader happened to pass by.

Sydney arrived in her paramedic outfit to load me into the borrowed ambulance, where Mason was waiting to Revive me. I don't remember most of it, of course.

I woke up freezing and wheezing, throat sore from whatever Mason used to dislodge the grape. My lungs burned from the sudden return of oxygen, and for the first few minutes, I was completely confused as to what had happened. Mason hugged me for the first time when he told me that I'd died again.

For that, I remember death number three, strangely, with a tinge of fondness.

"This probably goes without saying, but you have to be incredibly careful with new friends," Mason says, interrupting my thoughts.

"I know," I mumble around the grapes in my mouth.

"She'll want to know about your background...your parents...where you lived before."

I swallow my food. "I know what to say."

"I know you do," Mason says.

"Don't worry, okay? I won't blow the program."

Mason looks at me for a moment and smiles genuinely, then refocuses on driving. I turn and look out the window at the suburb inching by. Though not brand-new, the houses are massive, with sprawling front yards and the kind of grown-up trees you can barely stand not to climb. In one driveway I see a family loading into a minivan: Both parents are dressed in weekend casual, their older child is dressed like a princess, and the baby is still in jammies. A block later, we hit a stop sign and three girls with pigtails ride their bikes in the crosswalk, all in a row, like ducklings.

When the GPS lady tells us, "You have arrived," an unfamiliar jolt of what I realize is nervousness pokes me in the gut. Too quickly for me to will it away, Mason turns into the driveway of a brown brick plantation-style house. It's impressive, with columns flanking the front porch and everything. I want to stare, but Mason quickly opens his door to get out, so I do the same. Audrey must have been watching for us; she flings open the front door.

"Hey!" she says.

"Hi, Audrey!"

Mason walks toward the front porch and gets there before I do.

"This is my dad, Mason," I say as he opens his mouth to introduce himself.

"Hi, Daisy's dad," Audrey says. Her mom appears behind her in the doorway, and you'd think Audrey and I were getting married for all the hand-shaking that goes on.

"Joanne McKean," Audrey's mom says as she takes my hand in hers. "It's so nice to meet you, Daisy."

"Nice to meet you, too."

Mrs. McKean has manicured nails and soft skin and

50

smells a little like maple syrup. She's wearing a gold cross and a light blue cardigan with worn jeans and flats. Her blond hair is blown dry into a sleek bob, and she looks like she should accompany the dictionary definition of mom. Even though they are nothing alike, Mrs. McKean makes me miss Sydney.

We all chat until finally Mason takes my (overt) cue to leave—"Dad, don't you have to be somewhere?"—and Audrey and I go inside. She gives me a quick tour of the main floor of the house, which is a cross between an art gallery and a Pottery Barn catalog, before we retreat to her bedroom.

I like Audrey even more when I step into her space.

The wall behind her bright yellow lacquer headboard is painted with black chalkboard paint, and it's covered with doodles and drawings, sayings and notes, scribbled floor to ceiling. The bed's made with simple white linens, but there's a funky throw pillow on top that has a cartoony map of Nebraska embroidered on it.

The rest of the walls are white. On the one directly across from the bed is a modern low black dresser; the wall with the door holds a small white desk, with no-frills shelves hanging over it. There are photos as well, but most are of Audrey and her family; the few shots of friends show faces I don't recognize. I wonder again why Audrey doesn't have more friends. Then, happy to be here regardless, I move on.

In the corner near the largest window is a little seating

area with a small futon and a striped yellow, red, and black chair. Between the two seats is a see-through coffee table, where a stack of magazines seems to be floating in midair.

"Is that Lucite?" I ask, pointing to the table before settling in across from Audrey.

"I guess," she says.

"It's so awesome," I murmur. "Did you design your room?"

Audrey nods proudly, smiling.

"I'm into that, too," I say.

"Cool."

There's a pause while I wonder what on earth to talk about next. Have I entirely used up my conversation starters after only a few days?

Thankfully, Audrey keeps things moving.

"So, your dad seems interesting," she says.

I raise my eyebrows. "Really?"

"Sure," she says. "He talks to you like you're an adult."

"Yeah."

"And don't hurl, but he's hot," Audrey says.

"Where's your bathroom?" I joke, standing halfway up. Audrey laughs and I sit back down.

"I'm sure everyone tells you that," she continues. "He looks like George Clooney ... only not as old."

"I've never thought about that, but you're right. He sort of does."

"Totally. But your coloring is so much lighter. You must look like your mom," Audrey says.

"Maybe," I say before I realize what I'm saying. When Audrey gives me a funny look, I proceed with caution. There are things I can share; there are things I can't.

"I'm adopted," I admit, which is mostly true. What I don't admit is that I was an orphan when I died in a bus crash; that after the government brought me back to life, it wasn't quite sure what to do with me; that ultimately it gave Mason a lifelong assignment to raise a child... or at least until I turn eighteen. That if we're getting technical, the adoption isn't legal because the real me died in Bern, Iowa, eleven years ago.

"Really?" Audrey asks, clearly intrigued by the whole adoption thing. Her brown eyes are wide and sparkling.

"Uh-huh," I say.

"I don't know anyone who was adopted," she says. "Did you always know, or did they pull a Lifetime movie on you and surprise you when your birth mother needed a kidney or something?"

Laughing, I say, "I always knew. Like you said, my dad treats me like an adult. Same goes for my mom. We don't really have secrets." At least not from one another. I scratch my nose before remembering that some agents would call the gesture a "tell." I return my hand to my lap.

"Gotcha," Audrey says, not seeming to notice. "But don't you wonder about your birth parents?"

"Not really," I say honestly.

"Seriously? I think I'd wonder."

"The way I see it is that I don't want to know people who didn't want to know me. I don't mean that to sound bitter, because I know they had their reasons. I mean it like I don't want to spend energy worrying or thinking about people who aren't in my life."

"I guess that's a good way to look at it," Audrey says. "You seem incredibly well-adjusted about the whole thing."

"Thanks, I think," I say, laughing. I tip my head to the side. "I don't think I've ever been called 'well-adjusted' before."

Audrey chuckles, too, and despite my concern about whether or not I'm sticking to the script, it feels good to have someone ask about my past. I'm so into the conversation that when Audrey asks how old I was when my parents adopted me, I blurt out the truth.

"Four."

"Where did you live before that?" she asks.

Screeching tires and warning bells sound in my brain; I actually feel my fingers wrap around the armrests. For practical reasons, like if I have to go to the emergency room or something and my blood doesn't match my parents', it's okay to tell people I'm adopted. But the story is that I was adopted at birth. Where I lived before is not part of the dossier.

"I can't get over your mom letting you chalkboard

your entire wall," I say, looking over Audrey's head. I force my hands back into my lap. Apparently okay with the change of subject, Audrey turns in her seat and admires the décor, too.

"My mom lets me do what I want," she says in this weird way that doesn't sound egotistical. It sounds strangely...sad. Audrey shifts her gaze from the wall to her feet; there's a brief pause in the conversation. Then, just when I start to feel awkward, her head snaps up and her eyes are on me again. "Hey, you want a soda?"

"Sure," I say, thankful she's not asking any more about my adoption.

"Regular or diet?"

"Regular."

"Okay, I'll be right back," she says, standing to leave but then pausing in the middle of the room. "Want music?"

"Sure."

Audrey goes over to her desk, but when she gets there, she huffs and shakes her head. I wonder what she's annoyed about but don't ask because it feels intrusive. Instead I look around some more as she opens iTunes on her laptop, selects a playlist, and turns up the volume on the little speakers.

"This okay?" she asks.

"It's great."

"Okay, I'll be right back."

Audrey leaves me alone in her room. As I relax into the lounger, I can't help but think that it's cozy here, in this chair and in this house. And for a girl with no real roots, cozy feels a lot like home.

One of my favorite new songs comes on, and I'm so happy that I can't help but sing.

eight

eight

eight

Something shifts in the doorway. I stop singing mid (tuneless) note and drop my arms to my sides. I look, expecting Audrey, but instead it's none other than the guy I've been drooling over in English all week, Matt something.

"Wicked air drumming," he teases, smiling a fidget-inducing half grin. His villain's eyes are shining. Playful. He looks like he's happy to see me.

"Thanks," I say, at a loss for words because I'm confused about why he's here. Is he Audrey's boyfriend? Just a friend here to hang out, too? Then I realize that not only is he barefoot, but he's leaning on the doorframe like he built it. My brain clicks. He lives here.

Duh.

Matt is Audrey's brother.

"You should see my air cymbals," I joke, happy to have solved the mystery. "They're even more worthy."

"Actually, what I liked most was the singing," Matt says, smiling full-out this time. "The high note at the end was pure genius." He scratches his defined jaw with the back of his index finger. It's oddly sexy.

"Awesome, right?" I say, hoping I sound more casual than I feel.

He gives me a double thumbs-up and a totally cheesy smile. "I think you could easily get a recording contract."

We both laugh, and when it subsides, we're still for a few seconds.

"I'm Daisy," I say, in case he doesn't recognize me. "We're in English together?"

"I know," he says automatically. He looks down and away for a second, smiling a little to himself like he's embarrassed for having answered so quickly. Then his narrow eyes are back on mine. "I didn't know you were friends with my sister."

"Our lockers are in the same hall," I explain. "That's how we met. She told me she has a brother. I didn't know it was you."

"It's me." Matt nods again, shoving his hands in the pockets of his worn jeans. He looks conflicted, like he wants to stay but thinks he should go.

"Audrey went to get sodas," I say just to say something, hoping that if I keep talking, he'll stay put. It works, at least for a minute.

"How'd you do on that quiz?" he asks.

"Fine," I say. "I got an A."

Another nod. "Me, too."

We hold each other's gaze for a slightly uncomfortable but still glorious moment. I feel like I did that time I had to present my science project in front of the whole freshman class: exhilarated and apprehensive at the same time.

Matt pulls an iPhone from his right pocket and steps into the room only far enough to put it in the charger on the desk. His being that much closer makes me shift in my seat.

"Don't tell Audrey about this, okay?"

"Okay," I say, confused. "Don't you have your own phone?"

"Yeah, but hers has better music. One time, I accidentally—" Matt stops himself, as if remembering that he has to be somewhere. "Never mind. Long and boring story."

I want to say that I'll listen to any story he has to tell, but I manage to hold back. He returns to the doorway.

"Guess I'll see you in class," he says, hesitating before giving a slight wave and turning to leave.

"Bye," I say quietly. Just then, as if the playlist is the soundtrack to my life, a lighthearted love song starts. But before I have too much time to skip into fantasyland, Audrey's back.

"Sorry about that," she says, a little out of breath as she rushes into the room. "My dad called from work and was grilling me about my homework. I didn't mean to leave you alone in here for so lo—" She stops and looks at me curiously. "What's with the goofy smile?"

"Oh, I was thinking about a guy," I say cryptically, keeping my crush on her brother a secret for today.

"Does he look like Jake Gyllenhaal?" she asks. "Because Jake is the hottest guy on the planet."

"No," I say with a little head shake. *To me, Matt is even better.*

Audrey and I read gossip magazines and talk about celebrities we'd like to have dinner with. She shows me the shoes she told me about earlier this week and I doodle daisies on her chalk wall. After a while, her mom invites us downstairs for cookies, which makes Audrey roll her eyes and causes my stomach to rumble. No one bakes cookies in my house. We jog down the steps and saunter into the kitchen, then plop ourselves onto the bench next to the rustic wooden table. Mrs. McKean gives us two cookies each, saying, "Don't worry, I made the lower-fat option, and the milk is skim." Audrey nods and we both start snacking.

Then every happily relaxed muscle in my body tenses when Matt walks into the room.

"What's up," he says to his mom.

"Hi, Mattie," Mrs. McKean says before standing on her toes to kiss him on the cheek. He doesn't pull away, but he does look a tiny bit embarrassed when our eyes meet, and I wonder whether it's about the kiss, or being called Mattie, or both.

Matt goes to the cabinet and retrieves a mug, then pours himself black coffee from the pot and adds a touch of milk. No sugar. He grabs a cookie and sits down with me and Audrey at the table.

My stomach flips at the sight of the little wisps of hair behind his ears. They've become my English-class distraction. Being so close now, I fight the urge to reach out and touch them. As if he can read my mind, he looks at me curiously, like he's wondering if I just might do it.

"Mattie, you slept the day away," Mrs. McKean says from across the kitchen.

"'Cause he was out so late," Audrey says under her breath. They both glance at their mom to make sure she didn't hear.

"I stayed up late reading," Matt says to his mom. She turns her back to us to get more cookies out of the oven. When she opens the oven door, it makes the warm kitchen hot.

"The show ran long," Matt whispers to Audrey. "I couldn't miss the encore."

"What are you kids plotting over there?" Mrs. McKean asks, spatula in hand.

"Nothing," the siblings say in unison.

We munch quietly for a moment before Audrey starts harassing her brother again. She leans toward him, elbows on the table, eyes narrowed, and lips pinched.

"By the way, I know you used my phone again. Just because you're too lazy to charge yours doesn't mean you can steal mine whenever you please. Stop taking my stuff."

Matt rolls his eyes at her and then looks at me with an expression that straddles the line between annoyed and amused. "Thanks a lot," he says in a voice that could be sarcastic; I don't know him that well. Right when I decide he's teasing, he gets up from the table.

"Later," he says to no one in particular.

"Bye," I say quietly, wishing I could make him stay.

Audrey and I decide to go to a just-opened mall that she says is like shopping heaven. We okay it with her mom and with Mason, then take off in her sunshiny yellow car. While we shop, I balance my overwhelming desire to ask about Matt, Matt, and more Matt with wanting to get to know Audrey better. I don't want Audrey to think I'm only interested in her brother, so I decide as we walk through the temperature-controlled atrium that I'm restricted to asking only three questions about Matt.

As we meander down the aisles of Von Maur, GAP, Abercrombie & Fitch, and Hot Topic, Audrey and I chat easily about anything and everything else. After only thirty minutes, I know that she got her hair colored at the salon on the first level, loves glass elevators, wants to go to Paris someday but takes Spanish at school, prefers pretzel bites to sticks or full soft pretzels, and is a closet history nerd.

"I could have rocked the Victorian era," Audrey says as she fingers a ruffled, Victorian-inspired shirt at Anthropologie.

"I think you're right," I say. "But corsets? No thanks."

"I bet they weren't so bad after you got used to them."

I hook Audrey a look like she's insane and move to the other side of the rack.

"I love this song." I sing quietly as I flip through pants I can't afford; I used all of my allowance on stuff for my bedroom.

"Ick," Audrey says. "I totally don't get this band. You and Matt."

I suck in my breath, hoping she'll say more about her brother. She doesn't, so I decide to use question number one.

"What show did he go see last night?" I ask casually.

"Crunch Toast."

"Love them, too."

"Actually, I agree with that one. They're awesome. One time..."

Audrey tells her story and I try to listen but instead I zone out, pulled away by thoughts of Matt's hair. Of his tanned arms and the wide, industrial-hip watch that looks like it was made specifically for his arm. I think of the way he smelled faintly of cucumber and mint—both must be in his shampoo. I think of the sound of him sipping his coffee: not a gross slurp, but not silent, either. Like a little inhale. Of his easy smile. Of the way his worn jeans hang perfectly from his hips. I think of the fact that he has the nicest boy feet I've ever seen...not that I've seen a ton of them.

I wonder what he's doing right now.

Then I wonder if he's mad about the iPhone.

Then I wonder whether he's wondering about me.

"Hello?" Audrey says. "Are you even listening to me?"

I blink, confused.

"I'm sorry, what?" I ask.

"Do...you...want...coffee?" she asks, enunciating every word. She looks really tired all of a sudden.

"Oh, yeah, sure," I say, putting the shirt I didn't realize I was holding back on the rack.

We take the escalator to the coffee shop on the second floor. Audrey orders a nonfat caramel latte and it sounds delicious so I get the same. When we're settled at a table by the window, Audrey checks her phone.

"What time do you have to be home?"

"Five," I say, sipping my drink.

"Okay, we're doing all right, then."

Audrey's still looking down at her phone. I take the opportunity to bring up Matt.

"Why did Matt take your phone?" I ask. She rolls her eyes dramatically.

"Because he's an idiot."

I raise my eyebrows, and she continues. "He accidentally synced all of his music onto my phone instead of his, and it took forever, and he's too lazy to go back and do it again on his own. So if I'm around, he's always taking my phone. It's so annoying."

"I saw him bringing it back today. I think he thinks I ratted him out."

"I knew anyway," Audrey says. "He never puts it back in the right place."

"I think he's mad at me."

"Doubt it."

"He seemed like it," I say.

Audrey sips her latte. "You mean when he said, 'Thanks a lot'?" she asks.

"Yeah."

"Oh, he was just messing around. At least I think he was. Sometimes, lately, I can't tell."

"What do you mean?" I ask, realizing my question probably counts as number three.

"Oh, nothing," Audrey says, disappointing me with her answer. "He's just got some stuff on his mind."

Audrey is quiet then, clearly done talking about her brother. Kicking myself for using all my questions about Matt, I look out the window to the mall patrons cruising by with strollers and shopping bags. Movement near a planter catches my eye: A man in a blue button-down and jeans is standing there, waiting for someone. The funny thing is that he looks right at me when I look at him. He watches me for a second like a curious stranger might, then looks away, taking out his phone and typing on the keyboard. I imagine him texting his wife or girlfriend to hurry up, except something about him bugs me. He's got the same robotic look that Cassie has, that the agents in the cleanup crews have.

Unexpectedly, my cell rings. It's Mason.

"Everything okay?" he asks.

"Yes, why?" I ask back.

"No reason. Do you have your card?"

"Yes," I say; he's asking about the debit card that's linked to my allowance account.

"That's good," Mason says. "Have fun."

Click.

nine

nine

nine

For exactly five days, my life is so normal that I almost forget I might be faking it. On Monday, Matt waves at me at the beginning of English. On Tuesday, he asks how it's going—from across the room before class—making at least three girls seated between us breathe jealousy. Every day except Wednesday, when she has an appointment at noon, Audrey and I eat lunch together, either in the cafeteria or off-campus. Despite the fact that others say "hello" in the halls, I seem to be Audrey's only friend. She and I text every night, and she even starts reading my blog.

Thursday night, she texts:

Audrey: I love your post about the anatomy of mall crowds.

Daisy: Thanks!

Audrey: Sure. And your friend Fabulous is hilarious.

Daisy: That's Megan. You'd love her.

My life starts to feel like a prime-time sitcom.

Then, on Friday, the cracks start to show.

The morning is fine, but things begin to unravel at lunch. Audrey and I go to the taco place down the street from school for the Friday special: two hard-shell tacos, chips and salsa, and a drink. Right after we finish eating, Audrey runs to the bathroom and throws up (I hear it because we're at a table close to the restrooms). But when she comes out, she lies about it.

"Oh my god, are you okay?" I ask when she sits down. Her brown eyes are watery and her face is so pale she's practically translucent.

"Totally fine," she says, taking a sip of her soda. "I thought I was going to pee my pants."

"Are you sure?" I ask. "Because I thought I heard you—"

"Throw up?" she interrupts. Then she leans closer and whispers, "There was another girl in there hurling her brains out. Maybe she's bulimic or something."

I glance at the door, wanting to believe my new friend, hoping some super-skinny girl with the telltale round face will walk out looking guilty. Except that I don't believe Audrey, not at all. The story was fine—good, even—but when she leaned in to whisper, her breath gave her away.

Vomit.

When we get back to school, a tall blond guy halfway across the commons approaches us, eyeing Audrey. The way he looks at her is nothing like one typical teen checking out another: He looks sad. Maybe even more than sad. Wrecked. The guy stops in front of us and opens his mouth to say something to her. The pain in his eyes makes me want to listen, but Audrey grabs my arm and pulls me around him and quickens her pace. Kids all around us watch the silent scene with funny looks on their faces as we work our way through the post-lunch crowd.

"What was that all about?" I ask quietly when we've made it to the hallway where our lockers are.

"Just an old boyfriend," she says.

"Wow, he's gorgeous."

Audrey's quiet for a second. Then she says, "He used to be."

The bell rings, so I don't get the chance to ask what she means.

On the way home from school, Audrey asks me to go to a movie tonight, which I take as a return to normal after a confusing afternoon. But then I walk into my house, throw down my bag, and head downstairs to say hi to Mason. And he screws things up again.

"We're going to Kansas City this weekend," he says, barely looking up from what he's working on.

"I know," I say. "You told me this morning. Are you getting Alzheimer's?" I smile at my own joke, but Mason ignores it. He seems stressed. He meets my gaze.

"I told you that Cassie and I are leaving tomorrow, not that you're going with us."

"Noooooo!" I protest. "You're going to test Wade!"

Wade Zimmerman, formerly Wade Sergeant, is hands-down the most annoying of the bus kids. He's only a year older than me, but he tries to act like he's an adult. He has this condescending way of talking. But what bugs me the most about Wade is that he won't acknowledge our shared past. In fact, he won't talk to me about the program at all. It's totally weird.

"Wade is a nice young man," Mason says, shaking his head at me and writing something down. Cassie sneezes and I jump because I hadn't even registered that she was in the room.

"Wade's obnoxious," I say, ignoring Cassie's sniffles. "And you always let me decide whether I want to go with you to do the tests. Why are you making my decision for me this time?"

Mason sighs. "I don't know," he says. "Something's bothering me, and I can't put my finger on it. Call it instinct or paranoia. I'd like to keep you close this weekend."

Apparently, Mason is one of God's favorite Disciples because of Mason's (borderline eerie) sixth sense about things. Knowing Mason is worried about something makes the hair on my arms stand up.

"Can I at least go to the movie with Audrey tonight?" I ask.

Pause.

"Yes," Mason says, but the frown on his face tells me that he'd rather I didn't.

I go anyway, so the detour from Normalville continues.

Mason claims he was already planning to go out for groceries, so he insists on dropping me off at Audrey's instead of letting her pick me up at home. In the car on the way over, he warns me, again, about getting too close to my new friend.

"Daisy, I don't want you to think that I'm against you having friends," he says slowly. "But I do want to remind you what's at stake here."

"And I want to remind you that I've been in the program almost as long as you have," I retort. "I get it."

"I know," Mason says. "It's just that you haven't actually been around that many people who aren't bus kids or agents. I want you to keep your head on straight."

"It's on as straight as it can be," I say.

"I guess that's all I can ask of you."

The way Mason checks the rearview mirror when we stop makes me afraid for a moment, but I brush it off and hop out of the car. I wave goodbye to him, but instead of leaving, he just sits there in the idling car as I ring the bell and wait for someone to answer. I hear footsteps running to the door on the other side. Audrey flings it open with a big smile on her face. Finally, Mason drives away.

"Hi!" Audrey says. "You're late!"

"It's Mas—my dad's fault," I lie. Honestly, I was having a clothing dilemma: broken-in sweatshirt, old jeans, and sneakers for maximum relaxation, or cuter—and less comfortable—straight-leg jeans, embellished T-shirt, and flats, just in case...

"Matt's coming," Audrey blurts out. "I thought I'd let you know so you don't have to blush like..." She pauses to examine my face. "Well, like that in front of him."

"I don't know what you're talking about," I say self-consciously.

"Shut it," Audrey teases. "I know you like him."

"Do not."

"Then why are you blushing?"

"I'm not blushing."

"Um, yes you are. But no worries. Matt won't notice."

Audrey yells upstairs for Matt to meet us in the car, then pushes past me. I follow her to the driveway. Once we're inside the car but before Matt joins us, I ask Audrey in a whisper: "Why won't Matt notice me?"

Confused, Audrey stares blankly at me.

"You just said that," I say. "That Matt won't notice me blushing."

"Oh my god, Daisy, don't be so sensitive!" Audrey says. "I didn't mean that he won't notice *you*. I meant that he hardly notices *anything* these days. The other day he asked me where his hat was. He was wearing it."

"Maybe he has something on his mind," I offer, hoping Audrey will elaborate.

Audrey rolls her eyes. "Don't we all," she says. I want to ask what's on *her* mind, and about a zillion other questions, but Matt opens the door and climbs in the backseat.

"Hey," he says when I turn around to look at him. He looks like a model for Levi's in his perfectly faded jeans and maroon-and-gray-striped hoodie.

"Hi, Matt," I say back. "I like your sweatshirt."

"Thanks," he says, smiling a little. "Cool shirt."

Audrey stifles a laugh and puts the car in reverse.

"Yes, we all look awesome," she says. "Now let's go. We're going to miss the previews."

I face front in the passenger seat, take a deep breath, and smile to myself. Glancing down at my shirt, I can't help but give myself props for choosing to wear the cuter outfit. Even if the top button on my jeans *is* digging into my stomach.

The movie is a comedy, but I don't laugh much. Instead, I listen to Matt. He only reacts to the smart jokes, not the stupid ones that everyone else seems to find hilarious. But when something strikes him as funny, it's really hard for me not to smile. His laughter starts low and gets higher the longer it lasts. It's easy and warm, like his mom's chocolate-chip cookies, and it makes me want to snuggle up to him. It's the perfect sound.

In contrast, Audrey's breath sounds strangely labored. I wonder whether she's got the flu or something, with the barfing at lunch and everything.

"Do you feel okay?" I whisper in Audrey's ear.

"Shh," she says. "I'm watching the movie."

I look over at Matt and he's looking at me, and I'm zapped by a jolt of electricity. I conjure up my flirtiest smile, then sit back and resume my popcorn-tub war with Audrey.

After the show we head to the food court because somehow half of the world's largest container of popcorn simply wasn't enough for Audrey. Matt and I find a place to sit while Audrey buys pretzel bites. We awkwardly look anywhere but at each other until I can't take it anymore.

"Do you like Mr. Jefferson?" I ask.

"Yeah, he's okay," he says. "You?"

"He seems pretty cool."

Pause.

"I didn't tell Audrey that you took her phone," I say, instantly feeling silly for bringing it up. I doubt he even remembers.

Except that he does.

"I know."

Matt smiles, mostly with his eyes. Someone at the next table over squeals and, curiously, he turns to see what's happening. I take the opportunity to examine his profile. His skin is still tanned from summer and is perfectly even except for a tiny scar on his chin and a pen-dot mole near his jawbone. Matt's neutral expression is borderline dark, but when he looks back at me and smiles again, this time showing off his straight, white teeth, it's impossible not to feel it. I force myself to look away so I don't say something stupid, like, *You're gorgeous.*

"Thanks for not telling her, though," Matt says, about the iPhone.

"Of course," I say. I notice that I'm bouncing my knee under the table, which is something I do only when I'm extremely nervous. "I wonder what's taking Audrey so long," I say. Matt shrugs and taps his fingers lightly on the table.

The longer I'm alone with him, the more excitable I get. I pick up a napkin that someone left on the table and start twisting it for something to do with my hands. Then, thankfully, before I origami a crane out of a recycled napkin, Audrey returns.

For one second, at least.

"Crap!" she says as she sits down. "I forgot to fill my soda." She picks up and waves an empty cup. I notice a little sweat on her forehead even though it's cool in the mall.

"I'll do it," I say, standing quickly. I feel like Matt's the sun and I need sunglasses: I'm overwhelmed by him and need a moment to calm down. "You eat," I say to Audrey. "What flavor do you want?"

"Clear," she says before popping a pretzel bite into her mouth.

"Got it," I say. I turn and walk back to the fountain-beverage station by the pretzel place and fill Audrey's paper cup with whatever brand of clear soda they have. I take a deep breath and shake my head at my girlishness as I grab a lid and snap it on, then shove a straw through it. I walk back to the table feeling surprisingly more centered.

"Do I get a tip for that?" I ask Audrey when I'm about five steps away from her.

"You wish!" she says, laughing loudly.

"Fine, then I'll take it back," I say, pretending to turn around.

"Give me my drink!" Audrey shouts playfully. Her voice echoes off the walls, up to the skylight. People all over the food court look up from their greasy snacks. An older lady tsks at the scene we're making; two young girls giggle to themselves.

And that's when I see her.

Across the food court, Nora Fitzgerald from Frozen Hills is turning in her chair to see what's going on.

Like a deer who spies a hunter, I bolt. Only when I round the corner of the main part of the mall and duck into one of those side hallways that lead to the creepy walkway behind the stores do I realize that I'm still holding Audrey's drink. When I'm sure that no one's followed me, I set it down on the floor and text Audrey.

Daisy: SORRY! But I can explain. Meet me around the corner by Foot Find.

I hit send and wait. Audrey and Matt arrive in minutes.

"You could have just asked for some of my soda, Dais," Audrey jokes. She picks it up and starts drinking it. "What's the deal?"

Matt's standing between me and the main walkway. Instinctively, I stay directly behind him, like he's my shield. He looks at me funny.

"You look like you saw a ghost," he says.

More like Nora did, I think to myself.

"I saw a girl from my old school who...uh...hates me," I say. "Can we just go?"

Matt shrugs and Audrey nods. We make our way toward the movie theater's parking lot, Audrey chattering about mean girls, me looking over my shoulder for Nora, and Matt eyeing me like he knows I'm lying and wants to ask about the truth.

Thankfully, I catch a break: Matt doesn't ask.

ten

ten

ten

"It's only a long weekend," Mason says, glancing at me in the rearview mirror as we barrel down Interstate 29 in the dark.

"I know," I say glumly. "But we weren't supposed to leave until tomorrow. And wait—what do you mean by long weekend?"

"I thought I told you that we're staying until Monday night," Mason says. "To ensure enough time for Wade's test. We called the school and got you excused from Monday's classes."

"No, you didn't tell me that," I mutter, turning backward in my seat and watching the lights of Omaha fade into the distance. I already regret telling Cassie and Mason about Nora because it gave them a reason to leave town tonight. Now I'm even more annoyed because I won't get to see Audrey or Matt on Monday. "I'm not supposed to be on this trip."

"You weren't supposed to be seen," Cassie says without looking up from her computer. I'm surprised by her tone; she's not usually so snappy. The worst part is that she's right.

"Why was Nora even in Omaha?" I mutter.

"We checked her email," Cassie says. "She's staying with relatives. Something about a family reunion this weekend."

"Random," I say, shaking my head. "What's going to happen with her?"

"Depends on quite a few variables," Mason says, scratching his head.

"Like?" I look at him expectantly.

"Like whether or not she saw you. And if she did, whether she wrote it off as coincidence or actually believes you're alive."

"And?"

"And it depends on what she does with the information."

"If she goes public—" I begin.

Cassie interrupts. "Then our thirty-year research study is over."

"But hasn't this happened before?" I protest.

"To my knowledge, it's only happened one other time," Cassie says.

79

"Twice," Mason corrects. "There was that one in Missouri."

"I meant that one. What was the other?"

"Florida."

"Oh, right," Cassie says before refocusing on her computer. It bugs me that she's talking like she was part of the program back then. Recruited straight from college after the program had already started, Cassie's younger than the other agents. At first she was assigned to the main lab, but her boss thought she'd be better in the field. So when Sydney left, Cassie was reassigned to us. But sometimes Cassie talks like she was with the Revive project from day one.

"I believe that the protocol is watch and wait," Cassie continues. "A team is monitoring Nora now. If she forgets it and moves on, then we will, too."

"And what if she doesn't?" I ask.

"Who knows what he'll do at this point?" Mason mutters. Cassie shoots him a surprised look, which softens his tone.

"Whatever happens, we'll deal with it," he says in a way that makes me feel like he's talking to himself more than to me or Cassie.

"If Nora pursues this, will we have to move again?" I ask.

"Probably," Mason says honestly.

And only right then, when the sick feeling creeps into my stomach, do I realize that I haven't been faking it. I want to live in Omaha permanently. I genuinely like Audrey; my feelings for Matt are real. Only when I'm faced with the possibility of another move do I realize how much I want to dig in my heels. Only then do I realize just how much I want to stay.

It's after one AM when I begin to boot up my snail of a computer. I can't very well take sleek spy technology to school, so, unlike the computers that Mason and Cassie get to use, I have a few-years-old laptop that's as heavy as a boulder and as loud as an airplane on takeoff.

Our small, independent hotel has a weak Internet signal, so between that and my grandma's microprocessor it takes forever to get online. After it connects, I log in using my password, which Mason makes me change every month. When my IM program pops up, I check for Audrey's username—QueenMcKean—to see whether she's online. There's no little green dot; she's not.

I sigh and switch over to my email account. I open a new message and begin typing *Audrey* so her address autofills.

To: almckean@smail.com
Subject: random night
Hey Aud,
How's this for weird: I'm writing from a hotel room in Kansas City. My parents were planning to come for the weekend and leave me alone in Omaha but, at the

last minute, changed their minds. They must have watched a movie about a teenager who throws a party the second her parents leave for vacation and rethought their decision. Not that I'm like that.

Hey, sorry again for that thing with that girl tonight. You seemed sort of out of it on the way home: are you mad at me for something? I mean I know I made us leave early but I didn't think it was that big of a deal. But if I did something, I'm sorry.

Anyway, thanks for the fun night and tell Matt the same. And okay, fine, I guess hiding behind my computer screen I can admit that I do sort of like him. A little. Hope that doesn't make you want to upchuck. But you said my dad was hot so I guess now we're even.

Daisy

I hit send and watch the email move from my outbox to the ether. Then I scoot off the bed, retrieve pajamas and toiletries from my bag, and walk to the bathroom to get ready to go to sleep. When I return, despite it being the middle of the night, I'm disappointed to find that there's no reply. Audrey's emailed me later than this, and now I can't help but wonder whether she really is mad at me for some reason.

I crawl under the overbleached sheets, wired on soda and adrenaline, confused.

*　　*　　*

After only three hours of real sleep—which feels more like three minutes—my wakeup call sounds and I want to throw the phone out the window. Instead I roll over, pick up the receiver, and then slam it down again without answering. Then I go back to sleep. Ten minutes later, there's a knock at the door. The interior one, of course.

"Daisy, are you up?" Mason's muffled voice calls through the wall.

"Yes," I groan, exhausted.

"Doesn't sound like it," Mason calls back.

"I am!" I shout back. Mason doesn't answer.

Annoyed at the daylight, I throw off the covers and climb out of bed, tripping over the laptop cord on my way to the bathroom. I land with a thud on the hideous carpet and lie there, wondering what else could go wrong. Eventually I manage to shower and get ready, which makes me feel a little better, until I remember where we're going today.

To Wade's house.

The Zimmermans have upgraded to an even bigger house—for three people—since the last time I was forced to come to Kansas City, so the neighborhood we're driving through now is new to me. Compared to the McKeans' development, this one is a poseur. The massive houses are set back from the street, and there are kids out playing on the sidewalks. The difference is that here, the homes are new, matching, and only pretend to have character. I realize that there aren't individual mailboxes in front of the homes when I see a postal worker pull up next to a large metal community box with a locked section for each family. Something about not having your own mailbox bothers me.

As if reading my mind, Megan texts.

Megan: Where are you?

Daisy: KC.

Megan: NO!!

Daisy: Yes. Mason made me.

Megan: So sorry, girl. I know how you loathe Wade. Hang tough, okay? I'll do an extra great post in your honor tonight. I'm thinking a backstage pass to my closet. You like?

Daisy: Sounds FABULOUS.

Megan: xoxo

Daisy: Same to you

Right then, we pull into the driveway of a house I can only describe as a non-pink, walled version of Barbie's dream house, complete with a Porsche out front. The license plate reads KCHS FP.

KCHS...Kansas City High School?

"Is that *Wade's* car?" I ask loudly.

"Must be," Mason says. "There's a student parking sticker on the front window." Of course Mr. Observant noticed that.

I groan.

"Be nice," Mason says quietly as we walk to the front porch and ring the bell.

"Always."

Taller than Mason, and with a square head, jaw, and shoulders, Wade Zimmerman is a big block of a guy. He has decent skin, cropped hair, and white teeth that are mostly straight. His nose is a touch crooked, which would add to his appeal if he didn't love to tell the story of how he broke it getting bucked off a mechanical bull...well after eight seconds, of course. Girls who like chauvinistic pigs—or maybe even grown women who like young guys—might find Wade attractive. I, on the other hand, do not.

My crap radar goes off the second we walk in the door. Wade is wearing—I am totally not kidding—a sweater-vest. Not a sexy J.Crew sweater-vest; an old-man politician sweater-vest.

"Lovely to see you again, Daisy," Wade says as he offers his hand to me to shake. I fight the urge to roll my eyes or pretend to be British when I answer.

"Good to see you, too," I mutter.

"How are you enjoying your new school?" he asks. Why does he have to talk like he's forty-seven?

"It's fine," I say. "What's with the Porsche?"

"Oh, you like it?" Wade asks. "It was a birthday gift from my parents." Shrugging, he adds, "It gets me to and from practice."

"Funny," I say, not thinking so at all. Instead of pointing out that he's the cockiest guy I know, I ask about his license plate: "What's FP?"

Wade chuckles loudly—literally, it sounds like "Ha, ha, ha, ha!" because I guess he's not even himself when he laughs—then explains the hilarity.

"It means Franchise Player," he says. "It's the nickname the other players have given me for my skills as a quarterback. It simply means that I'm a valued member of the team. It's all in jest."

In jest?

Wade tries to appear embarrassed, but there's nothing remotely flustered about his expression. All that reads there is pride.

Overconfidence.

"Cool," I say, not really thinking so, but trying to be nice because Mason asked me to.

After a few more pleasantries, scones, and one too many stories about scouts coming to see Wade play, I'm shown into the Zimmermans' first-floor office to mess around online while Mason and Cassie go to work. I log on and check my email: no reply from Audrey. Trying not to obsess too much about it, I switch over to *Anything Autopsy* and blog about sensible versus nonsensical cars for teens, then do a "she said" reply to Megan's diatribe about the newest YouTube pop sensation. Just as I'm hitting publish, Mason puts a hand on my shoulder.

"Ah!" I shout, jumping out of the chair. Mason steps back and raises his palms.

"Sorry, thought you heard me," he says, holding back a laugh.

"You're like a ninja; how would I have heard you?"

This makes Mason laugh for real, and I find it's impossible to keep a straight face. His unfiltered happiness is a rare treat, like when comedians laugh themselves out of character while performing sketch comedy. It doesn't happen all that often, but when it does, it's contagious.

"I wanted to make sure you're okay down here," he says after we've composed ourselves, waving a hand at the computer setup.

"I'm fine," I say, sitting down.

"Okay, good. Because we're ready to start now and won't be taking a break for three hours," Mason replies.

"Great," I say.

Mason turns to leave.

"Hey, Mason?" I say. He turns around and looks at me expectantly. "I think I'm getting attached to Omaha." Admitting it feels good, like a weight off my shoulders. I feel even better when Mason responds.

"Daisy, you're an adaptable young woman, and that's a

great asset for the program," he says. "But if you didn't start getting attached to places or people at some point, I'd be worried. Honestly, hearing you say that is a relief."

"Let's hope we don't have to move again."

"I'll do everything in my power to see that we don't."

I smile and Mason leaves, and I sit at Wade's computer wondering about what Mason said. I appreciate the sentiment, but I'm not sure it will do any good. I've heard that God likes Mason, but ultimately, God is the one in control.

If God says we move, there's nothing Mason can do about it.

If God says we move, we move.

eleven

eleven

eleven

At dinner, the adults encourage Wade and me to hang out together tonight. I can see through Wade's forced smile and gritted teeth that he's as thrilled about the idea as I am. When Mr. and Mrs. Zimmerman stand to clear plates and get dessert, Wade starts texting under the table and Mason leans over and whispers in my ear.

"I really think you should do this," he says.

"I wanted to watch a movie at the hotel," I protest. "And you know how I feel about..." I jerk my thumb in Wade's direction so he doesn't perk up at the sound of his own name.

"That's the point," Mason says. "Maybe you just need

to get to know each other better. I think it's important that you have friends, and at least Wade understands your past. You can talk about it with him."

Mason looks at me pointedly, reminding me that I can't talk about the program with Audrey or Matt.

"Except that he's in denial," I mutter.

"It'll be fun," Mason whispers before straightening up, signaling the end of the conversation. Mrs. Zimmerman returns carrying a coffeepot and Mr. Zimmerman trails behind with pie.

"Who likes blueberry?" Mrs. Zimmerman asks. Normally it's my favorite, but right now, facing a night with Wade, and with Audrey and Matt back in Omaha, where I want to be, not even blueberry pie can make me happy.

An hour later, I'm riding shotgun in a car no teenager should own, listening to some weird rap-country hybrid on full blast, wishing upon wishing that I was a better debater when it comes to Mason. When there's a break in the noise, I reach over and turn down the radio dial. Wade looks at me like I just slapped him, but he doesn't turn it back up.

"So what are we doing tonight?" I ask.

"I thought we'd chill with my boys and my girl at The Field, and then hit up a party later."

I bite my tongue to keep from laughing at the personality one-eighty. Wade would make a great Disciple someday, if he weren't so ashamed of the program. Then again, I haven't talked to him about it in a while. I decide to try again.

"So, how's the test going?" I begin.

"Fine," Wade says. "You know. . . ."

"Yeah," I say. "How far did you get today?"

"Just through the physical," Wade answers. His tone is not necessarily encouraging, but it's not dismissive, either. I decide to dive in with one of the biggies.

"So, Wade, how much do you remember about the day of the bus crash?"

Wade's head snaps in my direction and he stares at me for so long that I'm afraid he's going to crash the Porsche. Finally he looks away.

"Nothing," he says flatly before turning the music back up. He ignores me for the rest of the drive.

As it turns out, The Field isn't some hipster hangout downtown — a play on "playing the field" — nor is it a great wide expanse of landscape. It's a soccer field.

And it's lame.

We're sitting with Wade's girlfriend, Brittney, and his friends Colin and Nate on the top two benches of movable bleachers flanking a community play space. In thin jeans and a short-sleeved T-shirt, I'm warm even though the sun's almost down.

"How do you know my boyfriend again?" Brittney

asks defensively before sipping something that makes her shudder.

"Our dads are friends," Wade answers quickly. He catches my eye and smiles, but underneath I can see a warning: *Don't go there.*

"Oh, right," Brittney says, tossing her satiny dark hair off her shoulder, hitting me in the face with it in the process.

Wade and Colin sit in front of Brittney and me. Nate, a little too broody for my taste, is sitting four rows down and to the side, by himself.

Colin turns to look at me and smiles. Muscular, blond, and blue-eyed, he's nice-looking, but nothing close to Matt. Colin's the guy next door you can't believe lives in your town; Matt's the one so striking you can't believe he lives on your planet.

The obvious way that Colin flirts with me grosses me out a little.

"I almost didn't come out tonight," he says in a low voice that tries too hard. I look over and realize that Brittney and Wade are actually making out. Right next to us. I turn away quickly. "But I'm glad I did," Colin continues, looking me up and down. "It's good to meet you."

"Thanks," I say as I inch away from him. I try to look at anything other than the PDA to my right, so I watch Colin take a swig from his cup. I don't even like the way he drinks.

Finally, Brittney and Wade come up for air, and though I'm happy that I don't have to listen to any more smacking, sloppy kisses, the silence is uncomfortable. And frankly, the night is boring so far.

I consider the blood-red contents of my cup. Mason would call it a cup full of brain damage, but being with Wade and his friends might be doing me more harm than the booze. And Mason's the one who forced me to come anyway. Shrugging, I down it all in one drink.

"More?" Brittney asks, seeming to like me a little better now. She holds up a thermos and shakes it a little.

"Sure," I say. "Hit me."

Who knows how long later, I wake up on foul-smelling carpet in a dark, red-lit room with walls that are oozing bass. I have no idea where I am, and for the first few minutes, I don't care. I don't care about anything other than how I feel right now. And how I feel is bad.

Gutter bad.

I'm freezing and sweating at the same time. If I could move my limbs, I would cover myself with a blanket. I would cut off my head, it hurts so badly. I would curl up into a ball and die, assuming I haven't already. I pinch the skin on my bare arm to make sure that I'm alive.

Then, in flashes, it all starts coming back.

Running around the soccer field with Brittney.

Doing a keg stand on a dare from Nate.

Singing Karaoke—"No Air," no less—with Colin.

Cornering Wade on the dance floor to confront him about the program.

"Why won't you talk about it?" I slurred. He wiped his face before walking away, and I'm mortified to realize now that I must have spit on him.

I groan from my place on someone else's floor. I lick my teeth and they feel furry, coated in sugar and alcohol and something else—maybe hot dogs. I smell puke nearby but don't want to move to see where it is. Just then, the bass gets really loud, like someone opened the door.

"I think it's in here," a guy's voice says. "Hang on."

Footsteps crunch on the carpet as the guy navigates the tiny room. I hold my breath because I don't know if I'm supposed to be in here. The boy steps so close to my right hand that my fingers touch his treads. He gasps when he sees me.

"Holy shit! You scared me!" he says.

"Sorry," I mutter. My mouth is dry as dust.

"What are you doing down there?"

"Resting," I say.

"How long have you been in here?"

I shrug.

"Uh...okay. Well, stay as long as you like," the guy says, inching his way back toward the door. "Or do you want me to call someone?"

"That's okay," I say. "I already called my friend Audrey."

I did? I don't remember talking to her.

"Oh, good," the guy says, backing away carefully so as not to step on my listless body. "I'll have the doorman watch out for your friend. I'll tell him to tell her where you are."

I don't answer because my eyes are closed.

Three minutes or three hours later, someone jostles me. I want to protest and roll into a ball and kick them away for disturbing my coma, but my mouth doesn't work. My body doesn't work. So, without any say in the matter, I'm carried into the night, tucked into a car, and driven far, far away.

twelve

twelve

twelve

"Daisy? Are you awake?" Mason calls from across the food court at the mall. He's sitting at a table with Cassie and Nora Fitzgerald, and they're all staring at me. He knocks twice on the table, like he's rapping out some kind of code. He knocks a third time, then looks at me expectantly like I'm supposed to know what he's saying.

"Daisy?" he calls again.

Confused, I look across the table. Matt is there.

"Hey," he whispers. "Answer him."

And then a firm hand on my shoulder pulls me from the dream.

I open my eyes to a startling but welcome sight: Matt

is lying on his side, facing me, in real life. I suck in my breath at the sight of him.

"Answer your dad," he whispers calmly. I furrow my eyebrows.

"Answer him or he'll want to come in," Matt explains.

Getting it, I try to call back, but nothing comes out. I clear my throat, which reminds me of Mr. Jefferson. I wonder if his issue is that he drinks. Finally, I manage to find my voice.

"I'm awake," I say loudly, cringing.

I stare into Matt's dark eyes; he stares into mine. I'd ask what he's doing here if words didn't hurt.

"Good," Mason calls back through the wall. "Cassie and I are going to get some eggs at the hotel restaurant before heading to the Zimmermans'. We need to be there at eight. Are you coming?"

I wonder for a moment if Matt thinks it's weird that my dad would call my mom "Cassie" instead of "your mother," but he doesn't seem to notice. Then my stomach sloshes in a very bad way and I quit wondering.

"Ask if you can stay here today," Matt whispers. I nod.

Concerned about dragon breath, I turn my head away from Matt when I speak.

"Would it be okay if I hung around here today?" I ask the wall. There's silence on the other side of the door. "I want to catch up on some reading," I add, trying to sound normal but feeling anything but. Mason doesn't answer for a bit, as if he's considering what I've asked. Finally, he says:

"Stay inside the hotel."

"Okay," I call out. "Thanks."

My stomach lurches again and I curl into the fetal position.

"Are you going to be sick again?" Matt whispers.

"I don't know," I whisper back.

"We'll be back at seven," Mason says through the wall. "We'll eat together."

Wishing Mason would stop talking about food, I gather all my strength to answer, "Okay, sounds good." My stomach lurches again.

"Want to go to the bathroom?" Matt says quietly.

"I don't want to move," I whisper. Matt smiles weakly and brushes a piece of hair off my forehead.

"Then don't."

I gasp awake, heart pounding, eyes wide. Matt's still here, next to me on the bed. He's on his back now, staring up at the ceiling. I watch as he turns toward me, concerned.

"Bad dream?" he asks.

"I don't know," I say, because whatever ripped me from slumber is already out of reach. Without moving to know for sure, I can tell that my body is on the mend. I smack my lips and deeply inhale and exhale.

"So . . . I called you last night?" I say.

Matt rolls to his side again, facing me, smirking. "You drunk texted me."

"What did it say?" I ask self-consciously.

"Something like 'save me from frat boys,'" Matt says. I see a flicker of annoyance in his eyes. Jealousy?

"What else?"

"I called you when I got the text and you said you went out with a gay guy named Wade and—"

"I said Wade was gay?" I interrupt, frowning.

"Well, you kept saying over and over that he needs to come out of the closet," Matt replies.

I laugh in a quick exhale. "I think I meant that about something else.... Anyway, keep going."

"Okay, so you gave me this totally cryptic description of where you were," Matt says. "You said you were at Freckler with the moose."

"What does that even mean?" I ask, embarrassed about my weird language and about getting drunk in the first place. It's not me.

"Eventually, I figured out that you meant *Specter* Hall," he explains. "They have holiday reindeer on their lawn, all lit up and everything. One is really huge and could be mistaken for a moose."

"It's September," I say.

"Yes, it is," Matt says back. "Anyway, that made it easier."

"I'm so sorry."

"No worries—it was sort of fun," Matt says. "I pretended I was on one of those reality challenges...like I only had three hours to get to you or I'd lose out on a million dollars."

"Did you win?" I ask.

"No," he admits. "But only by fifteen minutes."

"I wonder what kind of trouble I was getting in while you were driving from Omaha," I say.

"I think you were okay," Matt says. "I talked to you a couple of times on the way. You were in that red room alone most of the time, except when you were in the bathroom, puking."

Half-embarrassed, half-flattered that he took care of me, I keep quiet.

"You're lucky your parents got you your own room," Matt says.

"Yeah," I agree weakly.

"Otherwise, you'd be in it for sure," he continues. "That was pretty dumb of you, you know. Getting lit with strange guys in a strange city. You could have been..."

"I know," I say quietly.

"Or, hell, even—"

"I know!" I say louder. "Shut up already!"

Matt looks at me, surprised, and we both can't help but laugh a little. Then we grow quiet, staring at each other.

"Anyway, thank you," I say.

"No problem," Matt says. "But you should really be thanking me for washing barf out of your hair."

My eyes widen before I pull the covers over my head and hide. I hear Matt laugh before he pokes me in the arm.

"I'm ordering food. What sounds good?"

"A cheeseburger," I say quickly.

From my cocoon, I hear Matt call and order two cheeseburgers with fries and sodas.

"You ordered me regular instead of diet," I say after he hangs up.

"So?" he asks. "I know that's what you drink."

"How can you be so sure?"

"That's what you ordered at the movie."

My stomach twists into a knot at the simple fact that Matt is paying attention. He yanks the covers off my face.

"You should probably shower," he says. "It'll make you feel better."

His face is only inches from mine when he says it, which makes my stomach twist even tighter. We hold each other's gaze for a moment, then a cleaning person knocks on the door and startles me out of la-la land. I walk on shaky legs to the door and tell her I'm all set with towels, then go to the bathroom to shower, feeling like I'm going to burst the whole time. Despite waking up feeling like hell, the day is turning out okay. Not only did I get out of hanging out with Wade, but Matt is here.

I can't deny how much I like him. And if late-night reconnaissance missions and soda orders from memory are any indication, he might like me, too.

*　　*　　*

By one in the afternoon, I'm clean, fed, and almost human again. Matt starts a movie and we both sit back against the headboard to watch. I hug a pillow to my torso and try to pay attention during the first five, then ten, then fifteen minutes. But something is gnawing at me.

"Why hasn't Audrey called?" I ask, my eyes still on the TV.

"Shh," Matt says, waving a hand at me. I'm quiet for five more minutes, all the while wondering if I've royally screwed up my friendship with Audrey. But I can't for the life of me figure out how.

"Seriously, Matt, is she mad at me or something?"

"No," he replies without looking in my direction.

"How do you know?" I ask.

"I just know."

I try to focus on the characters in the movie, but my thoughts turn to Friday night at the mall. It was only two days ago, but it feels like a lifetime. I think of the ride home, and of Audrey's distractedness. If she's not mad at me, then what could it be?

Then I remember Friday's barfing taco incident, and the fact that she lied about it. And her raspy breath at the movie. Her sweaty forehead afterward.

"Is something wrong with Audrey?" I ask, grasping. Matt's face snaps toward mine.

"What do you mean?" he asks, more confrontational

than questioning. His defensiveness tells me that I've hit on something.

"It's just that her voice always seems raspy and she gets tired easily and Friday, after the movie, she looked super out of it and..." My voice trails off. It sounds silly when I say it aloud. Except Matt is staring at me as if I just ran over his dog.

"What's wrong?" I ask softly. Without thinking too much about it, I reach out and touch my fingertips to his. I'm surprised by my confidence, but I don't move my fingers from his. Matt turns his head away, but he doesn't move his fingers, either.

"I'm not supposed to tell you," he says flatly.

"Tell me what?" I ask, annoyed. "It's so lame when people keep secrets. I—"

And then he says it.

"Audrey has cancer."

thirteen

thirteen

thirteen

At three o'clock, there's a note waiting under Mason's door at the hotel in Kansas City, and Matt and I are more than halfway to Omaha.

We haven't spoken for miles, but it's a comfortable silence, not the kind when you're scrambling for something to say. I can't explain how it happened, but sometime between waking up with him in my bed and riding next to him now, my nervousness with Matt has faded. It's not quite automatic, like it is with Audrey or Megan, but when Matt and I talk, it's easier. And when we don't talk, it's easier then, too. Even though my chest feels full, my knee is still and my breathing is steady. Despite the heavy thoughts in my head, Matt's presence is making me calm.

The particular stretch of road we're on has a funny tread: The sound of the tires against the pavement makes me think of a zipper quickly going up and down, over and over. The strange rhythm lulls me into a zoned-out state where all I can do is listen to my internal dialogue.

Audrey's dying.

She's really dying.

I ran off without telling Mason.

I want to help Audrey.

There's nothing I can do about Audrey.

Wow . . . it all makes sense. The hurling. Her mom letting her do everything she wants. The sad looks at school.

Is it terminal?

It has to be terminal. Yes, Matt's face says it is.

I'm going to get in trouble.

Getting in trouble is insignificant compared to what Audrey's going through.

I've never been in trouble.

Stop acting like a child. Audrey's DYING!

Yes, but . . .

Wow. I have a warped view of death.

And finally:

I want to tell Matt about Revive.

The last thought startles me. I gasp, but the sound of the road blocks it from Matt's ears. Never in my life have I dared to consider telling anyone about the program, and yet it would be so easy to open my mouth and let it out right now. I could tell him that I'm not exactly normal when it comes to thoughts on death. I could explain that being part of a program that makes death optional is sort of like wearing a protective suit through life. That it gives me confidence that other kids don't have. Like when I was younger and I took swimming lessons, I didn't bawl on the side of the pool like everyone else did because I wasn't afraid of drowning. Sure, I didn't *want* to drown — I knew what it felt like — but there was no finality about it to me.

Not wanting to die is very different from being paralyzed by the fear of it.

I could tell Matt how conflicted I feel right now, that I can't believe my one non-program friend has cancer. That my instinct is to try to save her, but I know it's futile: Even if Mason agreed to Revive someone outside the program, it doesn't work on gunshot victims or cancer patients. But maybe...

My stomach twists tight at the thought of sharing secrets. My mouth dries out as I start to ponder the right words. Matt and I are all alone, with miles to go; I obviously like him and I think he likes me. I could do this. My heart begins to race as I seriously consider...

BUMP!

Like it was sent to stop me, the road suddenly mellows

to smooth, fresh pavement, and with the noise gone I can hear my conscience. And what it's saying is that exposing the program is not only wrong — it's stupid, too. I barely know Matt: How can I trust him with something as monumental as this?

I'm embarrassed for even thinking about it.

To distract myself from going there again, I break the silence.

"Tell me what happened," I say gently. "How did Audrey find out about her cancer?"

It's a minute before Matt responds.

"Are you sure you want the details?" he asks.

"I'm sure."

"Okay," he says. I glance at him long enough to watch him thumb his hair out of his eyes and turn the music down to a whisper. Then he shares the story. "Two years ago we were on a weekend trip to Fremont Lakes with our parents. We ate these super-spicy tacos and Audrey got a stomachache. But then she threw up and could barely stand and Mom and Dad freaked out; they thought she might have extreme food poisoning or something.

"Dad rushed her to the hospital, and the doctor looked at her, and it turned out it had nothing to do with tacos. The doctor thought maybe she had a hole in her stomach or intestines or whatever. He wanted to operate immediately to fix it."

I look at Matt and watch as he flexes his sharp jaw

muscles. There are no tears in his dark eyes as he speaks, but there's pain, pure and simple. I reach over and touch his hand to encourage him to go on. He does.

"When Audrey went into surgery, Mom and I went to the hospital to hang out with my dad, and then, when it was over, the doctor asked my parents to follow him to his office. I sat in the waiting room until they came out. When they did, my mom was crying and couldn't stop. It was..." His voice catches; he takes a breath and finishes. "My dad told me that they found tumors in Audrey's stomach and liver."

"Oh my god," I say, covering my mouth.

"I know," he says. "It was insane."

I'm quiet, so Matt continues.

"Then Audrey was in the hospital for five or six days. The first few she was on a ventilator. It was really weird because when she woke up, she couldn't remember where she was or how she got there."

"Sounds like me last night," I joke, instantly regretting making light of the situation. Matt laughs weakly.

"Yeah," he says. "Anyway, she kept falling back to sleep, and then she'd wake up confused again. We kept having to tell her the story over and over. Finally it stayed in her brain. The next time she woke up she remembered, and she just cried. It was horrible."

"I can't even imagine," I say, and it feels flimsy.

"Eventually, she was well enough to get out of the hospital. We went home and she saw a bunch of different doctors, who gave her a bunch of different options." Matt humphs.

"What?" I ask.

"Doctors," he says flatly. "There's no right answer. It's all opinion. And some of their opinions suck."

I think of the only doctor I know: Mason. He went to medical school, but did his residency in a very different way, as part of a covert team under the umbrella of the FDA. Shaking off thoughts of Mason, I ask about the only way I know to treat cancer: "Chemo?"

"No. I guess it doesn't work on what she has," Matt says. "Basically her treatment is giving her some experimental drug, waiting and watching. It's bullshit."

It reminds me of the program's stance on Nora. It feels weak.

"Isn't there more they can do?" I ask, instantly pissed at Audrey's doctors. "Surgery or something?"

"I guess her liver has too many little tumors to take out," Matt says quietly.

"What about a liver transplant?" I offer.

Matt looks at me with a sad smile. "They don't give healthy livers to cancer patients, Daisy." I feel childish for suggesting it, and I'm glad when Matt's eyes turn back to the road.

"How long did they give her?" I ask.

"Three years," Matt says. "It's been two and a half. She was okay for a while, but now she keeps having pain. She keeps going back to the hospital."

"Is that where she is now?" I whisper.

"Not anymore," Matt says. "But that's why she didn't call you back or whatever. After the movie on Friday, she didn't look so good, so my parents freaked out and took her to the ER. They ran some tests and then sent her home, like usual. But they gave her painkillers, and they knock her out. She's been sleeping all weekend."

I look back to the mile markers and watch them zoom past for a while. Somehow the landscape amplifies my feelings of sadness, anger, and helplessness. Again, I think of Revive; again, I'm reminded of its limitations.

When I was seven, Mason gave me a rabbit to make me feel better for falling out of a tree and breaking my arm. I named the rabbit Ginger and took good care of her. She lived in a very clean cage in my bedroom, and I let her out for hours every day to play indoors, and sometimes outside in our fenced backyard. I don't speak rabbit, but I believe she was happy.

But then Ginger got cancer.

At first, it was a small lump. In the end, her feet barely touched the cage floor because the tumor eating her from the inside out was so huge. She wobbled around like a balloon animal with no legs, which would have been funny if it weren't so sad. And then she died.

I pleaded with Mason to save her.

"Give her the medicine," I cried, facedown into my

bed so that I couldn't see the dead rabbit in the cage near the door. Mason sat next to me, patting my back.

"Shh," he said calmly. "I know you're upset. I know you loved Ginger. But unfortunately, I can't do it, Daisy."

"Why?" I wailed.

"Because it won't work on her," he said softly.

"How do you know? Have you ever tried?" I cried. Mason smoothed my messy hair and sighed.

"Daisy, the rabbit had cancer. Do you know what that means?"

"Yes!"

"Well, we're learning that there are certain limitations to Revive," Mason said, like he was giving a report to his superiors, not comforting his pseudo daughter.

"What does limitations mean?" I asked, still facedown.

"It means that the medicine only works on certain types of bodies."

"People bodies?" I asked.

"Yes, and rat bodies, too, but that's not what I mean," Mason said. "I mean that it only works on bodies that are healthy before they die. Bodies that die suddenly—not from a disease."

"What's a disease?" I asked, rolling over and looking up at Mason. My tears stopped when my inquisitive nature took over. Mason was quiet for a moment, probably trying to decide how to boil it down for a seven-year-old.

"A disease is a really bad sickness that—"

"Like a cold?"

"Shh, let me finish," Mason said, lightly touching my hand. "It's like a cold, but a lot worse, and usually it's not something you can catch from someone else or fix with medicine."

"Am I going to get a disease?" I asked, sitting up straight. "I don't want to die again. It hurts!"

"No," Mason said confidently. "You're not going to get a disease, and you're not going to die again. But Daisy, listen to me. Ginger had cancer. That's a disease. An incurable one, which means it can't be fixed. Hers is the type of body that cannot be saved with the Revive medicine. Understand?"

I looked at the cage near the door, at the motionless rabbit inside, and said nothing.

"Ginger had a nice life, Daisy. Knowing that should make you feel a little better."

"It doesn't," I said honestly.

Mason gave me a weak smile. "Someday it might," he said before leaving my room and taking Ginger the dead rabbit with him.

Matt and I stop at a gas station about thirty miles out. Matt pumps and pays, then says he's going inside for food. From the car, I watch him walk the aisles, scrutinizing the snacks. He holds up a pack of Twizzlers and I shake my head no. He waves some chocolate and I make a face. Finally, he holds up a bag of chips. I give him a thumbs-up and mouth *Coke, too,* but he doesn't get what I'm saying, so I text him. He reads it and we make eye contact and laugh, both of us grabbing on to something meaningless like texting about junk food because the meaningful stuff is too huge.

At around five, we pull back onto the highway. Just as I'm opening the chips, my cell rings. Even though he's not supposed to be finished with Wade for a couple of hours, I know it's Mason calling to check in. I'm not ready to talk right now. I don't want to lie to him about where I am, and if I tell him, he'll try to make me come back.

"You should tell your parents where you are," Matt says, reading my mind.

"They'll find out eventually; I left a note."

"Yeah, but you should tell them you're okay. Parents worry."

"Oh, really?" I ask. "Where do your parents think *you* are right now?"

Matt looks at me, then back at the road. "With you," he says simply. "They trust me."

"How nice for you," I say. I hear Matt laugh a little under his breath. "What, you said, 'Hey, Mom and Dad, I know Audrey's sick and all, but I'm taking off to go save drunk Daisy from a stupid situation.'"

"Something like that," Matt says. He's smiling fully now and, knowing all I do about Audrey and how sad his life is right now, his smile seems precious.

"What exactly did you say to them?" I ask, taking in

his profile. The golden sunset illuminates his features and makes everything else hazy. It's as if I'm seeing him through one of those filter apps that makes your pictures look old-school. I admire his thick black eyelashes and the straight line of his nose. I sit on my left hand to keep from reaching over and touching the scar on his perfect chin.

"I said that you're from a small town and got lost in a big city," Matt answers, pulling me out of my imagination. "I said that you were scared and needed help and I was going to go help you."

"That's it?"

"That's it."

"Weren't they mad that you weren't staying home to be with Audrey?" I ask.

"They get it," Matt says seriously. "There's nothing for me to do but sit and stare at her. That drives her crazy. She told us all to leave her alone."

"I can't believe she didn't tell me that she has cancer," I say. "That's a pretty huge secret to keep from your friends." I'm distinctly aware of the irony of what I'm saying.

Matt glances at me again, warmly.

"It's not like that, Daisy. It's not like some great gossip she didn't want to tell you. It's just that her old friends sort of freaked and stopped hanging out with her when they found out."

"That's so bad," I say.

"I mean, not all at once, but gradually. Everyone was

supportive at first. But then she quit track and some of the clubs she was in and stuff, and she stopped partying. People stopped calling. You *are* Aud's friend. In fact, I think you might be her *only* friend," Matt says.

"She's my only friend, too," I say quietly, thinking to myself that since Megan is more of a sister, it's not a lie. I turn to watch downtown Omaha materialize.

"Hey, what about me?" Matt jokes. "I'm your friend."

I smile but don't look at him. "Oh, right," I tease. "I forgot about you."

fourteen

fourteen

fourteen

It's been two days since I last saw Audrey, and in that time, she's aged. Matt and his parents let me see her alone, and when I walk into her bedroom, I have to fight off tears. Audrey's lying on her back, eyes closed, arms at her sides. Her face looks ghostly, even compared to the white comforter, and I have no clue whether to stay or go. While considering my options, I scan the writing on Audrey's chalkboard wall. There's a new addition; a proverb:

Fall seven times, stand up eight.

I smile sadly; the rest of me is a statue. I look at Audrey's face just before she opens her eyes.

"Hey," I whisper.

"Why the hell are you whispering?" Audrey says loudly with a jovial laugh from the nest in her bed.

"I'm sorry I woke you," I say in my regular voice.

"You didn't," she says. "I wasn't asleep. I was meditating."

"Ah," I say, nodding and wondering if she's joking. I shift from one foot to the other. I can't decide if she's putting on an act for me right now. I decide to cut to the chase.

"So, thanks for telling me you have cancer."

Audrey laughs again. Even though she looks weak, her laugh is normal. I step farther into the room and sit down gingerly at her feet.

"Whoops," she says.

"Whoops?" I ask.

Audrey shrugs. "For not telling you."

"It's okay," I say. "I understand. But don't worry, I'm not scared of you."

"Thanks, Daisy," she says softly.

"Are you feeling okay?" I ask.

"Actually, yeah. I'm feeling a lot better now. The hospital gave me some painkillers and I slept most of yesterday. Good stuff. Of course, even though I'm feeling better, my parents made me promise to stay in bed for another couple of days."

I nod, not sure what to say next.

"I read your email a little while ago," Audrey says.

"Sorry for not getting back sooner. That sucks about your parents dragging you to Kansas City. Oh, but of *course* I wasn't mad at you. How could you think that?"

"I don't know," I say. "I just..." My voice trails off. "Anyway, I'm back."

"I'm glad," Audrey says. "Speaking of which, did my brother pick you up in KC? What's going on?"

I crawl up and sit next to her, leaning against the headboard like I did earlier with Matt.

"We've got a lot to talk about," I say with a broad smile despite the circumstances.

Audrey sits up and gets comfortable, then looks at me excitedly. "Okay, spill."

Finally, when I can't procrastinate any longer, I dial Mason's number. I have a nervous stomach; this must be what normal kids feel like when they break the rules. I hear him pick up and brace for the worst. But the worst doesn't come.

"Are you all right?" he asks, concerned.

Surprised, I'm silent.

"Daisy, are you there?"

I clear my throat. "Yes," I say weakly. I clear it again. "I'm here."

"Are you all right?" Mason asks again.

"I'm fine," I say. "I wanted..." My voice trails off.

"You wanted to see your friend," he answers for me.

"Yes," I say.

"I understand," Mason says. Then, softer, "I wish you would have talked to me about it."

"I know, but you were at Wade's and I just found out and I felt like I needed to be with Audrey right away."

"How did you get there?" Mason asks.

"Audrey's brother, Matt, came and picked me up," I say, rationalizing that it's the truth; I'm just altering the timeline.

"Uh-huh," Mason says, like he's going to ask more about Matt.

"It's really upsetting," I say, bringing it back to Audrey.

"I know, Daisy," Mason says softly. "You let me know if there's anything I can do for you."

"Anything?" I ask.

"Within reason," Mason says hesitantly.

I look around to make sure I'm still alone in the McKeans' kitchen.

"Revive her," I whisper. "When it happens, I mean. Bring her back."

Mason actually laughs into the phone. "You know I can't do that, Daisy," he says. "As much as I'd like to, you know that I can't."

"Yes, you can. When she dies, you stick the needle into her vein. She'll come back," I say, tears threatening to crop up again. "Just like me."

"She's not just like you," Mason says. "When I heard where you'd gone and why, I looked into her medical history. Daisy, her body is broken. Irreparable. I can't give a two-million-dollar treatment to someone it has no chance of working on."

"Is this about money?" I hiss.

"Not entirely," Mason answers in a businesslike manner. Sometimes I wish he wasn't so honest with me. "Things would be different were she in good health to start, but she's not. Add on top the hefty price tag, and you've got two big strikes against doing it. And she's not even in the program!"

"Maybe God would make an exception," I murmur.

"You know God doesn't make exceptions," Mason says quietly. "No one in; no one out."

"That's so...wrong," I protest. "Revive helps people. Shouldn't it be helping more people?"

"Perhaps," Mason says thoughtfully. "But regardless of that, as you well know, the drug doesn't work on cancer patients."

"But when was the last time that theory was tested?" I ask, trying to keep my volume in check. "The lab is always updating the formula. Maybe the newest version will work. It's at least worth a — "

"Daisy?"

I stop talking, but don't answer.

"Daisy, it won't work," he says softly. Mason doesn't

have to finish his sentence; I know what he means. I get a sick feeling in my stomach, so I change the subject.

"When are you coming back?" I ask.

"Will you be okay if we stick to our original plan?" Mason asks. "Returning Monday evening?"

"Yeah," I mutter.

"Would you like me to ask the McKeans if you could stay at their house tonight? So you're not all alone?"

"Sure," I say, with little enthusiasm.

"All right," Mason says. "I'll take care of it. But check in with me tomorrow afternoon, okay?"

"I will," I promise.

"Oh, and Daisy?" Mason says.

"What?" I ask, just wanting to hang up.

"If you ever take off without telling me again, you're going to be grounded for the rest of your life."

fifteen

fifteen

fifteen

I'm glad, then feel guilty for being glad, when Audrey
goes to bed at eight o'clock. I jump in my seat when she
abruptly stands and dramatically bids Matt and me fare-
well, barely one second into the credits for the first movie.
After she leaves, we look at each other quizzically from
opposite ends of the couch.

"Want to go somewhere?" Matt asks, like he's been
waiting all evening. He's in jeans; I have on yoga pants.

"This late?" I ask in protest, even though my stomach
is flipping at the thought of going somewhere — *anywhere* —
with Matt.

"It's not so late, Grandma," he says with a gleam in his
eye. He stands up. "I'll go tell my mom we're going out

for a bit. Get dressed and meet me back down here, unless you want to go outside in your pj's.

"These aren't pj's," I correct him. "They are stylish loungewear."

"Do you want to go out in your stylish loungewear?" he asks.

"Not really," I admit.

Matt heads off to find his mom, and I rush to the guest room—I'm staying in here tonight instead of in Audrey's room, so I won't disturb her—and quickly change into jeans, then throw a light sweater over my red shirt. Then I remove the sweater and the red shirt, and put on a purple T-shirt with ruffle embellishments instead. It's one I borrowed from Audrey that, according to her, "pimps my eyes." I apply lip gloss, let down my hair, put the sweater back on, and meet Matt downstairs.

"Hey," he says.

"Hi," I say back.

"You look good," he says, turning toward the front door.

"Thanks," I say quietly, following him outside into the warm fall evening.

I climb into the passenger seat of his car. It feels and smells familiar, thanks to our ride from Kansas City. Matt starts the engine and plugs in his iPhone—or maybe it's Audrey's—then quickly turns down the dial from full blast to normal. I roll down my window halfway to let the fresh air into my lungs. Matt rolls his down, too.

My favorite song ever begins as Matt pulls away from the curb. A breeze sends a waft of Matt's shampoo my way, and that combined with the fresh scent of the fall air that still wants to be summer makes me want to inhale and hold my breath until I might die if I don't let it out. I look at Matt's profile again and he must feel my gaze because he smiles even though his eyes are still on the road.

The perfectness of the moment makes me think of Audrey and all the moments like this that she won't have.

It makes me mad at Mason, until I realize that it's not his fault.

It's the program's.

"What are you thinking about?" Matt asks.

Once again, I consider breaking my vows and Mason's trust and telling Matt about the Revive program. But then I remember Mason's uneasy feeling; I remember the strange call to Sydney, and the way that God wanted to move up the tests. Something is going on, and telling our secrets definitely won't help the situation.

"Nothing," I say. "I just love this song."

We pull into a public lot and Matt kills the engine.

"It's good that you brought a sweater," he says. "It might get breezy where we're going."

"I came prepared," I say.

"Let's go," Matt says.

Without thinking too much about it, I join hands with

Matt as we set off through the lot, and then across a wide street. There are trees, a path, and water.

"What's that?" I ask, pointing.

"The Missouri River," Matt says. "We're going across."

Deciding to let go of my worries for the time being, I smile as we head toward a walking bridge that spans the river. Even at night, I can see clearly the massive pillars jutting out of the water and high into the sky, with webs of cables stretching down from their tops to support the river walk's weight. From the bridge, I can see both the twinkling lights of downtown Omaha and the bright stars above. It's beautiful.

"Pretty cool, right?" Matt asks.

"Yes!" I say enthusiastically. "Thanks for bringing me here. I've never done anything like this."

"Really?" Matt asks. "There aren't any rivers where you lived before? Where was it again?"

Everywhere, I want to say, but don't.

"Frozen Hills, Michigan."

"Sounds cold."

"It was."

We're still holding hands. I can't help but marvel at the fact that there's nothing remotely strange about it. No sweaty palms. Neither of us holds on too hard or soft: Our hands instinctively know how to be together.

"Hey, thanks again for coming to get me in Kansas City," I say. "That was really cool of you."

Matt shrugs but doesn't answer.

"I'm serious," I say. "I don't know anyone else who would have done that."

"I'm sure that's not true," Matt says.

We walk in silence for a few minutes. A breeze picks up over the water and gives me goose bumps. I want to button my sweater, but I don't want to let go of Matt's hand. Instead, I walk a little closer to him.

"So, were your parents pissed about you leaving Kansas City?" Matt asks.

"No, not really," I say. "My dad got it."

"You never talk about your mom," Matt observes.

"Yes, I do," I say. "What do you want to know?"

"What's her name?"

"Cassie," I say.

"What does she do?"

"She's a professional mom."

"Like mine," Matt says. "That's cool. What about your dad?"

"He's a psychologist," I say, feeling a pinch of guilt in my side for the lie.

"He's a shrink?"

"Sort of," I say.

"Does he always try to figure you out?" Matt asks.

"Sometimes," I say, laughing.

"And that doesn't bug you?" he asks.

I shrug. "Not really. He's all right." I get the sense that

Matt's going to keep asking about my parents, so I abruptly change the subject.

"Hey, did you know that I'm an excellent gymnast?" I drop Matt's hand and move toward the railing.

"Uh, no," Matt says, curious and a bit confused.

"It's true," I say, kicking off one shoe, then the other. "I'm especially great at the balance beam." Before Matt can reply, I'm up on the river-walk railing, crouched at first, then, when I have my balance, standing. I stretch my arms out to the sides and begin walking forward, my toes turned out so I can grip like a monkey.

"What are you *doing*?" Matt shouts. I glance at him without moving my head; he looks genuinely afraid.

"I'm showing you my balance-beam skills, of course," I say, taking two more steps. "Want to see my turn?"

"No!" Matt says harshly. "I want you to get down. You're going to fall."

"No, I'm not," I say without meeting his gaze. "And even if I did, I'd be fine. It's not that far of a fall. I'd just get a little wet. It's not like I'm going to die or anything."

I hear Matt stop. Carefully, I pivot to face him. Matt is not impressed by my skills. In fact, he looks pissed. I think I even see a trace of disgust. I lower myself into a crouch, then jump back to the walkway.

"What?" I ask as I walk back to my shoes and slip my feet into them. Matt shakes his head at me. "What?" I ask again.

"Is this how it is with you?" Matt asks. "Are you always this careless?"

I feel exposed by his words, and silly for showing off. I only wanted to change the subject, to lighten the mood. I didn't think about what it might mean to him. I realize what an idiotic thing it was to do.

"Oh, Matt, I'm sorry," I say. "Here I'm being flip while Audrey is sick. I didn't mean to . . . I'm so sorry." He stares at me, angry. "Do you want to go home?"

More staring, then finally, he speaks: "If you can manage to stay off the railing, I'm good with hanging out here awhile longer, if that's okay with you."

Relief floods through me, but I try to play it off.

"I guess I can handle that," I say, moving to his side as he starts toward the opposite side of the river once again. After a few moments, Matt speaks again, his voice softer this time.

"Sorry I freaked out," he says.

"No, really, I'm sorry. I didn't think of how you might feel with all that's happening with Audrey. I feel like a jerk."

Matt doesn't reply, which makes me feel worse.

"How are you with all of this stuff, anyway? Are you okay?"

Matt shrugs. "I'm as okay as I can be, I guess," he says. He runs a hand through his shaggy, dark hair. "If you want to know the truth, I'm a little sick of her being sick. That sounds horrible, I know."

"No, it doesn't. I bet it's hard taking care of someone."

"It's not even that," Matt answers. "I don't even really take care of her. She doesn't want me to. She wants me to be normal. But there's just so much buildup. In the beginning, it was all drama and sadness and planning, and now I just feel like I'm ready. Like I'll be wrecked when it happens, and until then, I'll hang out with my sister as much as I can."

"You have a positive attitude about it."

"Not on purpose," Matt says. "It's just how I feel."

"Not me," I say.

"You don't have a positive attitude?" Matt asks.

"Not at all. I mean, I know this is new to me and everything, so I'm pretty naïve, but frankly, I want her to get well."

"She won't," Matt says, matter-of-fact, which really annoys me. He zips his sweatshirt, reminding me that I'm cold, too. I button my sweater, then let my arms swing, ready for him to take hold of my hand again, but instead he shoves his hands into his sweatshirt pockets. I try not to feel disappointed.

"Can we change the subject?" I ask.

"Sure," Matt says.

"Okay...tell me about you," I say. "I know you're good at English, hate public displays of stupidity, and save damsels in drunken distress. What else do you like to do? Who do you hang out with? What are your plans after high school?"

"Whoa!" Matt says with an easy laugh. "What's with the interrogation?"

"Fine," I say. "Start with an easy one. You probably know Audrey's my best friend.... Who's yours?"

Matt pauses, but right when I think he might play it cool and say something dude-ish about not having a BFF, he lets me in a little.

"Drew," he says. "He's in our English class."

"The guy you sit behind?" I ask.

"Yeah," he says. "We've been friends since kindergarten. Funniest guy I know," Matt says with a chuckle. "He's a great guitar player, too. He's in a band with some guys from Omaha South. He keeps trying to get me to join."

"What do you play?" I ask.

"Baseball," Matt jokes.

"No, seriously," I prod him. I try to think whether I've seen any musical instruments around his house. Just as I'm wondering whether there's a drum kit stashed in the garage, I remember the—

"Piano," he says quietly. "I'd play keyboard in the band."

"That's cool. You should do it."

"I guess," he says, shrugging it off. "So, what do you like to do, besides getting blitzed with frat boys?"

"Very funny," I say as a stall tactic, silently running through possible responses. What do I like to do? Nothing as cool as playing in a band. When too much time has passed to be comfortable, I reply honestly. "I like to read,"

I say. "I'm super quick, and often I read like four books at once. I know that's sort of nerdy."

"No, it's cool," Matt says. "I wish I read more."

"And I blog, too."

Matt looks away, smiling.

"What?" I ask.

"Nothing, I just...I know. Aud showed me. I've been following your posts. They're really funny."

My breath catches: *Matt reads my blog?*

"Is that weird that I read it?" Matt asks. "An invasion of—"

"Privacy?" I laugh. "It's hardly private. I just haven't ever met any of my readers."

"Seriously? What about your friends back in Frozen Hills?"

I pause for a moment, then say, "Hey, Matt? Want to know a secret?"

He looks at me expectantly.

"I didn't have any real friends in Frozen Hills."

Instead of calling me a liar or—worse—asking why, Matt mutters "their loss" and moves on.

"I hear you like Arcade Fire," he says before grabbing my hand once again, and reminding me that I want to be nowhere but here.

Unfortunately, we reach the other side of the bridge a few short minutes later. We stop, ponder our next move, and then decide to turn back. As we retrace our steps, the view is even better. With the vast city in front of us and the wide sky overhead, I feel free to say anything. Apparently, Matt does, too.

"I'm glad you moved here," he says, eyes on the skyline.

"I am, too," I manage to say calmly.

"I really like you," Matt continues. "You're like this good thing that showed up in the middle of the bad. You're sort of helping me remember that there actually is positive stuff out there."

I feel like there's a balloon inflating in my chest.

"That's the nicest thing anyone's ever said to me," I say.

"Yeah, well, it's true."

Matt squeezes my hand. I wonder if he's going to stop and kiss me, but he doesn't. I'm disappointed, but instead I choose to focus on his sturdy grip and the way it makes me feel strong, like I can do anything, charged, like I'm plugged in.

I'm completely content until we reach the end of the walkway: That's when I get anxious about our impromptu first date being over. As if he feels the same way, Matt slows his pace, then stops. We lean against the railing, admiring the view.

"Home?" Matt asks after a few moments.

"Late-night food?" I ask back.

"Even better," he says, sounding a little relieved. He

takes my hand and leads me back across the wide street, through the parking lot, and into the familiar passenger seat of his car.

"How is it possible that you don't have a girlfriend?" I blurt out on the way to what Matt says is his favorite diner, ignoring how completely stalker it sounds.

"Who says I don't?" he answers. I flip my face toward his, shocked and instantly jealous.

"What?" I say a little too loudly, which makes Matt laugh.

"Just kidding," he says through chuckles. "I did last year, but she started college this year. We felt like it wouldn't work long-distance. Well, I felt that way. She wanted to stay together."

Now, in addition to jealous, I feel inferior. My lanky fifteen-year-old self is no match for a college girl. Possibly reading my anxiety, Matt adds, "She's a bitch."

We laugh together, and it brightens my mood again. I look out the window at the old and new buildings, thinking the conversation's over. But then we stop at a red light and Matt turns to face me.

"Even if she wasn't at college, it'd be over," he says. "I like someone else now." I have to look away so Matt doesn't see the grin splitting my face.

When we arrive at the diner a few minutes later we find that despite it being a Sunday night, we're not the only ones with the greasy-spoon idea. We have to circle around and park a few blocks away, and when we get out of the car, I suggest cutting through an alley.

"This isn't the greatest part of town," Matt protests.

"Nothing will happen," I say with a shrug, taking off alone. His choices are either to let me walk alone or to follow. He jogs a little to catch up with me. Aside from a tense moment with a large rat, we reach the diner unscathed. When Matt and I walk through the door, he turns and looks deep into my eyes.

"What are you afraid of?" he asks.

The question catches me off guard and makes me feel vulnerable. So I swallow hard and overcompensate: "Nothing," I say carelessly.

Matt looks at me like he did after the bridge-railing-as-balance-beam incident.

"Okay, fine," I say, exhaling. "Bees. I'm afraid of bees."

Two hours later, full from too many fries and a too-big milk shake, I try hard to suck in my stomach as Matt walks me to the guest bedroom door.

"That was really fun," I whisper, keenly aware of his parents' presence just three doors down.

"Yeah," he whispers back, smiling. He steps toward me in that way that guys do in the movies when they want a goodnight kiss, and butterflies flit inside me like I'm at the top of a roller coaster, ready to drop. I raise my chin a little to tell him that it's okay.

Matt's lips taste like vanilla. His warm chest brushes mine. His arms stay at his sides, but his left index finger wraps around my right. It's a long kiss, but there's no tongue—only sweet softness. And then, too quickly, it's over.

I look up and admire his face at close range. In the low light, his dark eyes are black, but there's nothing sinister about them. Our fingers are still intertwined, but our chests are no longer touching. I'm glad about that because my heart is racing. He breathes out and I breathe in.

"I should go to bed," he whispers.

"Okay," I whisper back.

Neither of us moves.

"I don't really want to."

"Me, either."

Still, we stand, watching each other. The house shifts. A toilet flushes.

"Okay, I'm going now," Matt says.

"Okay."

"Night," he whispers.

"Night," I whisper back.

Matt takes a step away and our fingers detach. I get that quick panicky feeling like when a glass tips to spill, a rush like I want to reach out and stop it from happening. He takes another step, our eyes still locked. Two more, and I feel bound to move with him, but somehow I manage to stay still.

He walks backward all the way to his room at the end of the hall, his eyes holding mine the entire time. When he reaches his door, he smiles and holds up a palm. I hold mine up, too. He dips his chin once before stepping inside; the door barely audibly clicks behind him.

And then — only then — do I start breathing again.

sixteen

sixteen

sixteen

Monday is Hooky Day. Cassie already had me excused from school because of the trip to Kansas City, and Audrey's still technically home sick, even though she's out of bed and claims to be feeling better. Matt's the only one who has to go to school today. At breakfast, I fight off a perma-grin every time I look at him, with his still-dripping wisps of hair clinging to his neck. I want to reach over and blot them, just for an excuse to touch him. Last night is fresh in my mind; I can still feel his lips on mine, and I have to try very hard not to stare at his mouth.

At least he seems to be into me, too.

Every time I look at him, he's either looking at me already or he feels my stare and looks up. He's moving a little quicker than usual and his dark eyes are sparkling. It's hard to eat.

Then it gets even harder.

Audrey starts humming into her cereal bowl and immediately I recognize the tune to Ingrid Michaelson's "The Way I Am." At first I think she's merely chirping, but then I realize that it's much more.

"If you are chilly, here take my sweater," she begins to sing, swaying overdramatically. Matt scrunches up his face in confusion.

"Did you take too many painkillers this morning?" Matt asks. "Why are you singing to your Cheerios?"

Audrey looks at him with a weird smile on her face. She rolls her eyes and looks at me, amused. She tilts her head to the side and raises the volume, singing the next two lines with her hand on her heart.

Matt gets that Audrey is serenading us just as their mom cuts in.

"What a pretty song!" Mrs. McKean says, thankfully interrupting the hazing ritual.

"Oh, yeah, lovely," Matt says, blowing out his breath. He looks embarrassed but plays it off. "You should try out for show choir."

Blushing, I stuff a piece of toast in my mouth. I chew until Matt abruptly stands to leave, then I look at him, surprised.

"I have to meet Drew," he says in explanation even

though he's looking at his mom, not me. But then his eyes meet mine and we're locked there for a moment, silently saying goodbye. He breaks the hold when he turns toward Audrey. "Later, Thelma."

Audrey rolls her eyes at him again. Matt walks over and hugs his mom, then he's gone.

"Sorry," Audrey says after he's gone. "But I couldn't resist. You two are disgustingly cute."

"That's okay," I say, taking another bite. "What's with 'Thelma'?"

She shakes her head. "That's what my dad wanted to name me. Matt thinks it's the nerdiest name ever, so when I annoy him, he calls me Thelma."

Audrey and I look at each other for a beat before we both burst out laughing. The name isn't *that* funny, but it's one of those times when the other person's giggles make yours multiply. I think I'm still delirious from seeing Matt this morning after last night, and Audrey's silly in general. Five minutes later, we both have tears streaming down our faces. After trying to talk to us but getting nowhere, Audrey's mom shakes her head and leaves the room, which only makes us laugh harder. I feel a little bad, but I don't calm down; instead I clutch my side and keep rolling.

Because sometimes, laughter is what you need.

Audrey and I spend the morning watching talk shows and painting our toenails turquoise. After lunch, despite my general aversion to direct sunlight, she drags me to the pool in her neighborhood. It's late September yet unseasonably warm enough for us to lie in the sun. My fair skin is slathered in SPF 50 sunblock, and Audrey's is utterly exposed to the elements.

"I might as well die tan," she says lazily, an arm draped over her eyes.

"Don't say things like that," I reply without looking at her.

"Why not?" she asks. "I speak the truth."

"I hate the truth," I mutter. "And besides, you never know — someone could cure cancer tomorrow."

"Don't be ridiculous, Daisy," Audrey says. She removes her arm from her eyes and looks over at me, squinting at first. When her eyes adjust to the brightness, her gaze sharpens. "Look at me."

I do.

"I'm not afraid, Daisy."

You should be, I think but don't say. In my experience, dying isn't all that great.

"That's good," I reply, because I have no idea what else to say.

"No, seriously, it *is* good. I mean, it's not good that I have cancer. When I first found out, I felt so cheated. I was convinced there was some way to fight it."

"You can," I say with borrowed confidence. "You should still be thinking that way."

"That's the thing, Daisy: No, I shouldn't," Audrey says. "At some point, you have to realize that death is coming and be grateful for what you've had instead of pissed that it's going away."

"But you're barely eighteen," I protest. "That's pretty young to give up."

"I'm not giving up," Audrey says. "I'm accepting my fate."

"That's weak," I mutter under my breath. I'm angry at Audrey, and I'm angry at myself for feeling this way. I wonder what I'm trying to accomplish by arguing with her. Do I *want* her to be as upset about her cancer as I am?

I wish I could rewind a few hours and laugh with her again. Instead, I'm mute, and Audrey looks away from me and flops her arm back over her eyes.

"Actually, I think that letting go is pretty strong, Daisy," she says. "Everyone has to go sometime. Maybe this is my time."

I shake my head at her, annoyed at her calmness. Then I wonder, *What if it was me?* Mason told me he had problems bringing me back last time; if I was in Audrey's flip-flops, would I be this Zen?

Doubtful.

"How long are we staying?" I ask, changing the subject. "I'm getting burned."

"You're clock-watching," Audrey teases, putting me

more at ease after the tense conversation. "You know Matt will be home from school soon."

I simultaneously roll my eyes and shake my head at my friend, but inside I know that she's right.

And maybe about more than just Matt.

seventeen

seventeen

seventeen

Matt must have rushed out of school after the 2:50 bell, because he walks in the house at 3:07. Of course he doesn't look hurried; he's laid back, as usual.

"Hi!" I say — perhaps a touch too enthusiastically — when he comes into the living room, where Audrey and I are zoned out on an afternoon talk show. I try to control myself, but I'm sure the look on my face is pure sap. Before he arrived, I was in a vegetative state; now, as he strides across the room, I'm buzzing.

"Hey," Matt says, smiling at me. "Hey, Aud," he says to his sister with a slight wave. He drops his book bag on the floor and falls into the squishy chair. He scrunches up his dark eyebrows as he looks at the TV. Teens are confronting their parents about the adults' bad habits, like smoking, doing drugs, and dating twenty-year-olds.

"What are you *watching?*" Matt asks.

"Quality TV," Audrey murmurs. "Watch for five minutes and you won't be able to look away."

Mrs. McKean comes into the room wearing one of those mom sweat suits that works for the gym or the grocery store. She's rubbing her hands together like she just put on lotion; I can smell its lemony scent.

"Audrey, did you forget about your appointment?" she asks.

"Huh?" Audrey says, struggling but finally pulling her eyes away from the on-screen train wreck to look at her mom.

"You have a checkup at four, and we need to leave at three thirty to get there on time," Mrs. McKean says. She glances at the time on the DVR before looking at me. "Daisy, we can drop you off on the way if you'd like."

"I'll take her," Matt says, his eyes still on the TV. I hold my breath.

"Great, thanks, Mattie," his mom says. "Audrey, please go get dressed."

Audrey looks down at her outfit. At three in the afternoon, she's in pajamas; that's what she elected to put on after we went to the pool.

"Fine," she says. "But I feel great. I don't know why we have to go today."

"You know Dr. Albright always wants to see you after a trip to the ER," her mom says.

Audrey rolls her eyes and stands. "I'll call you later," she says to me before leaving the room. Mrs. McKean follows her out. Matt stands up and turns off the TV.

"Wanna go?" he asks.

"Sure," I say, a little bummed that he wants to get rid of me so quickly.

I'm in my head the whole ride to my house, so much so that it feels like we're pulling into the driveway only seconds after we left. I put my hand on the door handle and am opening my mouth to say goodbye when Matt surprises me.

"Can I come in?"

"Uh...yes?" I sort of say/ask.

"You sure?"

"Yes," I say, recovering. "Of course you can come in." My gloominess immediately fades: Maybe he wants to hang out at my house for a change.

We park and Matt grabs my weekend bag out of the backseat. We walk up to the front porch, and I unlock the door and swing it open. The house is stale after being uninhabited for a few days. Right away, I move across the entryway and open the windows in the dining room. Matt sets my bag just inside the front door.

"When are your parents coming back?" he asks, looking around at the living, dining, and sitting rooms, all visible from where he's standing.

"Not until after ten," I say. "Maybe later."

I watch him scan the main level and try to see it as he might. The living room's five-piece furniture grouping looks as if it's brand-new even though it's probably eleven years old. There's a brown leather couch, love seat, and chair set, and matching glass coffee and side tables. Everything is positioned over a muted patterned rug. There's a TV armoire on one wall, and an ornate mirror over the fireplace. The walls are covered in floral paper that was probably trendy when it was glued on and is now either cute or hideous, depending on your stance on vintage wallpaper.

The small sitting room contains nothing but three walls of books and two oversized toile wingback chairs with footstools in front and a side table between them. The only visible wall is painted forest green, while the bookshelves are a deep brown, making the whole room too dark for reading.

The dining room is furnished with an antique set: an eight-person table that I'm guessing has never seated more than four, an ornate sideboard, and a massive china cabinet with a hutch that I used to be afraid to walk in front of as a kid because I thought it was going to fall down and crush me. Hanging low over the table is a pretty chandelier that came with the house; underneath is a Persian rug.

As I look around now, I realize how meticulous the advance team was when positioning the furniture here. The house is decorated to be pleasant, but not eye-catching. To feel warm, but not make you want to rush out and replicate it. The only miss is...

"There aren't any photos on the walls," Matt observes.

"Yeah," I say. "Well, we only moved in a couple weeks ago. My mom hasn't gotten around to it yet."

"I thought maybe your parents weren't into that," Matt says. "You know, the humiliating baby photos and stuff. I was going to say you were lucky."

"No," I say, playing it off. "Unfortunately not."

I make a mental note to tell Mason that we have to get some baby photos on the walls, stat, and then offer to give Matt a tour of the rest of the house. We sweep through the kitchen—me ignoring the door that leads downstairs, because Cassie would blow a fuse if I took my boyfriend into her lair—and head upstairs. Only when I reach the creaky step at the top do I think about what's happening right now: I'm taking a boy—maybe a boyfriend—to my room.

I don't have a lounge area in my bedroom like Audrey does, so Matt walks over and sits down on the foot of my bed. I stop in the middle of the room and consider my options, then go and sit down next to him, leaving a couple feet of space between us.

"Cool room," he says as he eyes the walls. He points to an Arcade Fire poster and smiles but doesn't say anything about it.

"Thanks," I say. "I like to decorate."

"You and my sister," he says with a small laugh. "But you're pretty decent at it."

Though I'm sure Matt doesn't notice, I'm aware of my

tiniest body movements. My knees tip, my shoulders turn, and my chin tilts toward him, like I'm a potted plant on a windowsill, shifting positions to find the brightest ray of sunlight. The right side of my body—the side closest to Matt—actually feels warmer than the left.

"So, what did I miss in English today?" I ask, basking.

"Nothing much," Matt says. "Mr. Jefferson gave us a bunch of new vocabulary words to look up, so it was basically busywork all period."

"What were the words? Let's see if I know any of them."

"Okay, um, if I can remember any…" Matt lies back and stares at the ceiling. It feels weird to be sitting up when he's lying down, so I do the same. I'm careful of where I put my inside arm, totally aware of how close it is to Matt's.

"There was *banter*," he says.

"Which is what we're doing right now," I reply. I fold my hands over my stomach.

"And *exorcise*," Matt says.

"*Exercise?*" I ask. "That was a vocabulary word?"

"No, not like running on a treadmill, like exorcising demons."

"Oh," I say. "Okay. Do another one."

"*Inculpate.*"

"No clue."

"I think it means to blame someone for something," Matt says. "Or to teach? Or maybe the teaching one is *inculcate*."

"What else?"

"There were some about books," Matt continues. "*Prologue and tome.*"

"Too easy," I say. "What was the challenge word?"

Mr. Jefferson likes to give us a challenge word of the day. If we get it right, we earn points. Enough points equals a free period.

"*Halcyon*," Matt says.

"*Halcyon*," I repeat. "Cool word. No clue what it means."

"I didn't know, either," Matt says. "I guess we'll find out tomorrow when the answer's on the board."

"Or we could look it up." I sit up, shove off the bed, and walk across the room to the bookshelf. My books are cataloged by color, and my dictionary is in the red section along with a DIY book about home décor, two romances, a thriller, and *The Lord of the Rings*. I grab the dictionary and flip through until I find it.

"It's a mythical bird," I say. "Oh, or it's an adjective meaning calm, peaceful, prosperous, joyful, or carefree."

"Good word," Matt says. "I'll never forget it now."

"Really?" I ask, shutting the dictionary and joining him back on my bed. This time I lie on my side, and either I'm closer to Matt or it just feels that way because I can see him better. "How come?"

"Because *carefree, peaceful* . . . those words reminds me of you," Matt says without hesitation, surprising me with his frankness. He looks away from the ceiling and into my eyes; his gaze is like lightning. "That's how I feel when I'm with you."

In a flash, I know what I didn't before: His words are more than flattering; they're the answer to the questions I've been asking myself for days.

Does he like me as much as I like him?

Can I trust him?

Should I tell him?

Now I know. I have the answer.

Yes. Yes. Yes.

Wholeheartedly, absolutely, yes.

eighteen

eighteen

eighteen

"Uh..." Matt says, looking around Mason's office a few minutes later. "What are we doing in here?"

"Sit down," I say, gesturing to the chairs across from the massive desk. "Please," I add, not wanting to sound bossy.

As I ease into the desk chair, I swallow down my anxiety and breathe deeply to calm myself. I try to focus on the positive side of the situation—that I feel so safe with Matt that I'm willing to risk everything—but the negatives muscle their way into my brain, too. I'm about to reveal a government secret that could have implications for nearly everyone I know. I'm getting ready to tell the guy I like that I've been lying to him. And finally, I'm about to tell the brother of a dying girl that there's a drug that saves people... oh, but that his sister can't have it.

It feels so overwhelming that for the blink of an eye, I consider backing out. But then I remember what Matt said:

Carefree, peaceful... those words remind me of you.

He has the right to know who I really am.

"Matt, there's something I want to tell you," I begin. "It's about me. About my life."

"Okay," he says, eyeing me curiously. "And it's something we have to talk about in your dad's office?" he jokes, gesturing around at the stale white walls and brown furniture.

"Sort of," I say. "Yes. But I'll get to that part in a minute."

"Okay."

Pause.

"I'm not sure where to start."

"The beginning?" Matt suggests, still smiling.

I exhale loudly, then decide to go for it. "I'm sworn not to tell you what I'm about to say," I begin. Matt sits up a little straighter in his chair, his interest piqued. He nods, as if agreeing not to share my secret. "So, before a drug gets approved and can be sold to people, it goes through a bunch of testing. A lot of the time, the public knows about the drug while it's being tested, but sometimes, with really controversial drugs, the tests are done secretly. They can take years, often decades." I pause, giving myself one final out. Then I just say it: "I'm part of one of those programs."

"Cool. What's it for?" Matt asks without skipping a beat. The look on his face is so... excited. I wait a moment before continuing, holding on to that look for as long as I can. I feel like I'm about to crush him, but how can I keep hanging out with him if he doesn't know the real me?

"It's a drug called Revive," I say finally. "It brings people back from the dead." Matt's brows pinch together in confusion. "I died when I was four years old," I clarify. "The drug brought me back to life."

"That's... Are you messing with me?" Matt asks.

"No," I say seriously.

Matt's eyes look playful as they search mine for a trace of teasing. When he finds none, his expression becomes somber.

"How did you die?" he asks, concerned.

"I was in a school-bus crash in Iowa," I say. "The bus skidded off a bridge into a lake."

I can practically see the wheels turning in Matt's brain.

"Not the one they made the miniseries about?" he asks, taking it in.

I nod.

"So..." he begins, the pieces clicking together for him. His eyebrows knit tighter and he shifts in his chair a little. After a few moments of puzzling, Matt asks what I've been waiting for him to ask: "Audrey?"

He says only her name, not daring to speak the rest.

I shake my head, not wanting to go there at all. But I realize that I have to.

"It's not..." I say, my voice trailing off. I regroup and try again. "It doesn't work on people with diseases or really serious injuries. It can't regrow damaged tissue. It's more like an electric pulse to your entire system at once. It shocks you back to life from the inside out. Revive can't help bodies that weren't healthy when the person died."

Visibly processing the information, Matt says, "That's the weirdest thing I've ever heard." He's borderline monotone, distracted, looking from me to the desk to the walls and back, searching for answers. He swallows hard; I think he's shell-shocked.

"I know."

"And...I don't...I mean, I'm not sure if I even want to know about this," he admits. He fidgets, then wipes his palms on his pants. "I mean, what am I supposed to do with this stuff? If it can't do anything for Audrey, I mean, what good is me knowing about it? It's not really fair." Matt stops talking and looks down at his hands. The sadness in his eyes makes me wonder if I've done the right thing.

"I'm sorry for telling you," I say, a little hurt that he doesn't understand why I did it. "I just thought...Well, I wanted to give you something. Like a part of me. I felt like I wanted you to know the real me. But I understand why you don't want to know about Revive."

"No, I get that," Matt says, his eyes softening when he looks up and meets my gaze. "It's just that I'm conflicted, you know? I want to get to know you, but it's hard hearing about something like this without thinking about Audrey. Without feeling like crap because it can't help her, too."

"I understand," I reiterate. "Believe me, I agree with you," I say, standing. "Let's just go hang out in my room some more. I'm really sorry for bringing it up."

Matt watches me stand but stays in his seat.

"Daisy?"

"Yeah?"

He pauses, then forces a half smile that makes my chest feel like it's caving in.

"I want to hear it," he says. "Tell me about your life."

Thoughts jumbled, I'm all over the place in the beginning, jumping from our move to Omaha to the fact that the program is managed by the Food and Drug Administration to the rigorous annual tests and back again. I know from the look on Matt's face that he's having a hard time following the story, but when I start to describe the agents and their function, the wall crumbles and it seems like he's not only getting it, but he's genuinely interested, too.

"The program was formed about a year before the bus

crash," I say. "Basically, they were waiting for something to happen so they'd have human test subjects. The agents were handpicked across industries for their specialties, and I'm sure they were anxious to get going."

"Where did they come from?" Matt asks.

"Other branches of the government," I say, shrugging. "Or civilian jobs. Some were recruited out of school," I say, thinking of Cassie.

"What do they do?" Matt asks. "Now, I mean."

"Some are scientists in the main lab in Virginia," I say. "All those guys do is death science. Others are like bodyguards—watchers for the kids in the program. My friend Megan's watcher is also a computer expert. He trolls the Internet for any flags about the program. He's got the personality of a computer on a slow connection, but he's a genius. He hacked the FBI mainframe as a teenager and once sent an email from a former president's account, just because he could. I swear, if he wasn't part of the Revive program, he'd probably be in prison—"

"Wait," Matt interrupts. "Your friend Megan... you mean Fabulous? From the blog? She died in that crash, too?"

"Yep."

He shakes his head. "This is insane."

"I know," I say quietly. "It must seem so strange to you. But this is me. I'm only being honest."

"I'm glad you are," he says, but his expression is uneasy. He takes a deep breath. "Keep going."

"Okay. So, like I said, the agents all have jobs," I say. "Mason and Cassie both have medical backgrounds, so their job is monitoring the health and well-being of the bus kids—"

"Mason and Cassie?" he interrupts. "As in your parents? Your parents are government agents?"

I frown. "Sorry," I say. "I skipped that part."

Matt shakes his head again, then runs a hand through his hair. I wait for him to say something, but he doesn't, so I go on. I tell him about being adopted, which he says he knew from Audrey, and about living with nuns before the crash. I explain that no other bus kids live with agents, but since there was no family to relocate with me, they had to assign me to someone.

"Wait, they told nuns you were dead?" he interrupts again. I don't mind; I like that he's paying attention.

"They told the whole town of Bern that everyone on the bus was dead. The program is totally confidential."

"But nuns? That feels especially wrong."

"I guess lying to nuns is bad," I say. "The funny thing is that God lied to them."

Matt looks at me blankly until I remember that I haven't shared that part yet, either.

"Oh, sorry," I say. "I forgot about the nicknames. Because Revive brings you back from the dead, and that's a God-like ability, the core group of agents started calling the program the God Project. They secretly dubbed the guy in charge God; they called themselves Disciples; and eventually, when they had human test subjects, they named us Converts. The nicknames stuck."

"That is totally messed up."

"I guess," I say, shrugging. "Are you religious?"

"I believe in a higher power, if that's what you mean," he says. "But not necessarily religion."

I nod but don't comment. So much of religion seems to revolve around death and what happens when you die that being part of a program like Revive has made religion seem unnecessary to me. And come to think of it, not a lot of the science-possessed agents in the program are religious. But I still have faith. In that way, Matt and I are the same.

"Okay, enough God talk," I say, sensing that I'm losing Matt. "I brought you in here in the first place to show you some of the program's secret documents and stuff. To give you a better picture of what it's like. To be honest, I thought maybe you wouldn't believe me unless I showed you proof."

He looks at me, surprised. "You thought I wouldn't believe you?" he asks.

"I . . . I guess so," I say, slightly embarrassed.

"Of course I believe you," he says with a quiet intensity, holding my stare for a few moments. Electric currents seem to pass between us as we survey each other, and somehow the warmth I get from them makes this whole situation seem okay.

"But I still want to see the cool stuff," Matt says finally, breaking the tension and with an easy smile. I laugh a little, then wave him closer.

"Drag that chair over here behind the computer. I'm about to blow your mind."

nineteen

nineteen

nineteen

I wave my hand to activate the computer, then touch the monitor so it recognizes my fingerprints. It prompts me for a password and I say the first three-syllable word I think of: *xenophobe*. Matt chuckles because he probably thinks the password is real when, really, the computer just needs me to speak more than two syllables so that it can use voice-recognition software to verify my identity.

"Duck for a second," I say to Matt. He looks at me funny but crouches down a bit, enough for the computer's "eye" to scan just me. When it's satisfied that I'm Daisy and not some imposter, the computer lets me into the directory for Program F-339145.

The God Project.

"They let all the kids in the program mess around in the files?" Matt asks.

"No," I murmur as I navigate the welcome screens with my hands instead of a mouse. "Like I said, I'm the only one who lives with agents. Mason in particular is really open. He says that I'm almost an agent myself, and that I should be able to access information if I want to. He trusts me."

"That's so cool," Matt says, mesmerized. I don't answer, choking on the irony of my words.

I motion open the folder with the archived newspaper clippings from the Iowa crash. I choose the longest, most informative story, then scoot my chair aside so Matt can read.

I watch his chocolate eyes float back and forth across the screen. At first, they're wide and bright: He's engrossed in the story. Then they narrow, making him look pensive. Finally, when he winces and his face freezes in a pained, uncomfortable expression, I force myself to look away. With nothing else to look at, I read the story again myself.

TWENTY CHILDREN, DRIVER DEAD AFTER BUS CRASH ON HIGHWAY 13

By Jolie Papadopolis, Staff Writer

Thursday, December 6, 2001

The Iowa Highway Patrol has not yet released the names of the minor children confirmed dead yesterday after a Brown Academy bus drove over the Highway

13 bridge and plummeted into icy Lake Confident below, killing all aboard. Police have not determined the cause of the collision; bus driver Peggy Miller, 22, of Briarwoods, also died in the crash.

Though paramedics arrived at the scene in less than 15 minutes, none of the 20 children aboard, ranging in age from four to eleven years old, nor Miller, could be resuscitated.

"It's the worst tragedy this town has ever seen," said Phillip D. Grobens, chief of police for the nearby city of Bern, where Brown Academy is located. "My heart breaks for the parents of these children, and for Ms. Miller, too."

According to an eyewitness, the bus swerved to avoid an oncoming vehicle that had crossed over the center divider of the two-lane bridge. The witness speculated that icy conditions on the bridge could have contributed to Miller's loss of control over the school bus. Witness Lacy Pine, 18, of Bern, said, "The bus fishtailed and it looked like she got control for a minute and then the back end swooshed hard to the left and the bus was going too fast and it went over. Broke clean through the guardrail. It was horrible. The ice ate it up and there was nothing anyone could do. It just sank."

Despite Pine's and corroborating eyewitness statements, Grobens says the county will perform an autopsy on Miller to rule out substance abuse or illness that might have contributed to the accident. Miller had been driving buses for only six months.

"With this many families destroyed, we have to investigate every possibility," Grobens said.

The names of the children will be released once all of the families have been notified. According to Grobens, one child's parents were out of the country at the time of the accident and have not yet been reached.

One of the state's top private schools, Brown Academy matriculates children from preschool to senior high and has received accolades for both its high standardized test scores and its scholarship programs for low-income families. Brown Academy director Elizabeth Friend said in a statement: "Our hearts go out to the families and friends impacted by this most terrible tragedy. Every one of those children was special, and deserves a special place in our hearts forever."

Brown Academy is closed this week and is offering free counseling for students and parents, as well as a meal service for families directly involved.

Police ask anyone who witnessed the crash to notify the Iowa Highway Patrol at 555-2301.

"Whoa," Matt says after he finishes reading. "That's heavy."

"I know, but look at how it turned out. Nearly everyone was fine."

"How many weren't fine?" he asks.

"Uh," I say, swiping aside the newspaper file and opening the document that contains the list of people who were on the school bus. "Six kids died for real. And the driver. So, seven people."

Matt scans the names of the kids and I do, too.

Tia Abernathy, Michael Dekas(X), Andrew Evans(X), Timothy Evans(X), Nathan Francis(X), Cody Frost, Marissa Frost, Joshua Hill, Tyler Hill, David Katz, Daisy McDaniel, Elizabeth Monroe, Anne Marie Patterson(X), Marcus Pitts, Chase Rogers, David Salazar, Wade Sergeant, Gavin Silva, Kelsey Stroud(X), Nicole Yang.

I look at Matt and see that he's still scrutinizing the names.

"Your real last name is McDaniel?"

"Yes," I say.

"We would have sat near each other at graduation if you didn't change your name," he says, dreamlike. I can tell he's fascinated by the list so I don't wipe it off the screen just yet.

"You're a year older than me," I say. "We won't graduate together."

"Oh, that's right. I forget because you're in English."

"And if I didn't change my name—if I didn't die—I wouldn't be in Omaha."

There's a pause in the conversation when I really want to ask Matt what he's thinking despite it being probably the most cliché thing to ask a guy. When Matt still doesn't take his eyes off the names, I open my mouth to ask if he has any questions. He beats me to it.

"Where's Megan?" he asks.

"Oh, she was Marcus Pitts then," I say. "She was born a boy. Her dad took the accident as an opportunity to leave them, mostly because he couldn't take the transgender thing. After they moved, Megan's mom let her wear whatever — be whoever — she wanted. She dressed in girl clothes from then on out."

"But she was only, what, like five?"

"I guess when you know, you know," I say with a shrug.

"Oh," Matt says. "So are the X's —"

"The ones who died," I say, nodding.

"Were those kids brothers?" Matt asks. "The Evanses?"

"Yes."

"And they both died?" Matt says, horrified.

"Yes."

"That's so rough. Their parents must have been devastated."

"I'm sure they were."

"I'm sure they still are."

I glance at Matt: He's holding his jaw in his right hand, and his forehead is distorted and distressed. His dark eyes are clouded over like a rainstorm. He's affected by these people he's never met. Maybe it's because of Audrey, or maybe he's just empathetic in general, but Matt's reaction makes me question my own. I have to be honest: For all the times I've logged on and researched the program, I haven't often dwelled on the ones who died for real. In this moment I realize that I haven't thought of them much at all.

Have I taken on some of Cassie's robotic tendencies

after living with her all these years? Or is it just my developing scientific mind that makes me look at the program so coolly? Or is it the program itself? By teaching me that death is optional, has the program desensitized me to *real* death?

How will I react if Audrey dies?

Or should I say *when*?

Thrusting that morbid thought from my brain, I wave away the list. I hear Matt inhale next to me like he's been holding his breath for a while. I consider logging off but decide to keep going since Matt seems so sucked in. I open the folder where they keep the files on all the victims: one for each, living or dead. They're not numbered—they all start with F-339145, and then have a random letter after the program identifier—so it's hard to tell which folder belongs to which person. Matt watches as I play a silent game of eeny, meeny, miny, moe.

When I open "moe," I immediately recognize Mason's handwriting. The page is dated December 5, 2001: the day of the bus crash.

Back when the program started, apparently God was paranoid about the Internet and made agents take notes on paper. Eventually, he got over his technophobia and had all of the paper files scanned in and then destroyed. But the handwritten notes are the most real. As I look at Mason's harried scrawl, I actually *feel* how dire the situation was, much more than if I was reading a typed report.

"Wow," I murmur.

"What?" Matt asks.

"Nothing, it's just the handwriting," I say. "It's Mason's, and it looks so . . . crazy."

Matt nods, but he still looks confused. I point at the date.

"This was the day of the crash," I explain. "The agents had to take quick notes between patients. I'm sure it was chaotic. And it had to be so frustrating for them. Mason and the others were supposed to bring twenty-one people back to life with only a syringe, and that's it."

Matt lets my words sink in for a few seconds. "But if the drug didn't work, they tried other ways to save you guys, too, right?" he asks.

"No, that's the point," I say. "To truly test the drug, they could only use Revive. Like, they couldn't even do CPR."

"But . . ." Matt's words fade.

"Can you imagine being a doctor and knowing all these lifesaving techniques and not being able to use them?" I ask.

"Kind of like having a sister with cancer and knowing about a lifesaving drug that she can't have," Matt says, staring right at me.

"I guess so," I say quietly.

"Sorry," Matt says.

"Don't apologize. You're right."

Matt steers the conversation back to the screen. Or rather, he looks at the notes and starts reading. Not really knowing what else to say, I read, too.

CASE NUMBER: 16
NAME: KELSEY STROUD
AGE: 6

PARENTS: JONATHAN AND NANCY STROUD
(CONSENT GIVEN AT 9:17 AM)
LOCATION OF BODY: LODGED UNDER
SEAT EIGHT (MIDDLE LEFT)
PRESUMED CAUSE OF DEATH: SEVERE
HEAD TRAUMA (METAL OBJECT PENETRATED
HEAD JUST ABOVE LEFT TEMPLE; SIGNIFICANT
SUBSEQUENT BLOOD LOSS; GLASGOW COMA
SCALE RATING 1 FOR VISUAL, VERBAL,
MOTOR)
FIRST DOSAGE: ONE VIAL, 9:18 AM
REACTION: NONE
REPEAT DOSAGE: NONE

RECOMMENDATION: AUTOPSY TO DETERMINE
DEFINITIVE CAUSE OF DEATH TO COMPARE
AGAINST OTHER REACTIONS TO DRUG. TEST
TISSUE AND HAIR SAMPLES FOR RESISTANT
MARKERS DESPITE CLEAR INDICATORS THAT
POINT TO HEAD TRAUMA AS COD. RELO
PARENTS DESPITE FAILED ATTEMPT?

"Damn," Matt says quietly, shaking his head.

"Sorry," I say again. "I wanted to find one for someone who made it. I can't really tell which file is for which kid."

"What happened to her parents?" Matt asks, ignoring my apology. I swipe away the notes and open another file in Kelsey's folder. It's a signed oath. I close that and find the relo detail sheet: Mr. and Mrs. Stroud, who had no reason to go through a name change, now live in North Dakota. At last contact, in 2011, they were "functioning normally."

Except that their daughter's dead.

Matt doesn't say anything more, so I open another folder. The first file is similar to the page of notes on Kelsey, but it's for another bus kid, written by another agent.

CASE NUMBER: 20
NAME: NATHAN FRANCIS
AGE: 9

Presumed cause of death: Broken neck (X-ray confirmed cervical vertebrae crushed, consistent with vehicle accident; completely unresponsive)
   First dosage: None
   Reaction: None
   Repeat dosage: None

"Damn," Matt says again, more forcefully this time.

"I know," I say, quickly closing the file, then tapping the air to open another. Thankfully, it's for someone who responded to Revive: Gavin Silva, now Gavin Villarreal. I exhale loudly as I move my hands to page through details of his Revival and relocation to New York.

"I know him," I say. "He's super cool."

"Oh, yeah?" Matt says weakly. I can tell he needs to hear some good news as much as, if not more than, I do.

"Yeah," I say. "Revive worked for a lot of us. It gave us life."

I feel like I just walked out of a haunted house: My nerves are frayed and I'm post-stress tired. I pause to regroup. Then I try to explain to Matt the pros of the Revive program.

"So, this guy, Gavin, is twenty-two now," I say in a measured tone. "You'd like him; he's really funny. He's in art school and he does these insane drawings. He sent me one for my birthday last year. . . . It's that one of the face, in my room?"

"Yeah, I saw it."

"Anyway, Gavin's life is *way* better now. Mason told me a few years ago that back in Bern, Gavin's dad was physically abusing him. Like hitting him, but also putting out cigarettes on him." I pause, shivering.

"That's sick," Matt says with a flash of anger in his eyes.

"It is," I agree. "It's terrible. He had it really rough. But the Revive program saved him from that."

Matt's eyebrows go up like he wants to hear more, so I keep talking.

"So, Gavin's best friend was one of the ones who died. His name was Michael Dekas. Anyway, before the crash, I guess Michael's parents started to suspect something was going on at Gavin's house, but they could never get Gavin to fess up. Mason said they asked Gavin's mom about it but she denied it, then didn't let Gavin come to their house for a while.

"Anyway, then the crash happened. Michael didn't respond at all to the drug; his parents were obviously devastated. But then when the agents went to try to Revive Gavin, they found all these burns on his body. There was no one there to claim him—his parents were in Canada, I guess—and the agents asked if any of the families there knew Gavin. The Dekases came forward, and when they saw the burns, they made a snap decision to volunteer to relocate with Gavin...as their son."

"No way," Matt says.

"It's true," I say. "The program saved Gavin's life twice, in a way."

"Yeah," Matt agrees. "But you know, that's also sort of kidnapping. It might be worse than the nun thing."

"I guess," I say, never having thought about it like that.

"But I still think it was the right thing to do," Matt clarifies quickly. "I mean, how could they send a kid back to a guy who was using him as an ashtray?"

"Exactly," I say, but it lacks conviction. Matt and I both

get lost in our thoughts for a few minutes. On my mind are shades of gray. Many times, I've pondered the ways in which Gavin's life is so much better now, but the one thing I haven't considered before is his real mom, and what her circumstances were like then and now. It strikes me for the first time that the situation might not have been as morally black and white as I've always thought.

Maybe they should have found her and offered her a way out, too.

There's a gnawing inside me that feels like guilt: guilt for second-guessing the program that gave me a life and a home. I move on from Gavin's story, at least on the outside.

"There were others who really benefited from Revive, too," I say to Matt. "I already told you how Megan's life got better. And Tyler and Joshua Hill—they're identical twins. Both were Revived. They live in Utah. It would have been so terrible if just one didn't make it, but they both did. Oh, and Elizabeth Monroe's younger sister was supposed to have been on the bus that day but wasn't; she stayed home sick. But Elizabeth was Revived, so her sister will never have the guilt of being the lucky one. I mean, can you imagine having to live each day knowing that your sibling won't get to . . ."

I'm so concerned with running from moral dilemmas and trying to defend the program that I don't realize what I'm saying until it's out of my mouth. But then it hits me like a sledgehammer to the heart. Shocked by my own words, I look quickly, wide-eyed, at Matt.

He's the lucky one; Audrey isn't.

"Oh my god, Matt," I say. "I can't believe I said that."

"It's okay," he says quietly before moving his eyes from me to the ceiling. There's nothing of interest up there, but he stares anyway.

"No, it isn't."

The room is so still, it's frozen.

"Actually, Daisy, you're right," Matt says finally, sighing loudly. He pulls his gaze from the ceiling and looks at me with fire in his dark eyes. "It's not okay that a drug like this exists and it can't help my sister. It's not okay at all."

I'm not sure what to do. Anxiously, I turn back to the screen and start closing files. I hear a clock chime downstairs; my breath sounds like a windstorm.

"We can never tell Aud about this," Matt says flatly.

"You can never tell *anyone* about this," I say.

"I said I wouldn't," Matt snaps. "But I guess you'll have to trust me on that."

"I do trust you," I say softly. "It's just that I've never told anyone this stuff before. I've never felt close enough to anyone to even *consider* telling them. And it would be a huge deal if it got out. I mean, there would be riots. Everyone would want it. But not everyone could benefit from it."

"Like Audrey," Matt says dismally. The anger is gone as quickly as it came, and I realize that I almost prefer it to sadness. Anger is manageable; sadness is heartbreaking.

"Like Audrey," I echo.

Even though Audrey will never be in the Revive program, I think of reading her name in a case file. Of failed attempts at bringing her back scrawled in rough handwriting. Of her time of death noted like it's nothing.

I can't ignore the sick feeling in my stomach right now.

This little venture of mine into the world of Revive was meant as a gesture for Matt, but all it's done is make me question my life. Revive brought me back, but the program stole a child from his mother and didn't try other methods of saving seven people. Who knows what else might have worked on Michael Dekas or Kelsey Stroud? Maybe they needed surgery, not injections.

And beyond that, though I knew that telling Matt about Revive would be rough on him because of Audrey, I didn't consider that it would also be rough on me. But as I sit here, that's what weighs me down most.

Revive gave me life—it is my life—but it won't give Audrey a second chance at hers. And for that, Matt has a right to be mad.

And so do I.

twenty

twenty

twenty

The sound of the garage door opening downstairs startles Matt and me out of our chairs. Quickly, I close everything on the computer and go through the steps to log off. We run out of the office and across the hall to my bedroom. Right as I'm wondering whether having Matt in my room is better than snooping in secret government files, someone starts coming up the stairs.

"Go sit in the beanbag," I say. Matt bolts across the room. I sit on the floor, leaning against the bed. I take a deep breath seconds before I hear the knock on my door.

"Daisy?" Mason calls.

"Hey, Dad," I say. The *dad* must have alerted him to someone else's presence in my room—I only call Mason

"Mason" at home — because when he opens the door, he's all father. I can hear cupboards opening and closing in the kitchen downstairs; Cassie's probably baking a casserole after seeing Matt's car out front.

"Hi, sweetheart," he says to me. "Hello, Matt."

Matt waves.

"Hey," I say. "We were studying English."

At this point, everyone in the room knows it's a lie — there aren't even any schoolbooks around — but Mason doesn't know I told Matt about the program, and I'm determined to keep it that way.

"I see," Mason says. "I hope you got a lot done, but it's getting a little late for a school night. It's probably about time for Matt to go home."

I glance at the clock and realize that it's almost nine. Six hours with Matt have passed like six minutes.

Matt starts climbing out of the beanbag and Mason turns to leave.

"Good to see you, young man," he says. "I hope your sister is feeling better."

"Thanks," Matt says before Mason leaves.

"Sorry," I whisper. "They're home early."

Matt crosses the room and stops about a foot from me. "It's so weird knowing that he's not your real dad," he says. "He really acts like a normal father. He deserves an Oscar."

"Wait 'til you meet my mom," I say with a dramatic eye roll.

Matt laughs that perfect laugh of his and in that

moment, despite my confusion over the program, I'm glad that I told him everything. I feel closer to him than ever.

When he leans in and kisses me this time, there's something new between us. Instead of first-kiss-with-a-hot-guy giddiness, there's something deeper. I can feel it in my toes and in my belly button.

And in my heart.

When Matt leaves, I log on to my regular computer and see if Megan's online. I message her and tell her cryptically about the evening. At least the part with Matt.

Megan: You did WHAT????

Daisy: I know.

Megan: M's going to kill you.

Daisy: Maybe

Megan: Worth it?

Daisy: Yes, if nothing more than for the kiss at the end of the day.

Megan: Spill...

We chat for an hour, until Megan has to do homework and I have to update the blog. Before signing off, she writes:

Curious, I type in the address for *Anything Autopsy.*
Megan's post is called "The Autopsy of the Queue" and is
all about the personalities people reveal while standing in
line (the cutters versus the cutees and the oblivious people in the middle who should have stayed home because
they always seem so surprised when the clerk shouts
"NEXT!"). Megan's position is in defense of the cutter, who
is just trying to make the most of her day. I spend an hour
perfecting a platform for the cutee, which is built on the
idea of karma. Practice patience and be rewarded with extra
butter on your popcorn; cut and find yourself in the one
seat in the theater with chocolate melted into the fabric.

I post my rebuttal, then get ready for bed. When I get
back to my room, there's a text waiting from Matt.

Matt: Can you talk?

Smiling, I type back:

Daisy: Call you in five?

Matt: I'll be waiting.

I dial in the dark. Matt picks up after the first ring.

"I thought of something on the way home," he says
instead of hi.

"What's that?"

"I don't get why you guys moved here," he says. My stomach sinks. I'm not sure why the idea of telling him I've been Revived more than once feels so bad, but it does. I think he mistakes my nervous silence for hurt. "I mean, I'm really glad you guys moved here. I didn't mean it like that at all. I just—"

"Oh, I know," I interrupt. "I'm a little embarrassed to tell you why. But I guess I've shared a lot today, so why not put it all out there?"

"Okay..."

"I've died five times."

Now Matt's the one who's silent.

"Are you still there?" I ask.

"Yeah," he says. "Whoa."

"I know," I say, ashamed. "I mean really, it's more like four—I had to be Revived twice after the bus crash—but technically, five vials means five deaths. After that first day...well, I'm really allergic to bees, and I guess I'm accident-prone, too."

"No way," Matt says. "What...I mean, what's it like?"

"What?"

"Dying," he says.

"Oh."

"If you don't mind talking about it," he adds.

"No, it's okay," I say. "Um...I don't really remember that much about it, to be honest." It's a total lie: I remember many graphic details, but I don't want to cause Matt more pain than I already have. He might think death talk is fascinating right now, but later, when Audrey's time comes, he'll be haunted by my stories of being afraid and in pain.

"Oh, okay," Matt says, sounding a little disappointed. But he changes the subject anyway. "Are you going back to school tomorrow?"

"Yeah," I say.

"Audrey, too."

"Really?" I ask, excited.

"Yep, the doctor cleared her," Matt says happily. "Only he wants her to be with people at all times in case she has a problem, so my mom won't let her drive to school alone. We're going together." Pause. "Want us to pick you up?"

I smile at how normal the conversation is now, even though Matt knows a completely abnormal thing about me.

"Yes," I say.

"Okay, we'll be there at seven twenty."

"Awesome."

It's late and that's the logical end to the conversation, but I get the feeling that Matt wants to say something more. I wait patiently, my nervousness snowballing with each passing second. Finally, he speaks.

"Daisy..."

"Uh-huh?"

"That was one freaking weird afternoon," he observes. His tone is low, intimate. It makes goose bumps pop up on my arms.

"I know."

"But it was good," Matt says.

"It was?"

"Yeah," he says. "It was weird, but it was okay, because of you. Because I feel like I know you a lot better now. I feel sort of honored that you told me all that. That you showed me the secret stuff."

"Even though..." I say, feeling like I can't even mention Audrey's name.

"Yeah, Daisy," Matt says. "Even though."

twenty-one

twenty-one

twenty-one

I can't sleep at all, and at three AM, after my third trip to the bathroom, I find myself in the dark in Mason's office. I'm drawn to Gavin's file like I'm addicted. I don't want to think about it, but in a way, I need to.

I log on with my handprint. When the prompt for the voice password appears, I tiptoe across the floor and quietly shut the office door so as not to wake Mason or Cassie. Back in the desk chair I say *halcyon* so low that I'm concerned the computer can't hear me, but it does. I'm in.

I go to open Gavin's file, but with the coding system I can't remember which one it was. I brush my left hand over the icon for recent files and then expand the page so the details show. I sort by the time the files were last accessed and find what I'm looking for. But then I see something weird: A new folder was created yesterday. Even stranger still, though the folder is named like all the rest, it's marked as "hidden" so that when you look in the main directory, you won't find it unless you know it's there.

"What's this?" I whisper to myself, selecting the hidden folder, then the first file in it. Unlike the others, this one is typed instead of handwritten, but it's formatted the same way. I'm nervous that it's for another Chase—that one of the bus kids died again or something. I skim over the top and go to the "name" line, tipping my head in confusion when I see that it's listed as "Confidential."

A confidential name?

I read down the page and find that the drug worked: The subject was Revived and relocated to Franklin, Nevada, after the crash. Only it says "car," not "bus," so it was a different crash. Did one of the bus kids get in another accident?

I scroll up to the top to see which case number it is so that I can find the confidential Convert. It takes me a couple of frustrating seconds to locate it before finally I see that the file is for case number—

What?!

I suck in my breath. My hand flies to my mouth, and even though I'm alone, I murmur through my fingers: "That's not possible."

I know that I'm perfectly safe, in a locked house with

183

two gun-toting government agents down the hall, but I'm instantly afraid. The room is too dark. The night is too still. What's on the screen in front of me is too shocking. I'm so creeped out that I start to consider that I'm being watched. I log off like lightning and then hurry out of the office, across the hall, and into my bed.

Only then, when I'm burrowed down deep under the covers, do I think about what I saw.

There were twenty-one people on the bus.

I just met Case 22.

twenty-two

twenty-two

twenty-two

A car horn wakes me up.

Completely foggy, I turn my eyes to the clock on my nightstand. Somehow, despite my stupor, my brain registers that it's 7:32 AM. Suddenly, I'm awake. I fling off the covers, run to the window, and see Matt's car sitting in the driveway with Audrey up front. Right then a text message comes through from Audrey.

> Audrey: Almost ready? We're here.

> **Daisy: I heard...give me five?**

> Audrey: No problem

I run to the dresser and yank fresh underwear and a bra from the top drawer. I strip my pajamas off and pull on my skivvies, then grab yesterday's jeans from the floor. I rush to the closet and rip the first shirt I see off its hanger: It's a bright blue peasant top that falls off my shoulders a bit. I don't really love it, but it's what I'm wearing.

I glance at the clock. It's 7:34.

I slip into black flats and race to the bathroom, where I pee while simultaneously brushing my teeth, then pull my hair into a high ponytail that actually looks okay. I put blush on my cheeks and eyelids and then nearly poke my eye out trying to apply mascara too quickly. After a stop in my bedroom to grab my bag, I make it to the car at 7:38, breathless and a little sweaty.

"Sorry," I say to the McKean siblings as I slide into the backseat. It feels weird to be back here instead of in the passenger seat.

"No problem," Audrey says, smiling brightly.

Matt glances at me in the mirror as he backs out of the driveway.

"Did you oversleep?" he asks.

"Yeah," I admit. "Total insomnia. I probably got about two hours."

"Well, you can't tell," he says warmly, which makes both Audrey and me smile.

"Thanks," I say, feeling my cheeks turn pink.

Matt turns on the radio and it's an upbeat love song

that makes it hard not to smile the whole way to school. At least he's smiling, too.

I spend the day alternating between conflicting feelings. I'm optimistic about Audrey's high spirits and positively cheerful when I think of Matt's kisses and kind words. I'm panicked about Case 22, but exasperated because I can't put my finger on what exactly I'm afraid of. I'm relieved to have shared secrets with Matt, but ashamed because I know Mason would be disappointed if he knew about it.

But mostly, I'm lifted by the fact that Matt and I have a new, strong connection.

In English, I can feel that connection across the room. In the halls, we're in color and everyone else is in black-and-white. In the noisy cafeteria, I hear everything he says as clearly as if I'm wearing earbuds and he's my playlist.

Audrey notices it, too.

"Not to be gross or anything, but did you and my brother do it or something?" she whispers in the hallway between fifth and sixth periods.

"What?" I say, shocked. "No! Oh my god, no!"

"Okay," she says, laughing and holding up her hands. "I get it. You didn't. You two just seem overly gooey today."

"Oh," I say, turning to face my locker, embarrassed. "We had some nice conversations yesterday." I feel bad about lying to Audrey, but Matt's right: It's not fair to tell her about Revive.

"I see," she says, eyeing me skeptically. "Conversations about doing—"

"Audrey!" I shout, laughing. "Shut up!"

"Fine, fine," she says. "But for the record, I think you're lying."

"And for the record, I think you're nutso."

"Well, you're probably right on that one," Audrey says, flipping her lovely hair off her shoulder and beaming at me. Her teeth are bright white and her dark eyes are sparkling; her skin looks perfect against the lavender shirt she's wearing. She's the most perfect version of herself in this everyday moment.

It makes me queasy to think that she might not have much time left.

When Matt and Audrey drop me off after school, I grab a snack and head down to the basement to check in. With Mason and Cassie having been gone, and with my having rushed out of the house this morning, I haven't really talked to Mason in days. But when I open the door at the top of the stairs, I realize that the lights are out; nobody's home. Apple and energy bar in hand, I turn and run upstairs to the office: This is my chance for a closer look at Case 22.

Even though Mason's okay with me checking out the Revive files and Cassie tolerates it because she has to, I'm on high alert, feeling like I'm doing something wrong. And yet, I retrace my steps from last night, accessing the recently updated files from the directory.

I glance through the case numbers and open the last one accessed, but it's Gavin's, not Case 22. I go back and try again.

My stomach sinks even before my brain realizes what's happening.

I refresh the screen.

Then I refresh it again.

I navigate to another screen and then back.

Like a hacker on a mission, I work different angles until a door closes downstairs and I snap out of it. I log off and cross the hall to my room, confused.

I know what I saw yesterday.

I know the unsettled feeling it gave me today.

But as hard as I look, right now I can't find it.

Case 22 is gone.

twenty-three
twenty-three

twenty-three

It's been two weeks with no answers or even leads, and I've managed to bulldoze my worries about Case 22 into a corner of my brain. It's not that I'm not burning with curiosity; it's that I know that I'll have to ask Mason if I want to find out more. And the truth is that Mason's no dummy. If I tell him about Case 22, he'll want details.

What was in the file?

How did you find it?

When did you last see it?

"When" is what scares me the most. I'll have to tell him it was the night he came back from Kansas City and Matt was at our house. And then, Mason being the actual smartest person I know, he'll get what I did: He'll know I told Matt about Revive. So, instead of implicating myself, I decide to embrace my new life and try to ignore the program until I can figure out how to research Case 22 *without* Mason's help.

In the meantime, I'm starting to feel like I was born and raised in Omaha and have known the McKeans since birth. Matt, Audrey, and I carpool to school every morning and hang out every afternoon. Audrey and I can finish each other's sentences, and she even helps me come up with great blog topics like "What's worse: Sunday night or Monday morning?" and "Gym teachers: Friend or Foe?"

Even better, Audrey seems to be feeling good, which somehow makes it okay that I'm feeling *amazing*. Although Matt and I don't talk about Revive, the way he watches for bees when we eat lunch outside tells me that it's always on his mind. We hold hands in the halls at school and text or chat until late every night, and more and more, I know that our relationship is way beyond crush status.

I've got a best friend and a boyfriend, and it's fine by me that they've got the same last name.

On the Thursday before my birthday, Audrey and I eat lunch in the cafeteria because Matt's got a dentist appointment.

"I love my brother, but it's nice to have a break from him once in a while," Audrey says before taking a bite of yogurt.

"Yeah, it's nice to have some girl time," I say, smiling at her.

"So, Dais, do you love my brother?" she asks, eyes shining.

"You and your questions!" I shout. "Oh my god!" I redden as Audrey giggles. "And for the record, I only love my other boyfriend. You wouldn't know him; he lives in the Niagara Falls area," I joke, ripping off a line from *The Breakfast Club*, which Audrey and I streamed last weekend. We teased Matt about having Judd Nelson hair. Of course Matt's is way better.

"Oh, yeah?" Audrey plays along. "Is he hot?"

"The *hottest*!" I squeal. An entire group of girls one table over turns to see what's happening. When they go back to their lunches, we resume our conversation.

"What about you?" I ask seriously. "You never talk about any guys besides celebrities."

"What's the point?" Audrey says in a rare moment of defeatism. Then she bounces back. "Anyway, most of the true hotties graduated. Oh, man, like Bear Williams. He looks like a young Jake."

"You're Gyll-obsessed," I joke. "And *Bear*? That *can't* be his real name."

"It is. I swear."

"I don't know how anyone could take him seriously with a name like Bear."

"That's because you've never seen Bear Williams. Maybe I'll invite him to your birthday event."

I choke on a baby carrot.

"Excuse me?" I ask. "My birthday *what*?"

"Your birthday event," Audrey says. "Don't try to pretend that your sweet sixteen isn't on Saturday, Daisy West."

"What are you going to do?" I ask, a little afraid, but mostly flattered.

"You'll have to wait and see," Audrey says cryptically. "I mean, it's not a party or anything, but I think you'll like it."

"That's really nice of you," I say.

"Well, it's not all me," Audrey admits. "My brother might have told a little white lie about where he is right now."

My stomach flips as I start to ponder what the McKean siblings could possibly be planning for me.

Saturday morning, Mason makes me pancakes with candles and gives me an iTunes gift card and a voucher for driving lessons. Cassie hands over a store-bought greeting card with twenty dollars inside.

"Thanks, you guys," I say. "This is really sweet."

"Well, you only turn sixteen once," Mason says, smiling genuinely.

"Happy birthday," Cassie says before retreating to the basement to work. Mason calls after her that he'll be down in a minute.

"So, how's everything going?" he asks when we're alone.

"Fine," I say.

"You seem to be spending a lot of time with Audrey," Mason says. He coughs once. "And her brother."

"Yeah," I say, turning pink. Mason looks a little uncomfortable, but he presses on.

"Is he a good guy?" he asks. "Is he nice to you?"

"Yes," I say, fighting a grin. "He's nice to me. You'd like him. You should get to know him better."

"And Audrey?" Mason asks, changing the subject. I know Mason views people outside the program as audience members for his elaborate performance, not as friends. I can tell that he's still worried that I'm going to share too much. It makes me feel a little guilty that I already have.

"Audrey seems to be doing better," I say, shrugging it off. "She looks a lot better and acts like she has more energy." I smile, trying to make myself believe.

"That's good," Mason says. He opens his mouth to say something else, then closes it again. Having known him for so long, I can read his mind: I know he wants to tell me not to be naïve about cancer. But it's my birthday, so he holds back. Finally, instead he says, "Well, I should go down before Cassie blows a fuse."

I snort into my water glass at Mason's reference to Cassie, the machine.

"Good luck with that," I say.

"Thanks," Mason says, grinning at me. He takes a step toward the door before turning back. "Hey, kid, happy birthday, again. You've grown into...Well, I'm proud of you."

Mason walks over and kisses me on the head before quickly going downstairs, leaving me feeling full of love and admiration for the parent I would have picked any-way. Even if he wasn't assigned to me.

With everyone accounted for, I go to the office and search for the bazillionth time for the mysterious Case 22 file, reasoning that maybe since it's my birthday, I'll find it.

No luck.

So, I shower and get ready, then call Audrey.

"When's this event starting?" I ask.

"Whenever you're ready."

"I'm ready."

In honor of my special day, Audrey's mom lets her drive solo so we can have some girl time. Audrey picks me up in her happy car and takes me to the mall for coffee, pedi-cures, and the cute T-shirt of my choice (I select a super-soft tee with a pop art Einstein on it—which looks a lot cooler than it sounds). After that, we head back to Audrey's house to change for what she calls the *real* present.

"Put this on," Audrey says as she hits me in the face with an unidentified article of clothing. I'm brushing my hair at her vanity; she's buried in her closet, trying to find exactly the right outfit.

"Uh . . ." I say, taking in the royal blue tank dress.

"What?" Audrey asks. "It'll make your eyes pop. And you can't wear jeans. It's a special occasion!"

"I guess," I say, frowning at the dress.

"Don't you like it?" she asks. "It's one of my favorites."

"No, it's not that," I say. "It's really cute. I just don't wear a lot of dresses."

"Well, you should," Audrey says warmly before throwing silver leggings and a cropped black jacket at me. I give in and get dressed. She emerges with ankle boots in her hands, which, thankfully, she doesn't throw at me.

"See!" she shouts when I'm dressed. "The blue is awesome with your eyes." She grabs my shoulders and wheels me around to face the mirror. "You look like a model. Matt is going to die."

"Thanks, Aud."

"No problem," she says. "I'll be right back. I'm going to go borrow one of my mom's necklaces."

I sit back down at Audrey's vanity and use some of her makeup. Just as I'm applying a little light pink blush, I hear movement in the hallway. I turn to see Matt passing by on his way to the shower. He's carrying a towel and, as usual when he's at home, he's barefoot.

Our eyes meet.

"Wow," he says softly. We hold each other's stare for so long it feels dirty — in a good way. Neither of us says anything else, which makes it even more powerful. His eyes take in my hair, my exposed shoulder where the jacket is falling down on one side. We're a room away from each other and I can feel his eyes on me like fingertips.

"Move it along," I hear Audrey say to him from the hallway. "Drool later."

The bubble burst, Matt grins sheepishly and turns away.

The "real" gift is third-row tickets to Arcade Fire.

"It's like an eclipse," I say about the chances of my favorite band playing in town on my birthday. "Or a meteor shower."

"It's pretty awesome," Matt says as he watches the roadies set up.

Even though I thought she was joking, Audrey did actually invite Bear to the show. I glance over at them and silently agree that okay, fine, he *does* look a little like Jake Gyllenhaal.

But *still* he's not as cute as Matt.

"This is the most amazing birthday ever," I say in Matt's ear.

"You deserve it," he says in mine before kissing my neck and leaving me with head-to-toe goose bumps.

As the opening act begins to play, when the bass and the drums and the guitar and the screaming make it too loud to hear shouting let alone my whispered voice, I say, "I love you." I know he can't hear me, but I put it out into the universe anyway.

And for now, that's enough.

twenty-four

twenty-four

twenty-four

The next Friday, I realize that nothing can stay perfect forever.

Audrey goes home sick from school, and even though I talk to her after fourth period and she seems fine, I'm still concerned.

And then Matt and I have our first fight.

It happens after school, when I'm packing for a four-day trip to Seattle. I'm joining Mason and Cassie on their annual pilgrimage to the Northwest for Fabulous Megan's test. They'll poke and prod during the day, and Megan and I will have bonding time at night. As much as I love being around Matt and Audrey, I can't wait to just "be" with

Megan. There's something about spending time with someone who's known you forever. It's effortless.

Matt sits on the bed while I pack.

"It sucks that you'll be gone this weekend," he says.

"I know. But I'm really excited to see Megan. I haven't seen her since last year."

"I'll miss you," he says with a flirty smile that I feel to my toes. Smiling, I look back to the T-shirt I'm folding. He grabs one and folds, too.

"Hey, Dais?" Matt says. My stomach flits at the way he shortens my name. I love it.

"Uh-huh?" I murmur, folding happily like we're an old married couple doing the laundry together.

"There's something I've been meaning to ask you."

"Oh, yeah? What's that?"

"It's a favor." Matt looks away and, strangely, I don't take it as a warning. I'm too lost in my fantasy of us playing house.

"Anything for you," I say. "Ask away."

And then my fantasy crumbles.

"I want you to steal Revive."

To say I'm caught off guard is the understatement of the century: I'm a lottery winner who didn't buy a ticket. Except that would be a good surprise.

This is not.

I'm completely silent for at least three minutes. It

would be beyond awkward if there weren't so many thoughts barreling through my brain, not the least of which is a question: Over these past few weeks, when Matt's seemed to be falling for me, was it real? Or was he only buttering me up for this favor?

Finally, I find my words... at least three of them.

"There's no way..." I say, my voice trailing off. Matt looks at me like he's expecting something. Practically demanding it. I try three more: "Matt, I can't."

He stands up from the bed and steps so close to me that we could kiss.

"I know it will be hard, but I think if you —"

"No," I say decisively, taking a step away from him. "No. I can't do it. I signed an oath."

"But it's for Audrey," Matt says, touching me lightly on the arm. He looks at me the way he did the night of my birthday. It makes me feel sick.

"No," I say again. His hand recoils and he turns away from me a bit.

"Don't you care about my sister?"

"Of course!"

"Don't you want her to live?"

"Of course!" I say again, raising my voice a little. "But it won't work on her. Don't you remember what I told you? This isn't the way."

"That's what you've been programmed to say," Matt mutters. He crosses his arms over his chest.

"Matt, seriously, it won't work. It doesn't work on cancer. They've tried it."

"So you've said. What did they test it on? Rats?"

"Well, yes, but they're very good indicators—"

"Daisy, that's bullshit," Matt interrupts. "So, what, only you get the drug? No one else is good enough to have it, but you get it *five times*? Good thing you live with the Revive dealers."

"Hey!" I shout. "That's enough." I stare into Matt's dark eyes and wonder where the kindness went. Was it really all an act?

Feeling tears coming, I face the bed.

"I think you should leave," I say without looking at him.

"Good idea," Matt says bitterly before turning and slamming my bedroom door behind him.

twenty-five

twenty-five

twenty-five

Since Revive is staying at home, we get to fly to Seattle. I'm glad about it, but something about seeing people say goodbye to one another at the security gate sets me off. I bite the inside of my cheek to hold back tears, increasingly frustrated by what happened with Matt, worried about Audrey, and concerned about Case 22 and the program overall. Once I'm through the metal detector, I tell Mason and Cassie I'll meet them at the gate. Then I spend some time coming unglued and piecing myself back together in the privacy of the foul-smelling airport bathroom.

On the plane, I turn on my most miserable playlist and speak to no one the entire flight. In fact, I pretend to be asleep once we're in the air, and keep pretending through snack service and turbulence. Just before we land, I finally remove my earbuds and put away my iPod. The flight attendant says it's okay to turn our phones back on, and I'm happy to find a text waiting from Audrey.

Audrey: Matt said you guys are fighting. Everything ok?

With fresh tears popping into my eyes, I write back:

Daisy: Not sure. Hope so.

Audrey: Me, too.

Daisy: Are you feeling okay?

Audrey: Oh yeah, fine. I was just tired.

There is a pause, then Audrey texts again:

Audrey: I don't mean to downplay everything that's going on in your life, but I have good news. Do you want to hear it?

Smiling, I type:

Daisy: YES!

Audrey's giving me something to hold on to.

Audrey: Ok so I just found out that I'm getting surgery!!

I type:

Daisy: OMG that's great!!!

But something's nudging me, so I type:

Daisy: But, Aud, I thought they couldn't operate?

Audrey: New doctor = more optimistic. Maybe he can fix me.

I desperately want to be happy for Audrey, but something about the possibility of surgery now, when it's never been an option before, makes me feel skeptical. But I don't want to be a downer.

Daisy: He will! Think positively!

Audrey: I'm trying.

Daisy: I've got fingers and toes crossed for you.

Audrey: Thanks, Dais. Have a great time in Seattle. Miss you already!

Daisy: Miss you, too.

I put away the phone and Mason looks over at me quizzically. His tall frame is squished into the aisle seat. Despite her height, Cassie has room to spare in the middle.

"Everything okay?" Mason asks.

"I'm not sure," I say, pressing my head against the window as we pull up at the gate, incredibly thankful that my fellow travelers are a disinterested fembot and a man who's never been one to pry.

We check in to the hotel, have dinner, and bid one another goodnight. After posting a response to Megan's note about my theory that Monday morning is *clearly* better than Sunday night, I check my email.

There's nothing from Matt.

I start a movie, but it's a romantic comedy, and all it does is make me see how unfunny my life is. I turn it off and climb into bed hoping tomorrow will be a better day. Before I turn out the lights, I text Megan.

Daisy: Crap week. Can't wait to hang out.

Megan: Always here for you. Get some sleep and we'll fix it tomorrow.

Daisy: Love you

Megan: Love you more

*　　　*　　　*

In the morning, Mason is reading an email on his phone when I join him and Cassie in the lobby. He frowns at the text on the screen, and then shows it to Cassie.

"Interesting," she says as we walk to the car.

"To say the least," Mason mutters.

When we're all buckled in, I ask what's going on.

"God seems to be starting another lab."

"Why?" I ask. "Isn't the one in Virginia doing well?"

"It is," Mason says. "It was custom made for the program in its current iteration. The only reason I can think that he'd want another one is..." His voice trails off, like he's considering his words.

"What?" I ask.

Cassie lets out her breath sharply. Sometimes I think she gets annoyed by how much Mason shares with me. But Mason tells me anyway.

"Expansion."

I'm still wondering what Mason meant when Cassie knocks twice on the Holloways' door. When Megan's mom, Alicia, flings it open, I jump in front of my parental figures to hug her. The apartment smells like the world's best banana muffins, and instantly, I'm calmer.

They're halcyon muffins.

I smile at the thought of the SAT word, thinking that Matt would laugh. Then I remember our fight and eject him from my thoughts.

"Come in," Alicia says to the three of us. "How *are* you?"

She's one of those people who are so joyful that you fall in love with her instantly. Mason beams at her—sometimes I think he has a little crush—and even Cassie reciprocates when Alicia gives her a quick side hug.

"Now, where's that Megan?" Alicia says, looking around the open-air loft.

"Did I hear my name?" calls a lowish voice, and Megan rounds the corner from behind one of the few interior walls in the apartment. In a flowery dress, with enviable white-blond locks and the thickest eyelashes I've ever seen, my soul sister—born a brother is beautiful. I stifle a laugh as she overplays a silly, sexy walk; she reminds me of a Slinky. I rush her and crush her with a hug.

"Hi," I say into her pretty hair.

"Hi," she says, squeezing me back. "How's my girl?"

"Okay," I say, holding on. Megan's strong embrace reminds me a little of Matt's, and tears pop into my eyes. Suddenly I'm crying and laughing at the same time.

Megan lets go and steps back to examine me.

"I'd say we have some catching up to do."

I grin, so glad to be here.

twenty-six

twenty-six

twenty-six

After Megan's first day of testing, she and I stroll through Pike Place Market. Having lived mostly in smaller cities, I experience a bit of sensory overload surrounded by the crowd, but I love it. Megan and I have a tradition of buying salted caramels from Fran's, watching the fish throwers until it gets boring, then eating crab cakes at one of the restaurants that overlook the water.

"Can we skip the crab cakes tonight?" I ask as we turn away from the fresh catch. "I feel a little sick."

Megan grabs my hand and pulls me out of the market toward the city. We walk the block and a half to Starbucks and don't speak until we're both armed with caffeine and seated at a cozy table by the window.

"You've never passed up a crab cake in your life," Megan says. "What's going on?"

"Matt asked me to steal Revive for Audrey," I say.

Megan's jaw drops in shock. "No."

"Yes."

"Are you going to do it?"

"Megan, WHAT?" I ask.

She shrugs. "I mean, why not?"

"Um, it's seriously against the rules? I could get in major trouble. Like jail time."

"They'd never do that," Megan says, sipping her latte. "They'd be too afraid you'd rat out the whole program."

"I never thought of it like that," I admit.

"Listen, Daisy, I'm not knocking Revive or what it gave me and my mom. In fact, I'm grateful. But that doesn't mean I have to let them brainwash me into thinking that every little move they make is right. It doesn't mean I have to let them control me." She holds my gaze for a few seconds. "You shouldn't let them control you, either."

"So, what, you think I should steal it?" I ask, nervous.

"I think you should do what *you* think is right, not what God tells you to do."

The mention of God reminds me of the new lab. Expansion. Which reminds me of Case 22.

"I have to tell you something else," I whisper.

"Ooh, juicy!" Megan says, leaning in.

Minutes later, every secret I have is out.

*   *   *

"We have to find Case Twenty-two," Megan says when I'm finished. "The only way we can get the details is to ask the Convert directly."

"How on earth do you propose we do that?" I ask. My coffee's gone, and I'm sad about it.

"Get another one," Megan says when she sees me eyeing my empty cup unhappily. "You're on vacation."

I buy a second cup and a scone and come back to the table.

"So how do you propose we find out who this person is?" I ask.

"What else do you remember about the file?" Megan asks.

"Nothing much," I say. "I was stuck on it being the twenty-second case. I wasn't paying too much attention to the rest. Oh—it did say the name of the relo town. It's called Franklin, Nevada. I have no idea where that is."

Megan types it into her phone.

"That's because it's barely a town," she says. "Poor, poor kid has to grow up in a population of...oh my god, three thousand. Daisy, that's our break. All we have to do is ask someone. It's so small, surely anyone would notice the new family in town."

Within minutes, my genius friend has come up with a plan to call the night desk at the local newspaper. She'll tell whoever answers that it's her job to do a write-up for the school website about the new family in town, but she's so bad at journalism that she already forgot the family's last name.

It's so ridiculous, it works.

"That's right, Emerson!" Megan says excitedly into the phone. "Oh, Bill, thank you so much. You have a great evening, too."

"Now what?" I ask. "What do we do with just a last name?"

"We search Facebook, of course," Megan says, like it's the most obvious answer in the world.

"You should be an agent," I say.

"That's what David says, too," Megan says coyly. I know she likes her handler.

"Well, he's right," I say. "Let's go."

There's no one with the last name Emerson in Franklin on Facebook, and there are too many Emersons when we search the entire state of Nevada. I'm ready to give up when Megan calls David.

"Will you do me a favor?" she purrs into the phone. I'm a little embarrassed, but a lot curious about what she's going to ask.

Megan pauses to listen to David.

"Of course, but this should be no big deal. See, there's this kid I met at that online party last weekend. We bonded, and I wanted to get in touch on Facebook. The only thing is that I don't remember the first name."

Pause.

"Yes, totally. The last name is Emerson, in Franklin, Nevada."

Pause.

"Really? You know such random things. So anyway, they just moved to Franklin, so you could like figure it out with a newly hooked-up Internet connection or something, right?"

Pause.

"Hacking the city's water company is even better! You're a genius!"

Pause. Giggle.

"Sure, sure, I know you're busy. But I'll be forever in your debt, and..."

Pause.

"You know what? I'm not even sure!" Megan bursts out laughing, and I can hear David laughing on the other end of the line as well. When they recover, I hear David's muted voice say something else.

"Okay, great. Thanks for your help."

Pause.

"You, too. Bye."

"What was so hilarious?" I ask after Megan ends the call.

She smiles broadly. "He picked up on the fact that I wasn't saying 'he' or 'she,' 'him' or 'her,'" Megan says. "He asked whether he's looking for a boy or a girl."

I laugh, getting it as she says it.

"He knows I participated in an online party for transgender kids last weekend, so he totally bought it when I said that I honestly had no idea."

"You're brilliant," I say, hugging my friend.

"Ditto, Miss D."

I'm staying at Megan's tonight, like I always do when we're in Seattle. In flannel pajama bottoms and ironic T-shirts, splayed out on her fluffy pink rug with bowls of popcorn on our tummies, Megan and I watch TV, then argue for half an hour about the pros and cons of slutty Halloween costumes.

"Save it for the blog!" I shout at her as I leave the room to pee. When I come back, she's at her desk, typing furiously.

"I didn't mean that you should blog right *now*," I say as I flop onto the bed. I roll over on my back and laugh at the poster of Jake Gyllenhaal on the ceiling. Apparently, my friends make up the Jake G. fan club. I don't really get it. I mean, he's sort of *old*.

"David came through," Megan says excitedly.

"Did he call?" I ask, eyes still on the ceiling.

"Yes, he called! He found the name. And I just found our *girl*!"

I pop up off the bed and hurry to the desk. I look over Megan's shoulder: She's on Facebook, typing a witty comment to go with her friend request. I read it and laugh, then my eyes find the profile picture and my laughter is gone.

The hair is shorter and a different color, but the face is the same.

It's . . .

Oh my god.

Oh my GOD.

"What's her name?" I ask, monotone. They never change first names. This will confirm it.

Megan looks up from her note and smiles.

"Oh, it's so cute; she's a little Irish lass. Her name is Nora."

I lap Megan's bedroom three times before she gets me to sit down.

"Girl, you're tripping," she says, sitting facing me. "Now what's up?"

I sigh loudly, grabbing one of Megan's pillows and clutching it to my chest.

"I went to school with that girl in Frozen Hills," I say, pointing at the computer accusingly. "She's the one who spotted me in the mall."

"Daisy!" Megan says, rolling her eyes. "That profile picture is tiny by tiny — it could be me. You're freaking out for no reason."

"I'm not," I say firmly. "I know what she looks like. She lived down the street from me."

"Wait, what?" Megan asks. "How is this the first I'm hearing about her?"

"Because we weren't friends," I explain. "We weren't anything. She was popular and I was . . . well, you know."

"Wait, wait," Megan says. "I'm confused. Tell me the

whole story. Speak slowly; pretend I'm Wade." Megan winks and it makes me laugh, which takes away some of my anxiety.

"Okay," I say, hugging the pillow tighter. "Nora Fitzgerald lived down the street from us in Frozen Hills. She invited me to her birthday party when we first moved there, but I didn't go."

"Why not?"

"Totally irrelevant."

"Why not?"

"I felt inferior. She was rich and had an apron-wearing mom and wore clothes that matched head to toe."

Megan nods once like she understands.

"So anyway, Nora turned out to be popular, and I did my own thing. Then I got stung and we moved." I pause for breath; I feel like I've been running. "Then that night in Omaha, I went out with Matt and Audrey and I saw Nora — she was randomly visiting relatives or something — and she might have seen me. . . . But she might not have. Regardless, Mason kidnapped me that night and took me to Kansas City —"

"Poor Wade."

"Shut up," I say, tossing a pillow at Megan's face. She catches it. "On the way, I asked Mason what God would do about Nora, and he said they'd watch and wait and see what *she* did."

"What does that mean?" Megan asks.

"I don't know," I admit. "We didn't really talk about it

again. I found out about Audrey and went back to Omaha and sort of forgot about it."

"And then you got all lovey-dovey with Matt and *really* forgot about it," Megan teases.

"Yeah, but it makes sense," I say, ignoring her comment about Matt. "What if Nora did see me, and she told someone? What if God relocated her and her family so she'd keep quiet?"

"That's a little far-fetched, but for the sake of argument, why would they agree to be relocated?" Megan asks.

"Maybe they didn't," I say. "Maybe God threatened them."

"Or paid them off," Megan says excitedly. "Maybe he gave them millions of dollars in hush money."

"Maybe," I say, genuinely considering it. "Except you're forgetting the file."

"That you claim to have seen at three in the morning after you had a sweeps-week moment with the guy you like, and that mysteriously disappeared after you saw it."

"Are you saying that I imagined the file?" I ask seriously.

"Or dreamed it," Megan says, matching my tone.

"It was there," I say flatly, annoyed that she's challenging me on this.

"Okay, I believe you," she says, too quickly, which is even more annoying.

"If you're going to cave so easily, why argue in the first

place?" I ask, rolling my eyes at her. She doesn't answer, so I continue. "*Anyway*, the file for Case Twenty-two says that the subject was *Revived*. As in dead and brought back to life."

"Even if the file's real, that entry could be fake, to cover up the money."

"Or it could be real," I say.

Megan shakes her head at me. "So, let me get this straight in my Wade-sized brain," she says. "You're saying that Nora saw you in that mall and told somebody, threatening to expose the program. And you're saying that God found out about it and actually killed Nora so that he could Revive her and relocate her, all to make sure she didn't talk?" Megan lifts her perfectly manicured eyebrows expectantly. "*That's* your theory?"

"Yes," I say decisively. "That's my theory."

Megan's quiet for a few moments, considering. She squints her eyes at the ceiling and bites her pinkie nail. Then finally, she speaks: "I guess it could work."

"You're totally annoying," I say.

"But you love me."

"I do."

"What should we do now?" Megan asks. "I mean, if your theory is true and God's killing anyone who knows about the project..."

I suck in my breath so hard I think my lungs might explode. It makes Megan jump.

"What?" she asks, wide-eyed.

"Do you think Matt could be in danger?" I say, realizing what I might have done to the guy I like.

"No," Megan says reflexively to reassure me. But the concerned look on her face tells me otherwise. "And the difference is that if this is true, Nora was threatening to out the program. No one knows that Matt knows, and he won't tell anyone." She pauses. "Right?"

"No," I say uneasily. "At least I thought he wouldn't."

"He won't," Megan says quietly, as if she knows him. "You have good instincts with people. I'm sure you can still trust him, even if he's being a child right now."

"I hope so," I say, worried anyway. "But oh my god, what about Nora? If it's true, seeing me in that mall ruined her life."

"You can't take all the credit," Megan says. "People make their own decisions. Maybe she saw you. But she could have minded her own business and stayed right there in Michigan. And besides, I'm not even one hundred percent convinced."

"Look up Nora Fitzgerald on Facebook," I command, fed up with the back-and-forth. Megan crawls off the bed and searches for Nora.

"No account," she reports. "But maybe she's one of those dorks who's taking a stand against social networks. We should totally blog about that, by the way."

"She's not," I say. "But just in case, search for Gina Geiger. She's Nora's best friend."

"Okay, here's Gina," Megan says. "Whoa, check out that red lipstick. Is she a tranny?"

"Focus," I say. "Look through her friend list."

"Love to, but I can't without friending her. Want me to?"

"No, let's figure it out another way."

"Should I go back to the original plan of friending Nora directly?" Megan asks.

"Shh," I say, holding up a hand. "I'm thinking."

The room is still for a few moments.

"Just Google Nora Fitzgerald and see if anything comes up," I say as a last resort. I listen to Megan's nails clicking against the keys.

"Here's something," she says, clicking on a link. I climb off the bed and walk up behind Megan as the page is loading. I realize that we're looking at the Frozen Hills newspaper, then scan the rest of the page. Megan and I both gasp when we see the headline:

LOCAL TEEN KILLED IN DRUNK DRIVING ACCIDENT

"I guess you were right," Megan says quietly.

"Guess so."

twenty-seven

twenty-seven

twenty-seven

An unwilling night owl, I'm not asleep when I hear a knock on the front door at five AM. I wonder whether Alicia's expecting someone as I listen to her shuffle through the condo to answer. There's whispered conversation, and I'm surprised to realize that one of the low voices is Mason's. Footsteps approach and the door to Megan's room cracks open, spilling in a stream of light.

"Daisy?" Alicia whispers. "Mason's here to see you."

"Okay," I whisper before crawling over the sleeping Megan. I tiptoe across the carpet and close her door behind me. When I've joined Mason, Alicia leaves us alone. I'm light sensitive and squinting, with my arms over my chest and my hands in my armpits because I'm not wearing a bra.

"I'm going to take you back to Omaha," Mason says softly. "Cassie's going to finish up here. I'm so sorry to tell you this, but Audrey's in a coma. It's likely that she'll die very soon."

My jaw drops. I blink. I blink again.

How can he tell me this when I'm still wearing pajamas?

I'm not sure why I expected a filter from him. He deals in death: It's clinical, not personal. I'm not sure why I expected more of a warning from Audrey. I'm not sure why I expected anything at all. This is how people with no access to Revive end their lives: inconveniently and with no buffer.

They go into comas.

And die.

twenty-eight
twenty-eight

twenty-eight

I'm so concerned about Audrey—playing a loop of the last few times we saw each other in my head—that I'm barely even aware of the flight home. When we land, we get our luggage and find the car, then head straight to the hospital from the airport. But even as we're driving there, Mason tries to talk me out of going.

"Daisy, I brought you back so you could say goodbye to your friend, but I'd like you to consider something."

I don't speak, so he goes on.

"You don't have to go to the hospital. Audrey would understand."

"What are you talking about?" I ask, my voice hoarse because I haven't spoken for so long.

"I thought a lot about this on the plane," Mason says. "People flock to deathbeds because they think that it'll be better for them to say goodbye, to hold their loved one's hand. But Daisy, sometimes it isn't better. That image of them dying sticks with you. But still, people do it. And I'm happy to take you there if you want to go. I'm just saying that it's okay if you want to hold on to the image of Audrey smiling and laughing and remember her that way. Because she's not laughing right now. She's not awake. She's barely alive. A machine is breathing for her. Do you understand?"

I don't speak right away. I think of Audrey in the hallway at school that day, of the perfect picture of her. Fleetingly, I consider what Mason is saying. But skipping the hard times just so I can remember the good doesn't sound like the right thing to do. In fact, I'm not even sure Mason believes his own advice.

"I'm going," I say flatly.

"I'm not sure that's the right decision."

"But it's my decision, right?"

"Yes," he says.

"Then I'm going."

Walking under the arch leading into the hospital, I have knots in my stomach. I'm surprised that I'm actually afraid to see Audrey, like the permanence of her impending death might be catching or something. But I know in my heart that I need to be here.

We walk through the doors and across the vast lobby.

With its muted colors and three-story wall of windows, the light, bright hospital seems to be telling me to feel hopeful. But I don't.

We make our way to the ICU waiting room. There are tables arranged like a lounge, chairs near a TV, and couches along several of the walls. All of the furniture is either an unrecognizable shade of nothing blue—like that background color that comes standard as computer wallpaper—or something between peach and salmon. The room is bigger than our basement, but there are only five people inside: the McKeans—minus Audrey—Mason, and me.

When we walk in, Matt peels his eyes away from the window to look at me. The rest of his features are indifferent, but I can see wreckage in his eyes. Despite his behavior the last time I saw him, I want to run over and try my best to save him. He looks away before I finish the thought.

Mrs. McKean is stirring tea in a paper cup; Mr. McKean is pacing. I wonder who's with Audrey until Mr. McKean explains to Mason that visiting hours are over for the afternoon.

"That's too bad," Mason says. He glances over at me before saying in a hushed tone, "When would be a good time for us to come back? Daisy would like to see Audrey."

Mr. McKean looks at me sadly. He gives me a weak smile, then deals a blow to the gut. "I'm afraid that's impossible," he says to Mason. "Only immediate family is allowed in the ICU."

"I see," Mason says in his businesslike manner. Irrationally, I wonder if Mason called ahead and asked Mr. McKean to lie, but in my heart I know that Mason would never do that. He only brought up not saying goodbye in the car to protect me.

Feeling helpless, I trudge to a seat stationed against the wall farthest away from Matt and flop into it.

The men speak in hushed tones for what feels like an extremely long time. I try not to listen as Mason gently offers to help in any way he can. He even goes so far as to offer counseling to Matt, which irritates me even though I know he's simply trying to maintain cover. I bite my thumbnail. Matt stares out the window. The men shake hands. Mrs. McKean stares at her tea. Mason walks over to me.

"I'll take you back to the house."

"That's it?" I ask.

"That's it."

Exhausted and hating hospital policy, the second I walk inside our house, I go to my room and climb under the covers. Not long after that, Mason appears. He sits down at the end of my bed and lightly touches my foot through the comforter. Then he puts his hands in his lap.

"Daisy, would you like to go back to Seattle and spend a few more days with Megan?"

"I want to stay here, just in case they change their minds," I say.

"That's highly unlikely."

"Still."

"I thought that Megan might boost your spirits," Mason says. "You two seemed to be having fun. And then I could help Cassie—"

"Is this really about you wanting to go back and get the test done quicker?" I interrupt.

"No, but that would be a side benefit," Mason says honestly.

"Just go."

"I can't leave you here alone."

"You've left me alone a million times," I say, shaking my head at him. "Get someone to check in on me if you're so worried."

"I . . ." Mason stops. I can tell he's considering it.

"It's fine, Mason, really. I'll be fine. And besides, I sort of want to be alone, anyway."

Mason nods, understanding. Like me, he enjoys solitude.

"Well, if you really don't mind, perhaps I'll call James."

Two hours later, I'm alone in an empty house on the worst day of my life.

I'm startled awake, and at first I think I slept for twenty-four hours. Then I realize it's the same horrible day: the day that started in Seattle and ended with me alone in an empty house, forbidden to see my dying friend at the hospital.

I lie still for a minute, thinking of all that's happened

and all that's gone wrong. I sit up and rub my eyes, growing more and more agitated. Finally, when I can sit still no longer, anger and adrenaline catapult me out of bed and down the stairs. In the middle of the open area between the kitchen and the living room, I turn around, unsure what to do.

Because I have to do something.

And then the answer hits me like a hailstorm.

I run toward the basement door. I turn on the lights and gag on the smell of rat poop as I descend. At the bottom of the stairs, I make sure that every light does its job. I want to see everything: the medical equipment; the rat cages with furry, squeaky test subjects inside; the small, locked closet where they keep the firearms.

I want to see the black case.

Mason's voice saying *In case of an emergency*, runs through my head.

If this isn't an emergency, I don't know what is.

I reach the case but hesitate before opening it. Somewhere deep inside me, I know what I'm doing is wrong. But then I think of Audrey. I think of Matt. I think of God and the program and Nora. How God controlled Nora. And how, with rules and oaths, he's controlling me.

I think of Megan.

I think of taking control.

And then, with no more hesitation, I punch in the first code.

*   *   *

At six thirty, I stand alone on the river walk, watching the people move like ants through downtown after a long day at work. Mason and the other agents call them — the normal people — Unenlightened. More like untouched.

I hear the rhythmic thud of feet running toward me but I don't turn to look. They slow as they approach, and then stop. Raspy breath sounds next to me, but there's nothing else.

"I want you to know that I'm not doing this for you," I say, keeping my eyes on the skyline.

"You have your reasons," Matt answers gruffly. "Can we just do this? I need to get back to the hospital."

I turn to face him. Our eyes meet for the second time today. And for the second time, despite hating him, I want to hug him. But I don't. Instead, I reach into my pocket and pull out a tiny loaded syringe with a plastic cover over the needle.

"Burn the syringe after you use it," I say to Matt.

"Okay."

"I've never actually seen this done on a human," I continue. "But I think you just give her the whole dose."

"Where?" he asks. An evening breeze blows his long hair into his eyes. He shakes it out like he's mad at it.

"I don't know," I say. I try to think back. Once I had an IV when I woke up. Maybe twice. "Does she have an IV? You could put it in that. Or just into her arm."

"Okay," Matt says, sounding unsure.

"Matt, you don't have to do it if—"

"Yes, I do," he interrupts. "I have to. It can't hurt her. I mean she'll already be—"

"I know," I jump in, not wanting him to say it. "But I want you to know how big of a deal this is," I say, thinking of Nora's situation.

"I'm not going to get you in trouble," Matt snaps.

"I'm not talking about that," I say calmly. "There are worse things than me getting in trouble."

Matt looks at me, waiting for an explanation, but I stop talking and shove my hands into my jeans pockets. I don't want to scare him, especially right now. Because in my heart I know he'll do it anyway.

"Just be careful, okay?" My tone is pleading, and I can see in his mellowed gaze that I've gotten through.

"I will," he says quietly. He takes a step away. "Thanks for doing this."

"Of course," I say, but it comes out a whisper.

Please let it work, I think.

I watch Matt walk away. He looks back once, and when he does, there's a flash of something sweet in his eyes. But then he turns away again, and too soon, he's gone.

twenty-nine

twenty-nine

twenty-nine

In the middle of the next night, something awakens me. I look at the clock: It's 2:38 AM. Unsure about what pulled me from sleep, I listen to the sounds of the darkness. A tree brushes against the glass outside my window; car tires squeal in the distance. I listen for Mason's snores before I remember he's not home.

I feel alone, but I'm not afraid. I relax and listen to the world until the creaks of the house and the barks of the dog next door blend into the background and I manage to fall back to sleep.

When I wake again, my brain is muddy. It's daytime, but the world is too still. The sun is on the wrong side of the house. But also, there's something else.

Somehow, in the core of me, I know.

I reach for the phone next to me. I text Matt to confirm.

It happened in the middle of the night.

Audrey is dead.

thirty

thirty

thirty

Mason's on his way back from Seattle, again, but for now I'm by myself. Honestly, I feel like I have been this whole time. If James checked up on me, he did it invisibly. Guess that makes him good at his job.

I brush my teeth, think about the fact that Audrey is dead, and throw up. Then I brush my teeth again. I stare at myself in the mirror for a long while, not really seeing. I start to feel trapped in my own skin, like I need to move or I'll go crazy. I rush out of the house, not knowing where I'm going. I walk a few blocks, then text Matt.

Daisy: Where are you?

Matt: Home.

Daisy: I'm coming over.

No answer.

Maybe I called a cab; maybe it just showed up. I don't really remember. I give the driver the McKeans' address and remind myself to breathe the whole way there. I look down at my lap and realize that I'm wearing a pair of Audrey's jeans. I fold forward and sob silently for the duration of the ride. Lucky for him, the taxi driver doesn't look at me or ask whether I'm all right.

The Mini sits in front of the McKeans' house, smiling and waiting to *beep beep* around town with Audrey at the wheel. I want to kick the car or drag my key through the paint: It's too happy.

Matt answers my knock but says nothing. He opens the door wider so I can come in, and I do, even though I'm pretty sure he doesn't really want me to. I follow him to his bedroom, not caring who's home or who minds.

"I don't know why you're here," he says when we both sit down on his rumpled bed. This is the first time I've ever been in his room.

"I didn't want to be alone," I say honestly. I have no filter anymore. "And I wanted to know what happened. Did you do it?"

"Yes." He's looking across the room with flat, emotionless eyes.

"And?"

"And nothing," he says. "I injected it into her IV less than five minutes after they called time of death."

"And?" I ask again, as gently as I can. Matt's head snaps in my direction so quickly that it makes me jump.

"And what, Daisy?" he hisses. "What the hell do you think? Does it look like Audrey's sitting next to me right now?"

His hand is gripping the bedspread like he's afraid he'll fall off.

"I'm sorry I came," I say, standing. "And I'm sorry it didn't work."

"I'm sure you are," Matt mutters. My blood boils and all I want to do is scream at him. Tell him that I loved his sister, that I love him. Shake him and say maybe he did it wrong. Wrap my arms around him and lie on his bed and cry with him.

Instead, I leave.

An hour later, Matt's on my doorstep. He's sweaty and I wonder if it's possible that he ran all the way here. I let him in and we go upstairs to my room. It's exactly the same as when I went to his house, but in reverse.

Except it isn't.

We don't say a word to each other. I walk into my room first and he follows; halfway across the floor, he catches my hand and spins me around. He grabs my face in his hands and kisses me, unsure for a moment, then hard, aggressive, but nothing I don't want him to do. I feel like I'm drawing out his pain like venom from a rattle-snake bite and, for a few minutes, it makes me forget my own misery.

We fall onto my bed and hold each other so tightly that our hands can't really move to explore body parts or anything. Besides, this isn't about moving through the bases. This is so much more than that.

Clothes are somehow undone, and we're so close to . . .

Matt abruptly pushes back and stands. His jeans are unbuttoned and his T-shirt is rumpled and stretched out. His hair is wild, covering his left eye completely. I can only see the tears welling up in his right.

"I don't know what I'm doing," he says with a voice so pained it burns me. "I don't know whether to hold you or hate you."

I'm stunned into silence. Matt turns toward the door. "I have to go."

And he leaves like that, disheveled, but I don't say any-thing. He might run into Mason on the way out—who knows when he'll be back—or scare mothers pushing babies on the street. But I don't care what Matt looks like right now, and I know he doesn't, either. Because when someone dies—dies for real—things like how you look don't matter anymore.

In fact, what no one ever told me is that nothing does.

thirty-one

thirty-one

thirty-one

I stare at the ceiling of my bedroom, thinking or not thinking, floating or just lying there. I might have been at Matt's three days or three hours ago: Time passes in odd increments. The lamp on my nightstand buzzes so loudly I want to smash it but I'm numb all over. My arms are glued to the bed. I look at my phone and register the time; the instant I look away, it's gone from my memory.

Mason's back.

Cassie's back.

Someone brings me food that I don't eat. Instead, I examine it like a fossil, drawing conclusions from the plate's contents. The dish contains breakfast: It must be morning. There are blueberry pancakes: Mason's concerned. There's a vitamin on the tray: He's *really* concerned.

The second I start to feel amused by my archaeological approach, I remember that Audrey is dead. I'm sitting here counting the number of grapes on my plate like tree rings and Audrey will never eat breakfast again.

Suddenly blueberry pancakes are an insult.

I shove the tray to the end of my bed. I roll onto my side and clutch my torso and curl into the fetal position because it's too much. She's not going to pick me up for school. I'm not going to meet her for lunch. She's not going to tease me about liking her brother or about my taste in music, or lend me clothes or talk about Bear or Jake or anyone else.

She's dead.

My phone rings; it's Megan's tone. I don't answer it. I don't even look at it. Anger rolls through me: I shouldn't have been in Seattle when Audrey was dying. I should have known something was up. I should have stayed.

My chest caves in; my heart is crushed. I try to psychically ask Matt to come over and lie next to me. But not to kiss me or anything. Just to lie here. I imagine him staring into my eyes like in Kansas City, but all I can see are his tears for his dead sister.

I cover my head with my pillow, but the thoughts are still there.

I wonder if they'll ever go away.

*   *   *

I stay in bed until nighttime, then wander the house in the dark. For hours, I stare out the living room window at the desolate street, hoping to see Audrey's ghost there, waving at me. I retreat into my sour, stale room before anyone wakes up in the morning. I listen to showers running. To breakfast being made. My phone buzzes so many times that I turn it off. Mason brings more food; the hunger strike continues.

"You need to get up," Mason says. He walks across the room and throws open the curtains. He opens the window and the fresh outside air stings my nostrils.

"No," I mutter.

"You'll feel better after a shower," he says.

I laugh bitterly. As if a shower could wash away the pain of losing Audrey. "Not likely."

"Your choice," Mason says, moving to the door again. "We're leaving for her funeral in an hour."

Of course, I get up.

I stand on shaky legs like a newborn fawn and hobble across the room. I can feel the lack of fuel in my body, but the thought of food makes me want to hurl. I grab clean underwear from the dresser then check my phone, which is charging on the desk. There are several missed calls from Megan; there's a text waiting from Matt:

Matt: I'm sorry.

Just two words, and yet, they are monumental.

They give me enough kick to move.

I shower and dry my hair, then pin back my curls in the front. I stare at my blue eyes in the mirror for a long time, searching for recognition. My face doesn't look the same anymore.

I go back into my room and pull on a black skirt of Audrey's.

It might seem weird to wear a dead girl's clothes to her funeral, but to me, it feels okay. She was free with her stuff, and half the clothes in my closet are probably hers. And besides that, there's the note.

Mr. McKean brought it over the night she died. It seemed an odd delivery at the time — why not stay with your family? — but then I realized he probably needed to keep busy so he wouldn't be forced to sit and think about Audrey. He's like one of those sharks that will die if they stop moving. So he brought over the note.

I pick it up off the nightstand and run my fingers over Audrey's straight-up-and-down cursive. It looks so much like her to me. I reread the first half of the letter.

Daisy—

Promise you'll do two things for me.

The first is easy: Take my clothes. ALL OF THEM. Even if you throw them away, get them out of our house (but I have pretty good) taste—haha!—so you should just keep them).

You've seen those people who can't let go. They sob over old T-shirts that aren't worth anything. My mom is a pack rat; she'll obsess. My ugliest pajamas will break her heart. Take them, Daisy. Do it for me (and for your wardrobe ☺).

There is a knock at the bedroom door.

"Almost ready?" Cassie says quietly. Her tone is less robotic, more like how she acts when we're in public.

"Yes," I answer. I fold the letter and put it in my pocket, slip on some flats, and open the door.

"You look nice," Cassie says.

I don't care.

For a girl who, according to her brother, didn't have many friends, Audrey's funeral service is packed. I can't help but wonder whether school let out early for attending kids. Then I imagine Audrey's ghost reading my mind and immediately feel like crap for thinking that.

I inhale a breath of musty old church air. *It's a good turn-out,* I mentally say to Audrey, as if she can hear me. *Everyone loved you.*

I've never been to a funeral, so I have no basis for saying that this one seems typical. I don't cry, because when dozens of Audrey's classmates stand and talk about her, they cry enough for all of us. They sob. They weep. Dramatically, they proclaim to the sky that they will miss their best friend. Meanwhile, I think back to Audrey's room. I think of the faces in the pictures on her desk. I recognize very few faces here.

Again I feel awful for thinking such thoughts.

After the service, we caravan to a nearby cemetery. The day is bright, like Audrey's personality. The vibrant orange and red fall trees and the towering monuments look earthy and polished at the same time, just like my friend was. Everyone gathers around her grave; I try to listen and feel something without passing out from the lack of food. It's only a warm day, not too hot, but I'm sweating just the same, wishing that Audrey were here to make a joke about me forgetting to wear deodorant.

The crowd disperses following the burial, and very quickly the only people left are the preacher, the McKeans, and us. Matt stands apart from his parents, staring at his sister's grave. Mason and Cassie wait for Mr. and Mrs. McKean to thank the preacher, and then they offer their condolences. I watch Mason put his hand on Cassie's back like a loving husband and want to scream for him to stop pretending. Because this is real.

I look at Matt and imagine that I can see a halo of pain radiating from him. Despite everything, I know I love him.

Without thinking about it, I walk over, stand beside him, and grab his hand.

My eyes stay on Audrey's casket. I don't look to see for sure, but I assume Matt's do, too. He doesn't pull away; he holds tight and doesn't let go. What we both need is each other.

We stand like that, staring, forever. With her brother next to me, without the crying fakers pretending to be her friends, I let myself really feel the loss. I feel it in every part of me: in my hair and in my toes. I feel it like something is rotting deep down in my core, releasing bitterness and anger and pure sadness into my veins.

Standing here, holding Matt's hand, I want to say so many things to him. I want to tell him that I'm so sorry. I want to say that I feel horrible that Revive didn't work. I want to say that I love him and that I want to take all of his pain away.

But I can't. I can't speak. And I can't take Matt's pain, because I have too much of my own, and I have no place to put his.

As if it's mimicking my emotions, the afternoon sky clouds over. It smells like rain is on the way. I break from my trance and look to the clouds.

Are you up there? I think to Audrey. Nothing happens.

Because she's dead.

Dead.

I think of what that really means.

It is not like being gone—like my real parents or the

nuns or people in the cities we had to leave—because gone implies that you can come back if you really want to. Contrary to what I may have been taught, there's no coming back from death. Not really. Someday, I'll die for good. And then I'll be like Audrey.

Not gone.

Dead.

I shudder at the thought, and Matt squeezes my hand tighter.

I look back to earth and the gravesite. Only then do I realize that Matt and I are alone. I look at him.

His eyes are on me.

"Hi," he says, as if he's seeing me for the first time. He looks down at our clasped hands and smiles, and then moves his gaze back to my eyes.

"Hi," I say back to the boy I never want to leave.

"I'm really sorry," Matt says.

"Me, too."

Eventually, we leave the cemetery. We drive in heavy silence to Matt's house. Cars are parked everywhere: in the driveway and out front, across the street and around the corner. Matt eases into a small space down the street and as we approach on foot, I try not to look at Audrey's happy car.

Inside, there are piles of food on every available surface, and every room is crowded with people wearing black and navy blue, talking in hushed, respectful tones as if they're afraid they're going to wake the dead. I feel like

I have cotton in my ears: When people talk to me, I have to ask them to repeat themselves.

"What?" I ask Mason after he mumbles something to me.

"I asked if you'd like some food," he says, looking at me with concern.

"Oh."

My thoughts snag on something I don't remember five seconds after I think it, and when I look back at Mason, he's not there. I'm not sure whether or not I answered his question. Maybe he's gone to get food; maybe he's just gone.

I stand in one spot until I start to feel paralyzed, then I move to make sure I still can. That's when I realize that Matt and I are never more than a few steps away from each other. After we arrived, we split up, but we never really split apart. Bound by an invisible chain, I move into the kitchen, thirsty, and he's already there, his nose in the refrigerator. He sits on the sofa and I check out the photos on the living room walls. I lean against the piano, desperate for this day to be done, and he lightly brushes my shoulder as he passes. I realize that we're giving each other strength using all we've got left: our presence.

Matt is sitting on the hearth across the room when Mason walks up and tells me that it's time to go. I'm beyond exhausted, and it could be eight or midnight: Either would make sense in my new, strange world.

Fifteen feet between us, Matt and I stare at each other, neither of us moving but both of us knowing it's going to get more difficult before it gets better.

"Okay," I say, still watching Matt. I'll see him at school when he comes back. But it will be different. Leaving now feels like saying goodbye to our old selves, to anything light and carefree.

Goodbye, halcyon.

My eyes well up with tears, and they stay locked on Matt's until I reach the doorway of the room and am forced to turn a corner. Even when I look away, I can feel his stare. I'm not sure how my feet are capable of walking away, but they do, and when I reach the back of the SUV, I collapse on the seat and fall asleep in an instant. Mason zombie-walks me into the house when we arrive, and I sleep in my funeral clothes, even my shoes.

thirty-two

thirty-two

thirty-two

Four days later, I shoot upright in bed at four in the morning. Heart thundering in my chest, I listen for signs of what startled me awake. There is movement down-stairs: I hear two pairs of footsteps rushing around the house.

I jump out of bed and run down to the lab to see what's going on.

"Go back to bed," Mason says when he sees me. "Everything's okay."

"What are you doing?" I ask. My heart sinks when I see him standing beside the black case.

"God wants us to try something," he says. He looks

incredibly uneasy. Cassie shakes her head as she leafs through a file.

"Where are those forms?" she asks.

"I'm not sure we'll need them," Mason says quietly. "How many vials do you think we should bring?"

"The most we'll use is three, but bring five to be safe."

"What are you going to try?" I ask.

"There's been a car crash," he says. "A man coming home from a night shift," he explains in broken sentences like he's preoccupied. "A janitor. Car's totaled. God wants us to try to Revive him."

"But it hasn't worked on adults," I say, shocked.

"I know," he says. "Not yet, but they've made improvements."

Not enough, I think.

"And it's the middle of the night," I continue.

"I know."

"And the test group is only the bus kids, and——"

"I know!" Mason shouts. He flips around and stares at me. He looks angry, but somehow I know it's not really directed at me. "Don't you think I know all of this? The program is supposed to be *controlled*. It's not supposed to be like this. Now he expects us to . . ." He stops talking midsentence and takes a deep breath. "It's going to be fine, Daisy," he says. "We heard on the scanner that the locals are on the way. If we don't make it before they do, we won't be able to try it."

I watch as Mason goes through the process that opens the Revive case, as his hand moves to choose five vials from the fifty. Wildly, my eyes flit over the vials. Forty-nine of them might save this man; the one filled with water most definitely will not. My temperature rises. I don't remember which one it was. I think it was some-where in the—

"Don't take that one," I blurt out without thinking. Mason's hand freezes in midair. Cassie and Mason both turn to face me, their expressions shifting from confusion to shock to anger.

"Why not?" Mason asks.

I don't speak.

"Why shouldn't we take that one?" he asks again.

I'm frozen solid.

"What did you do?" Mason snaps. I recoil. He's never talked to me like this before.

Strangely, Cassie is the one who rushes to my side. "Daisy, as you know, time is of the essence here," she says calmly. "We can talk about this later," she continues, shoot-ing Mason a look. "But if we need three vials right now, which part of the storage box should we take them from?"

I point to the leftmost row, and the row on the bottom.

"You're sure there's nothing wrong with those?" Cassie says as Mason starts grabbing vials.

I nod, not wanting to betray myself by speaking. In

truth, I'm only *pretty* sure. Not a hundred percent sure. Not bet-my-life-on-it sure.

Bet someone else's?

"Go upstairs," Mason says flatly as he closes the travel container. He doesn't meet my eyes when he moves past. I listen to him storm out to the car. Silently, Cassie goes, too.

thirty-three
thirty-three

thirty-three

A few hours later, I walk through the doors to Victory High a completely different person than I was just a few weeks ago. I haven't showered, and I'm wearing the T-shirt I slept in. My untamed dishwater curls are wrapped into a knot. I don't have on any makeup, not because I might cry and wash it away, but because it takes too much energy to put it on in the first place. I had three bites of a banana and a Coke for breakfast. I can't remember whether I brushed my teeth.

Inside school, it's too loud. Too bright. People are staring at me, whispering behind my back. They look like the unfocused background in a photograph: They're there to show contrast, but for nothing more.

I walk up the flight of stairs to the second level and work my way to my locker. Some girls are chatting at the locker next to mine. They stop talking when I approach and step aside so I can get through.

"Hi, Daisy," one of them says quietly.

"Hi," I say. I don't know her name.

I swap out my books and try very hard not to look at Audrey's locker as I walk away, but it doesn't work. I see it, and I imagine her standing there, smiling at me on the first day of school. Complimenting my shoes. Asking me to lunch.

Breathing.

Living.

As if I have emotional food poisoning, all of my tears and snot and even a shrill scream come out of me at once. Everyone in the hallway stops and stares. I run to the nurse's office and get excused from school.

The hall pass reads, "Distressed."

I block out the world for two days, or at least I think I do. When Mason's had enough, he picks the lock on my bedroom door.

"You have a visitor," he says. I have a pillow over my face so I can't see him or anyone else.

"Tell whoever it is to go away."

"You'll have to do that yourself," Mason says. I hear him leave the room. Someone else comes in. Whoever it is sits on the end of my bed but doesn't say anything. I don't move the pillow: I breathe into it and wait. The moisture of my breath, trapped between me and the fabric, makes me feel like I'm in a sauna, but I don't move. And still, silence. Eventually, I start to get perturbed. Why come into my room and just sit there? Frustrated, I toss aside the pillow. And then I see someone I never thought I'd see again.

"Sydney?"

"Hi, sweetie," she says in the voice that always made everything better. "I hear you're having a tough time."

The acknowledgment of my pain brings it all out again; I begin to sob. Sydney moves closer—right next to me—and wraps her arms around me. She's wearing a gray sweater that I'm pretty sure I ruin with snot, but she doesn't seem to mind. We sit there like that, her smoothing my ratty hair and me crying on her shoulder, until I don't have any tears left.

After that, we talk for hours. I tell her all about Audrey—every minute I remember. I tell her a lot, but not everything, about Matt. I share that I feel guilty for being with Megan when Audrey was dying. That I think there's something going on with the program that's stressing Mason out. That there's even more that I don't want to talk about right now.

"You've got the weight of the world on your shoulders," Sydney says. "I can see why you needed some time to yourself."

"I wish Mason was as understanding as you are," I say.

"Oh, Daisy, you need to give him a little credit," she says. "He may not have known what to do, but he knew enough to call someone who might. And I think he's more in tune with what you're going through than you might think."

"Maybe..." I say, not really believing it. Mason's a science guy, not a feelings guy. "I just don't know what to do now. I don't know how to *be* without Audrey. What should I do?"

"Daisy, I wish I could fix everything for you," Sydney says. "I'm so sorry to see you hurting. But the hard truth is that the only thing that can mend a broken heart is time."

I'm quiet, frowning because she sounds like a condolence card. I tell her as much.

"Well, it's good advice," she says. "That's why it's on so many cards."

I half smile at her; she takes my hand.

"There are little things you can do," she says.

"Like what?" I ask, craving a prescription that will cure my heartbreak.

"Well, like first thing in the morning, when you wake up and remember that Audrey's gone, instead of dwelling on what she won't get the chance to do, think of something really great that she *did* do. Honor her a little, and then move on."

"Easier said than done," I say. "What else?"

Sydney shrugs. "Take a shower. Go to school. Pay attention. Do the things you used to like to do; eventually, they'll get fun again. Call Megan and talk to her about your feelings. When he's ready, try to reconnect with Matt."

I'm quiet, so she continues.

"Unfortunately, there's no formula for making the pain of death go away sooner. No matter what, you're going to carry this with you for the rest of your life. But how you carry it is up to you. You can choose to dwell on the sadness of losing Audrey, or you can choose to celebrate the time you had with her."

"You sound like her," I say.

"She must have been a smart girl," Sydney jokes.

For the first time in days, a small laugh comes out of me.

"Are you going to get in trouble for coming here?" I ask.

"What God doesn't know won't hurt him," Sydney says. "And besides, my best girl needed me. You may not know it, but I'm always here for you, Daisy."

Sydney leaves after dinner, and it's like she takes some of my angst with her. By talking openly about Audrey, I feel like I've released a lead balloon. I'm a little bit lighter. A little bit better.

I go to bed at nine and sleep like a baby. When I wake up in the morning, the memory of Audrey's funeral slams into my brain. I push it aside, choosing to think instead about the time she thought she saw Jake Gyllenhaal outside Starbucks downtown. Sad and happy tears stream down my face as I laugh out loud about her reaction: She *really* thought it was him.

"You're totally Gyll-obsessed," I say aloud to Audrey, wherever she is.

And then, I go take a shower.

I walk to school, hoping that the fresh air and vitamin D will help perk me up even more. On the way, I dial Megan's number.

"I'm sorry for not calling you," I say.

"Don't apologize to me," she says. "Your best friend just died. I'm impressed that you're even functioning."

"I wasn't there for a few days," I say.

"I know," Megan says quietly. "Mason called my mom for advice."

"Sometimes I think they love each other," I say, smiling.

"Same."

"It's a good thing we love each other, too," I say. "Just in case they ever own it and get married or something."

"We're already sisters, anyway," Megan says.

We're quiet for a few seconds.

"Hey, Megs?"

"What's up?"

"I feel ... guilty," I say.

Megan is quiet, encouraging me to go on.

"I feel like I've been given so many chances, and Audrey didn't even get one," I say. "I feel horrible about it."

"You have survivor's guilt," Megan says softly. "It's normal."

"Yeah, but it's more than that," I say. "I feel like I should have done more for her. I feel guilty for being in Seattle when Audrey was going downhill. I feel like I abandoned her or something. I actually feel bad for being with you."

Megan is silent for so long I think the phone might have lost service.

"I can see how you might feel that way," she says finally.

"You do?" I ask.

"Of course," she says. "But stop worrying about things like that. You didn't give Audrey cancer, and you couldn't make it go away, either. Audrey knew you loved her, and you guys were good. There's no way you could have predicted when it would happen. It's not your fault."

When Megan says those last four words, my heart implodes. Not until this moment have I realized that I've been blaming myself. I mean, sure, Audrey had cancer, which was totally out of my control. But in a way, I thought—I hoped—that my friendship was helping her to stay strong.

"You're right," I say quietly. "It's not my fault."

"I'll tell you what is your fault, though," Megan says, a little tinge of teasing in her voice.

"Oh, really?" I say, okay with thinking about something besides death for a while.

"It's totally your fault that our blog is lopsided right now because of a serious lack of coverage out of Middle America."

"I might be able to solve that problem," I say.

"I can't wait to see what Flower Girl has to say."

Feeling lighter after my call with Megan, I reach Victory with a little time to spare. As I walk through the doors, an idea pops into my head. Before classes start, I go to the computer lab and print out the lyrics to "The Way I Am." It's the song Audrey sang to Matt and me when she was joking around about our crush. But I realize that it sums up our friendship, too.

With a bunch of curious students watching, I tape the lyrics to the front of Audrey's locker, then, smiling, head to English alone. Matt's chair is still empty, but I know he'll come back soon.

When I visit my locker again before lunch, there are more lyrics taped to Audrey's. By the end of the day, her locker is completely covered by handwritten and printed scraps of songs tacked on in Audrey's honor. As I read through the lyrics, I finally understand.

Everyone misses Audrey; they weren't faking it.

I'm not alone.

thirty-four

thirty-four

thirty-four

A little over a week later, responding to Megan's fantasy Grammy speech, I blog my gracious Oscar acceptance. Then, back on earth, I check Facebook. It's not something I do a lot. Having to start a new profile every time I change my name, I never have very many friends, so there's not much activity on my pages. When I last checked in Seattle, I only had sixteen friends, and most of them were bus kids.

That's why, after typing in my password and checking my notifications, I'm surprised to find thirty-two friend requests waiting for me, all from kids at Victory. Most of them are straight-up requests, but a few have sweet notes about how awesome Audrey was and how cool it was of me to start the lyric tribute.

I accept every single one without hesitation, then check my wall for new posts. Nicole Anderson, formerly Nicole Yang, a bus kid who lives in Atlanta, posted a "positive energy" message in light of Audrey's death. I smile about both the note and the fact that Megan's obviously looking out for me. A girl in my history class sent me a virtual hug. I scroll down and get a jolt when I see a post from Matt.

I miss you.

I don't know why, but I don't write back right away. I'd rather call him. See him in person. Look in his eyes and really connect with him.

For the moment, I move on.

I notice that Megan's online the second before she sends a friend suggestion. It's for Nora Emerson.

I sigh deeply, considering what to do. The night in Seattle when Megan and I found Nora feels like years ago, but two weeks have passed. So overwhelmed and exhausted by everything with Audrey, I've been pushing thoughts of Nora away. But it's time to deal with this. The need to know what happened to Nora—to know for sure if she's Case 22—overtakes me.

I click to add her as a friend and type a cryptic personal

message to her: "I want to hear your story. I'm like you."
As if she was waiting by the computer, she friends me immediately. Since she's online, I open the messaging program.

Nora, it's Daisy from FH. Call me if you want to talk.

I type in my cell number and hit return, then watch the clock. The phone rings before two minutes have passed.

"Hello?" I say.

"It's Nora," the voice on the other end of the line says. Unsure, she adds, "Emerson." Her voice is the same as the day she brought me the birthday invitation, except she was more confident back then.

"Nora, it's okay," I say. "This is Daisy. You knew me as Appleby. You probably thought I was dead until you saw me in that mall."

"Oh my god I thought I was going crazy!" The words tumble out of her mouth before she exhales loudly into the phone. "They showed me pictures from your autopsy."

"They did what?" I ask, appalled. Is this what the program is turning into—a ring of deception? Nora's quiet, so I clarify. "I don't know where the photos came from, but they were fake, Nora. I'm very much alive."

"I knew it," she admits. "Even when they showed me the photos. I knew it was you in that mall. You look exactly the same, only ... better."

"Thanks," I say quietly. Neither of us speaks for a few seconds. "So, who showed you the photos?" I ask gently.

"Two policemen," she says. "I told my mom about seeing you, and she called the police. The next day two of them came to our house."

"I see." I know that those "policemen" were agents, but somehow, even after being relocated, Nora still thinks they were cops. Is it possible she thinks that her car wreck was an accident? Is it possible that it was, and that the agents just happened to be trailing her because of me? Is it possible that they jumped on an opportunity to both save and silence Nora?

"But like I said, I didn't really believe them," she continues, interrupting my jumbled thoughts. "I had this feeling. I knew it was you. I told my mom, and even though she told me that I should let it go, I talked her into promising that we'd go to the station the next day and talk to the chief. Then that night I went out with Gina, and on the way home, I got in a car accident. That sort of over-shadowed everything."

Her voice wavers like she's going to cry, but she sniffs loudly and holds it together. I stay still, remembering what Mason says about people being allergic to uncomfortable silences. According to him, the best way to get someone else to talk is to hold your tongue. His strategy works.

"I woke up in this tiny town with my parents thanking God for saving my life and telling me stories of a Good Samaritan who pulled me from the car. But then they said that we had to live in Franklin and use new names and not tell anyone who we were before, and at first they wouldn't answer any more of my questions. I thought I was going mental...."

"Are you okay?" I ask after her words trail off. I can't help but feel sorry for Nora. Being Revived at this point and having closed-off parents who won't tell you anything has to feel terrible.

"I had some bruises," she says. "They're healed."

"That's not what I meant," I say.

"I know," she says, but she doesn't elaborate or answer my question. "It's...I don't know. I don't really want to talk about the accident. It's still too fresh."

"Okay, then let's talk about the drug," I say.

"What drug?" Nora asks, genuinely clueless.

I scrunch up my face, confused. Didn't they tell her anything? It strikes me that I might completely freak Nora out if I drop the whole Revive program in her lap at once. I decide to let her steer the conversation.

"Um...didn't they use some kind of a drug to save you?" I ask.

"Huh?" Nora asks. "Oh, no, the Good Samaritan did CPR for, like, twenty minutes, until the ambulance came."

"Do you remember it?" I ask.

"No," Nora says. "I passed out when I was still in the car."

Or *died*, I think to myself, but don't say. This is all too weird.

"So, why do you think you're in Franklin?" I ask.

"Oh, I *know* why we're in Franklin," Nora says. "My parents eventually fessed up to that much."

"Why?" I ask.

"Daisy, you don't have to be embarrassed," she says, confusing me again. "I know our dads worked with the same family back in Frozen Hills. Yours counseled their son, and mine did the accounting. Their former employer is on trial for racketeering and a bunch of worse crimes."

"Okay," I say when she pauses. My mind is spinning. What the hell is she talking about? Then, without me having to ask, she fills in the blanks.

"That's why you said 'we're the same' when you messaged me," Nora says. "Duh, we're both in the witness relocation program. And I'll tell you one thing, my relocation sucks."

Unable to contain myself, I pretend to be called to dinner a few minutes later, promising to reconnect in the next day or two. Then I dial Megan and tell her everything that just happened, word for word.

"What the *what*?" Megan says when I'm finished.

"I know! I mean...This is so... What's *happening*?"

"Okay, so let's think rationally here," Megan says.

"Okay."

"So Nora sees you, agents disguised as police try to deter her from telling anyone—"

"And maybe bug her house in the process?"

"Maybe," Megan agrees. "Which is how they knew that it didn't work."

"And why they were still following her that night."

"Conveniently."

"Too conveniently," I mutter.

"Then there's a crash, either accidental or intentional," Megan continues piecing it together. "If it was accidental, then the agents jumped on the chance; if it was intentional, then—"

"The program is jacked up."

"Yes," Megan says. "Okay, so either way, what, the agents go to Nora's parents like they did with the bus kids and say that we'll try to bring her back if you agree to a relo?"

"And they agree, but they decide to lie to Nora about why they're really there?"

"But they didn't make up that story on their own," Megan says. "The agents had to have fed it to them."

"Why not just tell them about the program, now that they're in it?" I ask.

"That's the million-dollar question," Megan says. "Maybe they were still concerned that Nora would tell, so they didn't fully pull back the curtain. Maybe they are keeping them in the dark, forcing them to lie to Nora so she's *really* in the dark and can't do more damage."

Neither of us speaks for a few moments as we collect our thoughts.

"I guess it works," I say. "I guess I understand why they'd want to keep Nora clueless. But I still feel sorry for her. Unlike us, she has no network."

"Except you, her fellow wit-pro buddy." Megan laughs.

"Funny," I say without laughing.

"Stop obsessing," Megan says.

"I'm not."

"Yes, you are," she says. "You want to know whether it was an accident or not."

"Don't you?"

"Honestly? Not really. I already think the program is a little dark side as it is; I don't need to be spooked about killer agents."

"Dark side?"

"Of course, Daisy," Megan says. "You know it better than anyone."

"I know," I say. I guess I am obsessing.

"All I'm saying is that if you decide to go digging in the cemetery," Megan says, "be careful."

Casually, over bacon-wrapped meat loaf and garlic mashed potatoes, I ask Mason what ended up happening with Nora. He looks at me funny at first, then remembers what I'm talking about.

"Oh, nothing," he says, setting down his fork and taking a drink of water. "If I remember correctly, the briefing said that she let it go, so we did, too. The agents were pulled out and reassigned."

"Oh," I say, pushing my food around on my plate with my fork.

"Sorry I forgot to circle back on that one," Mason says.

"No problem," I say as lightly as I can, knowing that even though Megan's not up for digging, I'm going to need a shovel.

thirty-five
thirty-five

thirty-five

Matt comes back to school on a Thursday.

I only find out he's coming back when he walks through the door to our English classroom. It stings a bit that he didn't tell me—that he didn't want to ride together or meet up before class—but I knew things would be different.

I just hope they're not different forever.

In the halls, people look from me to Matt and back again with funny expressions that I can't read. It feels like we broke up even though we were never official, except that when we catch each other's eyes, we talk without speaking.

I wish they'd stop staring.

Everything's going to be okay.

I still care about you.

We're only a few feet apart, but there's a wall between us, both of us unable to deal with the enormity of our feelings toward each other right now. Somehow I know that eventually we'll fall back into step, so the pain is the low hum of detachment rather than the screaming stab of the end.

I try to busy myself with other things, namely Nora.

After Matt's first day back, I call her like I have three other nights this week, but I need it more this time. We chat about school, she buzzes about boys. It's like we're old friends, except that we aren't. Not really. Talking with Nora makes me miss my *real* friends. Megan. Matt.

Audrey.

When it approaches bedtime, I decide to try again on the whole accident thing.

"A girl at my school got into a car accident," I lie. "She said it was the scariest thing that's ever happened to her."

"I can relate," Nora says. "I thought I was going to die."

"You did?"

"Of course," Nora says. "I was already creeped out by the dark road—the streetlamps were out in a couple of places because there was an electrical storm earlier in the day. Then when the truck came around the bend with its high beams on, I got this sinking feeling, like I knew it was going to swerve into my lane before it actually lost control."

I hold my breath; this is more than she's shared in any of our conversations. I don't want to call attention to her story by speaking, in the hope that she'll keep going. For now, it works.

"I cranked the wheel to get out of the truck's way. Half of my car went off the pavement onto the gravel, so when I braked, the loose, wet gravel sort of grabbed the car and pulled it more off the road, but my wheel was still turned so the car..." Pause. "It flipped."

"Oh, Nora," I say quietly. "That's horrible."

"Yeah," she says.

I get the sense that she's going to change the subject, so I ask a question to stay on topic.

"What was it like?" I ask, cringing for making her relive it.

There's another pause, when I wonder if I've pushed too hard. But then...

"Loud," she says. "It happened really quickly, but I remember it like I was in slow motion. I had this CD case on the seat next to me, and I remember watching it float around the car like there was no gravity or something. My water spilled all over me. I hit my head, but I didn't feel any pain. Then the car landed upside down. I was still strapped in, so I was just hanging there. Bleeding."

"That must have been so insanely terrifying," I say honestly. "I mean, to be out there all by yourself, thinking you're going to die."

"Except that I wasn't by myself," Nora says. "I saw the

truck driver before I passed out. He was the Good Samaritan. He walked in front of my headlights, and then crouched down next to my window. It was open because all the glass was broken."

"And he pulled you out?"

"Yes," Nora says. "But not right away. At first he checked on me. Then he called someone."

"Nine-one-one?"

"I guess, but it sounded more like a normal conversation. Maybe he was asking a friend what to do. I'm sure he didn't know whether he should move me or not."

"I'm sure," I echo, wanting to shake her for being so clueless. "What did he look like?" I ask, channeling Mason and Cassie.

"Uh..." Nora says, warily. "Just normal," she says, and I don't press it. In fact, I don't say anything at all. "Anyway, then he came back over and said, 'Help is coming,' and I passed out a couple seconds after that."

It hits me again that Nora doesn't know she died.

"Wow," I say, because it seems safe.

Nora's quiet, except I can hear her inhale and exhale like she's breathing through the trauma. Finally, she laughs a little.

"What's funny?" I ask.

"It's just weird what you remember."

"Like what?"

"Like the guy," Nora says. "It's mean, because he saved me and all, but he reminded me a little of Daffy Duck."

"Huh?" I ask. "He looked like a duck?"

"No," Nora clarifies. "He reminded me of him. It was his voice. He had a lisp. It wasn't as pronounced as Daffy's, but…"

Nora keeps talking about cartoon characters, but I don't hear her. I'm lost in thought, time-traveling back to when we first came to Omaha and I visited the aquarium. I remember the unsettling stranger who talked to me and then disappeared.

The otherwise nondescript stranger with a lisp.

Even though lisps are incredibly common, I feel it in my bones that this is more than a coincidence. But why would the same agent who was there to Revive Nora— who possibly caused her death—be at the aquarium? And why would an agent be so covert while speaking with me? We're one big network, all working together. Everyone knows one another. Everyone except…

The hairs on my arms stand up; a shiver dances down my spine.

"Are you there, Daisy?" Nora asks.

"Sorry," I say. "I've got to go."

I end the call before she says goodbye, and then I sit in shock.

Finally, because I've got to tell someone, I dial Megan. The second she picks up, before she has the chance to say anything, I spill.

"Megs," I say, fear in my voice, "I'm pretty sure I saw God."

The floorboards creak outside my door and I stop talking for a minute to listen. When no one comes in, I continue in a whisper.

"Even though Nora hasn't confirmed that someone had her killed, I know it's true," I say. "And that is just... off-the-rails crazy. And then they hid her, but didn't tell her about the program, and now they're Reviving new Converts? It's all too much. If this is how things are going, I'm even more worried about Matt. I'm going to pull together notes on everything I know and share them with Mason tomorrow," I say. "He'll know what to do."

"I think it's the right move," Megan says. "You're taking control."

"Love you, Megs," I say.

"Love you more."

When I finally go to bed, I imagine Matt's car being driven off the road and have to shake my head to fight off the thought. I toss and turn for hours, thinking of one gruesome scenario after another. I lie on my left side and the thoughts are there. I switch to my right—no escape.

Finally, I force myself to remember that Matt isn't Nora: He won't tell.

Then again, I think as I flip to my stomach, it seems that God paid me a visit, so maybe he's watching me. And if he's watching, then maybe he already knows, anyway.

thirty-six
thirty-six

thirty-six

In the morning, anxiety slams into me. Then I think of Audrey singing to Matt and me at the breakfast table and I smile. I climb out of bed, shower, and go to find Mason before school.

Unfortunately, he and Cassie are on their way out.

"We need supplies," he says. "We're headed to the store. Want to come?"

"Not really," I admit.

"I'll let you drive," he offers.

"Sold."

Cassie sits in the back and I buckle into the driver's seat. I've only had two lessons, but I have my learner's permit now, so I sort of know what I'm doing. Even so, easing the tank out of the driveway is no easy task: I run over a patch of yard in the process.

I do better on the main roads, and somehow I manage to get us to the supermarket in one piece. Mason and Cassie put on parent faces as we walk inside, and I bounce along after them, giddy from driving.

The store is unusually busy and the lines are so long that I start to worry that I'll be late for school. We split up to shop and manage to do it pretty quickly. Then, even though we're pressed for time and it would be faster if Mason drove back to the house, I don't pass up the opportunity to pilot the return trip, too.

More confident this time, I have no trouble at all, not even with the sharp turn onto our street. But just when I blinker to pull into the driveway, Mason's hand flies to my knee.

"Stop," he commands.

"What?" I say, slamming on the brakes. I look at the street in front of me and behind. I'm afraid I've run over something or someone.

"Shh," he hisses.

Confused, I look at Mason's face. And that's when I want to scream.

Mason is a different person, one I've never seen before. Every muscle in his body is tense. His eyes are narrow, piercing. His jaw is clenched. And even though I didn't see him grab it — didn't know he had it on him — he's holding his gun.

"Back down the street," Mason says. Suddenly, I can't remember how to put the car in reverse. I fumble with a few things before Cassie pops up from the backseat and pulls the gearshift down to R. Slowly, I manage to creep backward a few dozen feet away from the house.

"I'll go," Cassie says to Mason. "You stay with her."

"No, I'll do it," Mason says. "Drive away. Check in ten."

Cassie nods once.

In seconds, Mason is inside the house, I'm ducked down in the back, and Cassie is driving a little too fast for residential streets. Only when I peek out the window at the house as we're speeding away do I realize what freaked Mason out in the first place.

The front door is wide open.

thirty-seven
thirty-seven

thirty-seven

"Are we moving here?"

"No, it's just a safe house," Mason says.

I'm standing in a dirty living room in Hayes, Texas, frowning at my surroundings in disbelief. I feel like I was teleported here when, really, it took thirteen hours by car. And still, I know nothing. Mason and Cassie were engrossed in their too-quiet conversation or calls from other Disciples the whole way. And with no one to talk to, the weight of too many nights with too little sleep got to me. The only scenery I saw was the backs of my closed eyelids.

"Why would God tell us to come here?" I ask, feeling the need to cough because of the thick layer of dust in the house.

"He didn't," Mason admits. I spin around. Cassie glances up from her tiny computer, then looks down again.

"Mason, what are we doing here?" I ask, starting to get anxious.

"We're retreating into the shadows," Mason says. "We're not sure what happened today—who broke in and why they did it—so we're taking a step back for a while. We're going to watch and wait."

"But…didn't that directive come from God?"

"No, it came from me," Mason says, standing tall. "God is acting out of character lately. We don't know who broke in. It could have been him."

"WHAT?" I ask. "You think God broke in to our house?"

"It's possible," Mason says. "But it's just as possible that someone completely unassociated with the program did it. That's why we're stepping back."

"And watching," I say.

"Yes."

It reminds me of the approach God recommended for Nora. Even if Mason doesn't, I know how well that worked out.

"So, how are we watching?" I ask.

"Several ways," Mason says as he removes his computer from its case. "James and David are flying to Omaha as we speak to do a sweep for bugging devices and to conduct a more thorough check for missing items. As you know, I was in a bit of a rush."

"Speaking of which, where's my book bag?" I ask. "You got it, right?"

My notes on Case 22 are in my backpack, tucked inside my math textbook.

"I'm sorry, Daisy—I only packed your clothes and your computer. I didn't get your schoolwork."

I shake my head at him. "Will you ask someone to send it overnight?"

"You want a government agent to FedEx your backpack?" Mason asks, a smirk on his face.

"Yes," I say flatly.

"Maybe," he replies. "We'll see if one of them can get it out."

Instead of making a snide remark, I change the subject. "How long are we staying here?" I ask.

"A week," Mason says. "Probably no more."

"Probably?" I ask. "What about school? I'll be held back for all I've missed between Audrey and this." The mention of Audrey's name slugs me in the side.

Mason pauses and eyes me in a way that makes me nervous. He shifts his shoulders so he's fully facing me; his expression is somber but sympathetic. It's the mask you'd wear while breaking the news about Santa's existence to a hopeful child. I half expect him to crouch down to eye level.

"I wanted to talk to you about that," he says quietly. And then, he deals me yet another of many blows today: "We're thinking of homeschooling you for a while."

Instantly on fire, I open my mouth to protest, but Mason's phone rings again. He holds up his left index finger—*just a minute*—while he answers with his right hand. Deflated, I blow out my air and run both hands through my hair, pausing in the middle of the movement to consider ripping some out. I look at Cassie, who's still typing away. Then I look at Mason, who, seemingly energized by his conversation, is talking loudly, offering opinions, and arguing with animated gestures that the person on the other end of the line can't even see.

And me?

I stand here in the middle of a strange living room, wishing I could go back two months and start all over again in Omaha.

But would I be able to change anything at all?

When he feels me staring at him, Mason covers the phone with his hand and whispers to me.

"Go start getting settled," he says. "It's only temporary, but you can still arrange the bedroom how you like."

He winks at me then, like this is some big joke. It only makes me more irate; there's no one to listen to how I feel about homeschooling or safe houses or any of the rest. I storm out of the room. And as I walk down the hallway in search of a bedroom, the kind of pissed that slamming doors and screaming doesn't even help, I realize that for the first time in my life, I feel like giving my dad the finger.

*   *   *

In the morning, we go out for supplies. Residual anger still stuck in my teeth, I don't speak to Mason unless I absolutely have to. Instead, I check out our temporary hometown.

As it turns out, there's nothing nice, appealing, or even remotely interesting about Hayes, Texas. Even in November, it's hot. It's small. It makes you feel like you sprinkled dirt on your cereal, then ate more for dessert. Women wearing curlers in public look at us funny at the hardware store. They cluck at Cassie because she's beautiful and they're in house-coats. The man at the grocery store asks where we're headed, as if there's a NO VACANCY sign at the edge of town and he'd like us to move along as soon as possible.

We do our shopping and return to the house, then Mason and Cassie are back to work. I meander from room to room aimlessly. Helpless. In the kitchen, I sit at the Salvation Army table and stare at the wall over the stove. After a while, I notice the grease splatters. I look at the floor and realize that it's a different color under the table than in the high-traffic area.

I stand abruptly, mission accepted. I may not be able to control much else, but I can clean. And what I figure out after four hours is that scrubbing floors, washing windows, and—vomit—cleaning toilets has a way of working the fury out of me. When they happen to cross my path, Mason and Cassie look at me like I've completely lost it. But as I start tidying the final room, I am completely clear. Without emotion or concern, I mentally outline what I'm going to say to Mason about Case 22 when the notes arrive.

I plan how to convince him to go after God.

Later that night, Cassie spends an hour "fixing" my computer. I know she's trying to be helpful, but really, I just want her to leave me alone. Now that I'm not mad anymore, and with a plan firmly planted in my head, there's nothing left to think of but Matt. I want to contact him, but Bot Girl's taken over my mainframe.

"What are you doing to it?" I ask, leaning over her shoulder as she types code faster than I can speak.

"Making it so no one can track your footprints," Cassie says. The quiet cadence of the keys tapping under her fingertips is surprisingly calming.

"So I can use it when you're done?" I fidget a little, considering what to say to Matt.

"Yes," Cassie says, not looking at me. I move around her and sit on the edge of the creaky bed. From across the room, the glare of the screen bounces off Cassie's glasses, making her look like she doesn't have eyes.

I'm startled when she pushes back from the desk.

"All done," she says in her sweetest accent.

"Thanks," I say to her back as she leaves.

After she's gone, I force myself to write a blog post and check in with Megan before I can write to Matt.

When finally—*finally*—I do, the words pour out of me like they've been waiting to hop onto the blank page.

Matt,

Even though it feels like we're on different planets now, I think of you constantly. I can only hope our orbits cross soon. I miss you like I never thought I could miss anyone.

Love,

Daisy

I hit send and wait awhile for a reply that doesn't come. Then I fall asleep in a bed that's probably infested with bedbugs, thinking that it would be all right if only Matt was here next to me.

thirty-eight

thirty-eight

thirty-eight

"Who are you talking to?" I ask Mason when I walk into the kitchen the next day. He has his cell pressed to his ear and a coffee mug in his left hand. He scowls at me for the interruption and shakes his head.

"If it's David, please ask about my backpack," I whisper. Mason is a killer multitasker: he hears and gives me a thumbs-up. I pop bread in the toaster and wait, then, because there's no jam, I use a butter-like substance that I hope doesn't kill me. I sit down and start eating, watching Mason and trying to will him to ask about my backpack with my mind. Right when I think he's forgotten, he comes through.

"Thanks for the lab inventory," Mason says. "Can I ask

one other small thing?" He pauses to listen. "Great, thanks. Daisy needs her school backpack. It's red, with a black-and-white patch on the front. I think it's in her room....Hang on."

He looks at me.

"Yes, on the right side of my desk, on the floor," I say.

Mason repeats the directions and then agrees to hang on while David goes to look for it. "No, the right side." He pauses again. "Yes, do that," he says.

I take another bite of toast, waiting for confirmation that the bag is on the way. Instead, Mason looks at me while he speaks to David.

"I can't believe it," he says. "Nothing else is missing in the whole house but a teenager's backpack? Guess that rules out involvement from the program."

Except that it doesn't, I think to myself as my stomach sinks. I put down my toast, no longer hungry.

I know it was about Case 22.

And *that* has everything to do with the program.

In fact, it has everything to do with God himself.

When Mason hangs up, I catch him before he rushes out of the room.

"I need to talk to you," I say seriously. It gets his attention. "And Cassie, too."

"Okay," Mason says, a concerned look on his face. "Is everything okay?"

"Not really," I say. "Let's get Cassie, and I'll tell you what I mean."

When my guardians are settled at the table across from me, I begin my prepared statement.

"I believe that God killed Nora Fitzgerald," I say directly, looking Mason, then Cassie, right in the eyes. Mason's eyebrows scrunch up in confusion; Cassie looks as surprised as she is capable of looking.

"That's quite an accusation, Daisy," Mason says. "Why do you think that?"

"Well, a few days after Nora spotted me at the mall, I was on the system and stumbled across a folder for a twenty-second case." I leave out the part about Matt.

Mason looks at me like I've just claimed that the earth is flat.

"But there are only twenty-one cases," he says.

"I know," I say. "But this was number twenty-two. I was curious, of course, so I opened it, but the name was confidential. The relocation town was listed as Franklin, Nevada."

"Okay . . ." Mason says.

Distracted, Cassie checks her watch and shifts in her seat. I know she'd rather be working.

"I told Megan about it," I say. Suddenly, Cassie attacks Mason with her eyes, probably annoyed that he's given me access in the first place.

"Daisy, you need to keep what you see in there to yourself from here on out," Mason says.

"Fine," I say. "But Megan's not the point. Anyway, she and I were messing around online and we found an article from Frozen Hills that said that Nora Fitzgerald had been killed in a car accident. But then we found her alive, on Facebook." Cassie looks confused this time: I wonder if she's going to call me on what I'm saying. I'm messing up the timeline and leaving out David's involvement, but basically, it's right. I speak quickly so she won't question me.

"Anyway, I've been talking to Nora," I say. Mason's jaw drops. Cassie inhales sharply.

"You've been talking to a girl who thinks you're dead?" Mason asks, sitting straighter in his seat.

"See?" Cassie says to him. "You give her too much freedom. Now look at what she's done."

"You guys are totally missing the point," I say forcefully. "The point is that Nora was killed—on purpose—then relocated because she knew about me. Except that she wasn't told anything real. She thinks that her family's in the witness protection program."

Cassie rolls her eyes, then stands abruptly.

"I've got real work to do," she says. "I'm going to let you deal with this mess, Mason."

She leaves the room and Mason stares at me for a long time before speaking again.

"Daisy, I can tell that this is really bothering you," he says. "So I want to understand. It sounds to me like maybe the agents following Nora because of the sighting took advantage of the situation when she crashed. They made the call to fix the problem by Reviving and relocating her.

It stands to reason that they wouldn't want to divulge pro-gram secrets, so they kept it from her. I'm not seeing how God fits in here."

"I was getting to that," I say. I take a deep breath and try to explain my hunch to Mason. "When we went to the aquarium when we first moved to Omaha, there was a guy who talked to me in the big ocean exhibit. He was there, asking questions, and then he disappeared. I couldn't remember a thing about him other than that he had a lisp."

I take a gulp of air.

"Anyway, when Nora told me about the crash, she said that the Good Samaritan who saved her sounded like Daffy Duck. Like he had a lisp. And when she described the situation, it sounded really weird. Like the guy didn't move or react quickly, and he called a 'friend' instead of nine-one-one. It got me thinking.

"I wondered if it was the same guy. At first, I thought he was an agent, but in that case, why didn't he identify himself to me that day at the aquarium? The only person I can think of who might talk to me anonymously, then kill Nora, is —"

"God," Mason says pensively.

"Right," I say.

There's a flash of something in Mason's eyes.

"What?" I ask.

"Nothing. The lisp thing just reminded me of . . . Noth-ing," he says. Then he shakes his head. "Why would God be in Omaha? He has no connection to Omaha other than me and Cassie, and he never meets with agents in person. There's no reason for him to be there."

"Who knows where God goes or what he does?" I ask.

"Well, he doesn't kill people," Mason says in a way that makes me feel like he's trying to convince himself.

"He didn't used to," I say. "But you've said yourself that there are upsetting changes happening to the program. Like the new lab, like God wanting you to Revive new people—"

"I did say that," Mason interrupts. "But this is over the top. We're testing a drug that gives people life—we don't take it away. There's no way Nora's accident was at God's hands."

"Then how do you explain that the one thing stolen from our house was my book bag, which contained a file detailing all of this and more?"

Mason looks away and smiles a little, then says, "Maybe you left it at school?"

"I didn't," I say flatly.

Mason's phone rings again. He answers and talks for so long that I think of going upstairs and giving up. But I've come this far. When he hangs up, I try again.

"Mason, what did the lisp remind you of?" I ask.

He sighs. "It reminded me of the bus crash," he says. "The local news interviewed an employee at a gas station a half mile from the bridge. Police were looking for the worn red truck that eyewitnesses said ran the bus into the lake. The gas station worker claimed to have seen the truck ten minutes before the incident. He said the driver stopped in to buy a lottery ticket. Apparently, the driver said, 'I think it's my lucky day.'"

Mason pauses; I look at him expectantly.

"The guy couldn't describe the man other than to say that he had a lisp," Mason says. He jumps when I inhale.

"Are you serious?" I say loudly.

"Daisy, calm down."

"It's not a coincidence," I say. "What if God caused the bus crash, too?"

"Stop," he says, startling me. "If that's true, then the work I've done for eleven years is all for nothing. God would never — could never — purposely kill twenty-one people. Twenty children. It didn't happen."

"Fine," I say. "But will you at least do me a favor?"

"What's that?"

"Ask David to look for the file on Case Twenty-two," I say. "If it exists, he'll find it. And if he finds it..."

I let the words hang in the air.

"Promise you'll let it go if David doesn't find anything," he says.

"Only if you promise to do something about it if he does."

Mason calls David and I make my way upstairs. Once there, feeling edgy, I pull out Audrey's letter. Something about the smooth handwriting calms me: I've started reading it every time I feel upset.

Daisy—

Promise you'll do two things for me.

The first is easy: Take my clothes. ALL OF THEM. Even if you throw them away, get them out of our house (but I have pretty good taste—haha!—so you should just keep them).

You've seen those people who can't let go. They sob over old T-shirts that aren't worth anything. My mom is a pack rat; she'll obsess. My ugliest pajamas will break her heart. Take them, Daisy. Do it for me (and for your wardrobe ☺).

The second thing: Take care of my brother.

He tries to be this strong, tough guy, because I think that's what he believes is expected of him. But he and I are so close.... This is going to wreck his world. I know he cares about you; I want you to be there for him.

There are so many other things to say, but I have to go to the hospital now. I hope you'll never read this, but just in case, I want you to know that you are unique and beautiful and funny and

*I'm glad to have called you my friend. My best
friend.*

> *Love,*
>
> *Audrey*

Beyond the clothes thing, I can't help but think that
I'm not doing too well with Audrey's other request. I text
Matt and when, after thirty minutes, nothing comes
through, I wonder if I've waited too long to reach out to
him. I wonder whether he's already gone.

Not six hours later, Mason knocks at my bedroom door
and tells me that he's flying to Washington, D.C., tomorrow. Cassie will stay here with me while Mason goes to
the top about God's recent exploits.

When I turn out the light, I picture Matt lying next to
me, and the idea of him makes me a little less restless.
Still, with bus crashes and faceless men in my mind, it
takes me forever to fall asleep, which is why I sleep until
eleven o'clock in the morning.

By the time I wake up, the house is quiet.

Everyone's gone.

thirty-nine

thirty-nine

thirty-nine

As I crunch through a bowl of old-people cereal, I grow increasingly anxious about Mason's trip to Washington. I drum my fingers on the table as I consider the possible outcomes.

Worst case, God will be found guilty of heinous crimes, no one will want to step in to run a dysfunctional program already in progress, and the world as I know it will crumble. The God Project will die; Revive will be the basis for a study with new, willing participants. Disgruntled bus kids will speak out; newspapers will accuse the government of hiding a superdrug; the government will lie about the drug's existence. Revive will become nothing but a myth; no one will have access.

Not even me.

And with no program to keep us together, what will become of me and Megan? Or of me and Mason, for that matter? Where will I live?

Shaking off thoughts of homelessness, I consider the more positive scenario.

Best case, God's actions will be easily explained and the program will continue as it has been. The rest of the bus kids and I will remain in the God Project for another nineteen years, after which point — assuming there have been no major issues — the FDA will approve Revive and make it available on a very small, controlled scale, probably first to the military. Carefully and quietly, it will trickle out to the public, and new lives will be saved.

Except I can't shake the feeling that the best case isn't that great. The past few months have been eye-opening for me; knowing what I do now about the program, will it ever really be the same? When I look through the files of those who didn't respond to Revive, will I dwell on the fact that they weren't given other lifesaving measures? When I visit Gavin in New York, will I be able to love his parents as much knowing that they took him from his birth mother? When I think of Audrey, will I always feel that I kept something monumental from her?

When I look into Matt's eyes, will I ever feel like he's safe?

With no right answer to comfort me, I shiver in my sleep shirt despite it being hot here in Hell, Texas. I get up, rinse my bowl in the sink, and decide to try not to think about Mason's trip. He's not even on the plane yet; his meeting's not until tomorrow. There's plenty of time to worry about him later.

For now, I choose to focus on Matt.

I check to confirm that he hasn't responded to my email or text. Then, I dial.

"Hi," he says, as if he was expecting me.

"Uh, hi," I say, surprised. I thought my call would go to voice mail; I glance at the clock and realize it's the beginning of lunch period at school.

We're both quiet for a minute. I wonder whether he's thinking of the last time we saw each other, because that's what I'm thinking about.

"Where are you?" I ask. It's too quiet in the background.

"In my kitchen," he says. "Where are you? You haven't been in school."

"Texas," I say.

"*What?* Why?"

"Long story," I say. "Something's going on with the program. I don't want to talk about it right now, okay?"

"Fine with me."

Pause.

"Matt, I wanted..." I stop talking because I'm not sure *what* I wanted. Instead, I ask, "Did you get my email?"

"Yes," he says quietly. "Text, too." And then, just when

I think he's going to make an excuse for not writing back, he simply says, "Thank you."

"You're welcome."

"Thanks for doing that thing for Aud, too," Matt says. "The lyrics."

"I didn't really mean to start a trend," I say. "I wanted to give her something."

"I know," Matt says. "I know what you mean."

"I miss her," I say quietly. He doesn't reply. His mom says something to him in the background.

"Listen, I've got to go," he says. "Can I call you back?"

"Sure," I say, my voice blatantly disappointed.

"Okay, I will. Bye."

Matt hangs up before I have the chance to say goodbye.

forty

forty

forty

I check the time on my phone: Mason's flight is taking off in a few minutes. At least Cassie will be back from the airport soon to rescue me from loneliness. Then again, having her around doesn't necessarily feel like company.

Frustrated by the feeling that I'm losing Matt more by the day, I grab a book and jog downstairs. I consider flopping onto the dingy couch in the living room, then turn instead toward the back of the house. Through the picture window, I see a line of trees acting as a fence for the property line. The middle one has a lovely reading spot beneath it. Fresh air calls.

I grab a blanket, bang out the back door, and stomp across the patio and the grass. It's snowing in other parts of the country and here it's still seventy degrees out; it's strange to be in such a season-less place. As I walk farther away from the house, the grass gets more and more overgrown until it's up to midcalf, just before the tree line. I throw down the blanket and ease to a sitting position, my back against tree bark.

I open my book and try to read, but I'm distracted by everything; the words don't make sense. After rereading the first page three times, I give up. I set the book down on the blanket next to me, lean my head back, and close my eyes. Right when I'm starting to unwind, my ringtone makes me jump. I pull the phone out of my pocket; my stomach flips when I see that it's Matt.

"You called back," I say.

"I said I would," Matt says softly. "You didn't think I was going to call?"

"I...no," I admit.

"I'm sorry," Matt says. "I'm sorry for not replying or calling. It's been hard. But I realized after I talked to you earlier that you're the one person on earth who makes it better."

I cover my mouth with my fingers and speak through them: "Wow," I say.

"What?"

"Sorry," I say, moving my hand back to the blanket. "I said 'wow.' I mean...that's how I feel about you. Like if we could be near each other all the time, it would make it better."

"I know," Matt says. "I mean, you have the craziest life

of anyone I've ever heard of, but you're the only one who makes me feel calm and sane."

We listen to each other breathe for a few moments.

"Do you want to talk about Audrey?" I ask.

"Not really," he says. "My parents are making me go to a counselor. All I do is talk about Audrey."

"I understand," I say, wanting to change the subject. "So . . . are you on your way back to school?"

"Not yet," Matt says. "I came home to take my mom to an appointment. Her car's in the shop. After I pick her up I'll head back. I'll miss a little of next period, but no biggie. Half of another class after all I've missed won't matter."

"Yeah," I say quietly.

There's a lull in the conversation before he adds: "When my mom calls, I'll have to go again."

"Okay, no problem," I say quickly.

"But I promise to call back," he says, a hint of playfulness in his voice.

"You'd better."

Pause.

"So, I know you said you didn't want to talk about it, but is everything okay with you?" Matt asks. "You guys randomly took off again, and now you're in . . . Where are you again?"

"Texas." I groan. "And yes, I'm fine. Everything's okay. It's some heavy stuff, but it's all going to be sorted out soon. Thanks for asking."

"Sure," Matt says. I think I hear a little disappointment in his voice, like he wanted me to open up. Then he moves on. "So, what's it like in Texas?"

"The lamest," I say. "At least where we are."

"I thought Texas was cool?" Matt asks.

"Parts of it, yes," I say. "But Hayes? Hayes is the opposite of cool."

"Hot," Matt jokes. I wipe my forehead with the back of my hand.

"It is definitely hot!" I say with a laugh. "I'm sweating like a pig right now!"

Matt laughs, too, the laugh I love so much it hurts, and for the moment at least, the mood is lifted. We chat about whether pigs really sweat that much and it's so easy and normal that I blurt out what I really want to say: "I want to be your girlfriend."

"I want to be your boyfriend," Matt replies easily, without hesitation.

"What do we do about that?" I ask.

Matt pauses, thinking a moment. "I guess what we just did? I mean, if we want to be together, then we are, even if you're in Texas."

"So we're dating," I say, trying it on for size.

"Honestly, I think we have been for a while," Matt says. "At least since that first kiss." My stomach turns somersaults and I smile a smile that makes my cheeks sore.

"I miss that kiss. And the other ones, too."

"Me, too."

"But, Matt?"

"Yeah?"

"I'm glad we didn't...you know..."

"I know," he says. "Not that it wouldn't be awesome," he adds quickly. "I'm just glad we didn't do something so huge on a day that was so bad. The experience would always be a little bit...tainted."

Matt's words are exactly what I need to hear. I want to run to him, but I have no way to get there. Instead I settle for telling him I love him, because suddenly I need to say it out loud—so he can hear me this time.

The moment I open my mouth, Matt's phone beeps.

"Hold on a sec," he says. "I bet it's my mom."

"Okay," I say. He switches over to the other line and I consider how I should say it—*Matt, I love you,* or *I love you, Matt*—while I move my feet to the beat of his hold song. A fly buzzes near my exposed ear and I brush it away lightly. Feeling airy, I sing quietly along with the song, wondering what he and his mom are talking about right now. It's been a few seconds but I don't mind. I'll wait all day for him.

Just then my other line rings, too. I switch over excitedly, expecting Megan and wanting to update her on the good news with Matt before I have to flip back over.

"Hello?" I say enthusiastically.

"You should keep your room tidier, Daisy."

I hear the lisp immediately; it sends chills down my spine.

"Who is this?" I say, feigning bravery despite the terror surging through me.

"Give it a think, Daisy," the voice says. "I'm sure you know."

"Is this..." I stop. "Is this God?"

He laughs a low, thin laugh. I suck in my breath.

At once I'm thankful for Mason's keen instincts: He whisked us out of Omaha and hid us in Texas, away from everyone, even God. And he was right to do it: God's clearly lost it if he's rummaging through my bedroom right now.

I feel myself relax the tiniest bit...until he speaks again.

"I've just finished reading the heartfelt letter from your dead friend," he says. "So sappy, and yet so touching."

My safe little world comes crashing down.

"You're in Texas?" I ask.

"Oh, no, no," God says, laughing. "I don't do heat. But I have eyes everywhere, Daisy." His tone changes to an evil hiss. "Don't for one second think that you're alone."

I stand abruptly, panicked. The fly buzzes my head again and I brush it away. I look up to the house and am horrified to see a silhouette in one of the windows. My window.

"Who is that?" I ask, staring.

"I guess you could say that it's Jesus," God says lightly.

"What's happening?" I ask.

"Silly girl, I think you know," God says. "Mason's

headed to D.C. to ruin my life, thanks in large part to you. We're hitting the road, but first I thought I'd gather some supplies. And, of course, return the favor."

I don't want to know what he means by that, so I focus on something else: Mason's not here to protect me, but Cassie will be back from the airport soon. All I have to do is stall him until she can get here.

"Where are you going?"

"Daisy, you're not a stupid kid; why do you ask such stupid questions?" he says. "But you know, I could live anywhere. I could be anyone."

"I know who you are," I say, taking a huge chance.

"You're lying," God says. "You have no idea who I am."

"Yes I do," I say. "I talked to you at the Omaha Aquarium."

The line is silent for so long that I start to shake with fear. He could tell *Jesus* to come right out here and kill me on the spot.

"Nice try," the voice says.

I know he's lying. He can wear all the disguises in the world, but he can't shake the lisp. I can hear it crystal clear, just like that day. Still, I don't provoke him. In fact, I don't say anything for a moment. I cover the phone with my hand so I can take a few deep breaths and try to calm my racing heart. As I do, I watch the window for movement. Then I hastily look around the wide-open acreage, trying desperately to remember in which direction the closest house lies. I take a step to the right, considering running....

"Daisy?" the chilling voice addresses me again.

"Yes?" I ask hoarsely.

"Jesus is excellent at many things," he says. "Sharp-shooting is one of them."

I freeze. There's a pause: I think I hear the tap of a keyboard.

"There we go," he says. "That's better. Now sit back down on your pretty little blanket. I do want you to go in out of the sun and meet my friend, but not yet. Wait for my word, will you now, dear?"

"Yes," I say, trapped.

"And stay on the phone with me," God says. "I'm loving our little chat."

I drop to my knees, then sit. I think of clicking over to Matt, screaming into the phone for help, but it's been too long. There's no way he's still holding for me. He's probably on his way to pick up his mom right now.

The fly that won't go away buzzes close this time, and when I brush it away, the back of my hand makes contact. The fly is too big to be a fly.

I freeze again, for another reason.

I hear what I didn't before: the hum in the background.

I look up, and there it is.

On a branch directly above me, I see it.

The hive.

*   *   *

"I have to move," I say into the phone.

"What's that?" God murmurs. It sounds like he's preoccupied with something else.

"I said I can't stay where I am," I say. I'm not sure what he's planning for me, but it might not be death. That's more than I can say for the bees.

"Why not?" God asks curiously. "Just a moment." I hear tapping, then nothing for a few seconds. I watch the silhouette appear in the window, then disappear again. A few seconds later, I hear two more taps, and then a small laugh.

"Oh my goodness," God mutters to himself, amused. "That is too good. Ironic, if you think about it."

"I'm moving, okay?" I say, standing slowly. "I'm walking toward the house. Tell your friend not to shoot me or anything."

There's a long, drawn-out pause. I can hear him breathing into the phone, through my ear and into the fear control panel in my brain.

"I told you to sit still." His voice is humorless and frigid. Terrifying.

"I can't," I say. "The bees will sting me."

"I assure you that worse will happen if you move," God says.

In the end, I don't debate it that long. Rationalizing that God would have instructed his lackey to shoot me in the beginning if he'd wanted me to die that way, I take a step.

Then I take another.

I hear tapping.

"Bad move," God says. "What a colossal waste of Revive you were."

Ignoring him, I take one more step, and the silhouette—Jesus—appears in the window. He props open the glass, and even from this great distance I can see the weapon aimed in my direction. I close my eyes and hold my breath, willing it to be quick.

There's a funny sound behind me, like a pebble hitting a pillow. Confused, I turn to look. And that's when I realize what he's done.

Jesus didn't shoot me; he shot the hive.

Angry bees spill out of the gaping hole in their home, seeking vengeance on anyone stupid enough to be standing nearby. I turn back to the house and see that Jesus is gone from the window. Even though I'm unsure where he is, there's no question now that I have to move. I take three steps before I hear the bees swarming above my head. Tears fill my eyes and fall down my cheeks; I don't move to wipe them away. In fact, other than my feet, the rest of my body is still. No. Sudden. Movements.

Step.

Inhale.

Step.

Exhale.

It's not that far.

It's not that far.

It's not that far.

I realize that the phone is still pressed to my ear. I'm afraid to move my arm, but I'm not going to sit on the phone with God while he and his puppet watch me die. With my thumb, I hit the call button; miraculously, I hear hold music.

I'm still on hold with Matt!

The music drives me to take another step. And another.

I don't think I've been stung yet, but the adrenaline in my body could be masking the pain. A single thought runs through my head: *Reach the EpiPen*. There's one in my bag, in the kitchen. All I have to do is cross our yard and the patio and go inside. It's right there. I can do it.

Don't think about the man in the house. He doesn't know where it is.

I can grab it before he knows better.

More and more bees swarm my body. Carefully, I step onto the shorter crunchy brown grass and start across. It can't be more than fifteen steps to the patio. Then only a few more to the door.

My mind jumps to the morbid thought that I'm trying to push away: *There is very little Revive in the house, and surely Jesus has already taken it to boost God's stash*. Even if there was a spare syringe, there's no one sane to administer it. I'm alone.

A bee lands on my forehead as I step onto the concrete patio. I can feel it crawling across, finding the perfect spot to inject its venom. I manage to stay calm until, suddenly, a person appears behind the sliding door. The sun is reflecting on the glass so I can't see more than a shadow, but still it terrifies me. I gasp and stop moving.

And that's what sets them off.

Bees on my arms, cheeks, head, and neck start sting-ing at once, like they're synchronized. In the second before I close my eyes, the reflection on the door shifts and I real-ize that it's Cassie.

She's home!

A wave of relief rushes through me despite the fact that bees are wreaking havoc on my body.

"Cassie!" I scream. The bees try to crawl in my mouth, so I slam it shut. I walk, covered with bees like a bee-keeper but without the protective gear, two more steps.

Elated that I've reached the door, I extend my hand to open it.

Cassie reaches over to help.

I hear the lock click shut.

Baffled, I try the door. It's definitely locked.

Confused, through blurred vision, I stare at Cassie. Maybe she doesn't understand. Maybe she thinks she unlocked it. Except . . .

Her face is normal. Neutral. Robotic. But there's also a hint of curiosity.

I realize that Cassie's actually typing something into her phone. How can she be working at a time like this? My other line beeps. Even though I know who it is, I decide to answer, hoping God will show me mercy. I flip back over.

"Now you see the error of your ways," God says, enjoying this. When I don't speak, he continues. "Well, I guess the cat's out of the bag now," he says jovially. "Daisy, meet Jesus. You might also know her as Cassie."

My eyes widen as I look in disbelief at the woman I've lived with for six years. The woman I've pretended to love like a mother. I get it now: She's been in communication with him. Today. Maybe always.

Fruitlessly, I tug at the door again. Cassie shrugs a shoulder at me and smiles. Then, like it's nothing, she turns and walks away, my school backpack slung over her shoulder and cases in both hands.

"Don't feel bad, Daisy," God is saying in my ear. "The problem is that you're too smart for your own good. You and Mason were never going to survive this day. The bees just gave us some extra fun. Enjoy!"

God disconnects and the rage rushes out of me: I scream as loud as I can. A bee stings my tongue. More sickened by that than by the external bites, I chomp down hard and spit it out. Desperately, I flip back to Matt, but he's not there. I drop the phone and run over to the garden hose. Somehow, through already puffy eyes, I manage to turn on the water and scare off the majority of the bees.

But it's too late.

They've done their worst.

I fall to the concrete, wheezing and swelling, dropping the hose next to me. I cry out even though my face, tongue, and neck are expanding, making it increasingly difficult to speak.

"Cassie!" I shout. "How could you do this?"

I know it's fruitless; she's already gone. I try to shout a generic "Help!" to draw in the neighbors, but I'm wheezing now and the word is nothing but a whispered "hup."

Then I stop trying, and I know it won't be long.

Seconds later, my throat closes up completely.

And just before the bright day goes dark, I think of Audrey.

forty-one

forty-one

forty-one

I open my eyes, but not all the way.

My field of vision is limited. It's as if I'm looking through my hands curled into O's, like mock binoculars. I hear movement and have to turn my head because I have no peripheral vision.

Mason is sitting in a chair next to my hospital bed.

I blink at him. He smiles and takes my left hand, and in his hand mine feels funny. Not numb, but... wrong. I look down at my arms: They're bloated like they've been pumped with air, red and blotchy. My left arm is attached to an IV and I can't help but wonder how they found a vein through all that marshmallow skin. I don't have to look in a mirror to know that my face looks the same way; instinctively, I touch my puffy cheek.

Mason's eyes are watery, and he's blinking like he's trying not to cry.

"Hi, Daisy," he says warmly. I look around, squinting, trying to make my eyes work properly. Mason takes it as me not knowing where I am. "You're at the hospital. You were attacked by bees, but you're okay now. You're safe."

I let go of Mason's hand so I can pat an itch on my forehead, knowing well enough not to use my fingernails—I don't want scars. I pat another on my right arm as a nurse breezes in to check on me. She tips forward a little as she walks, like she's about to fall over. She has punk-rock hair—a bleach-blond boy cut—even though she's the age of a grandmother.

"Welcome back, young lady," she says as she puts a finger on my wrist and looks at the clock. Her words are kind, but her face is all business.

"Thanks," I say, managing to talk even though my lips are stuck together. "Did you..." I whisper to Mason. He shakes his head and glances at the nurse. She does something behind me, then writes on my chart. Mason waits for her to leave before he answers me.

"Matt saved you," he says. "He called nine-one-one. And..."

"What?"

"He also contacted Megan."

I stare at Mason for a second, realizing that he knows I told Matt about the program. But breaking the rules might have also saved both of our lives. Mason's not saying more about it, so I decide to gloss over it, too.

"How?" I ask. Pat, pat.

"Through the blog," Mason says. Pat, pat.

"That was so smart of him," I say, amazed. I wipe at nothing under my right eye, and it's then that I realize what's blocking my vision: skin. My own swollen skin.

"Yes," Mason says, bringing me back, "it was clever."

"Cassie..." I say, shaking my head in disbelief. When I do, I feel the sting wounds on my scalp rubbing against the pillow. Aware of them now, I pat my head.

"I know," he says. "I can't believe that she was watching our every move all this time. Plotting with God. I can't fathom how or why...." His voice trails off and, for a second, he looks distractedly out the window.

"So did I die?" I whisper, because who knows where the nurse went.

"Yes," Mason says, his green eyes back on me.

"Tell me what happened," I say, mostly because I want to know, but also because I need a distraction. I've been stung by bees before, but it's never been this bad. It's like having PMS bloat throughout my whole body instead of just in my midsection; I have to wiggle my fingers so they don't go numb from losing circulation. That, coupled with the itchy, burning pain of my body rejecting the venom, is making me feel like I'm going to freak out.

Mason looks at me wearily; he can tell I'm not feeling well. "You need your rest," he says.

"Tell me what happened," I command.

"Okay, Daisy," he says, patting my hand, but not hard enough to take away the itch. "Okay." He pauses and leans closer to me so I can hear him despite his low tone. "Matt told Megan that he heard you say something about Cassie —"

"He heard that?" I interrupt, remembering lying on the concrete. Dying.

"Apparently so," Mason says softly. "Anyway, Matt relayed that to Megan, who in turn got David involved. David tracked Cassie's cell location and recent calls, which led him to God's location. He sent teams after both and focused on you."

"But Cassie cleaned out the Revive," I say. "And no one was around to administer it."

"David grounded my plane in the middle of a field and had a car waiting for me," he says.

"I bet that was scary."

Mason makes a so-so gesture with his hand. I pat, pat my cheek. "The civilians were frantic," he says. "They thought it was terrorists. I got an in-flight message from David, though, so I knew what was happening. It's a good thing, too; God had something planned for me when I landed in Washington."

"How long did it take you to get to me?" I ask, shifting to a more comfortable position.

"Thankfully, the flight path took us east, so I was only about twenty miles away."

"That's too far out," I say, shaking my head. Surprisingly, I can't feel the stings this time. "You couldn't have brought me back from that." Suddenly I feel spacey, like I'm watching the scene from outside my body. I realize that nothing else is bothering me anymore, either. I move my head again to make sure.

"Did the nurse give me something?" I ask.

Mason nods. "We've been sedating you to keep you calm," he says. "You were stung more than a hundred times."

My head falls back to the pillow but I fight sleep; I need to know what happened. I shake my head more forcefully to clear the fog.

"How long was I dead?"

"Twelve minutes," Mason says seriously.

"Wait, what?" I ask, my eyelids drooping. "But you said you were..."

"Shh," Mason says. "Get some rest now. I'll explain later."

I refuse to close my eyes. "Explain now," I demand, but it lacks conviction.

"Daisy, you died, but Revive didn't bring you back," he says.

"What did, then?" I ask, finally closing my eyes, barely hanging on to consciousness.

"Blah, blah, blah," I hear Mason say, except I'm pretty sure that's not actually what he said. I force open my eyelids one last time.

"What saved me?"

This time, because I can see his lips, I get it.

"CPR."

forty-two

forty-two

forty-two

When I'm feeling better and looking less like Frankenstein, instead of taking me back to Omaha like I want him to, Mason flies with me to Washington State. That same day, he boards his second plane in a week bound for Washington, D.C. Even though God and Cassie are in custody, Mason wants me under a watchful eye until he's sure it's all over. Still jumping at shadows, I'm okay with being watched.

For two weeks, Mason checks in on the phone or through email every night, but he never says very much. I try to keep it light and enjoy my time with Megan, but I have questions that need to be answered before I can fully move on.

And there are things to say, too.

My second to last night in Seattle, I dial Matt. I've spoken to him twice since the accident, but both times it was too brief and stilted: Mason was in the room the first time, and Megan was hovering the second.

"Are you alone?" I ask. It's late; Megan and her mom are sleeping.

"Yeah, just listening to some music," he says. "How are you feeling?"

"Pretty good," I say. "I'm back in regular clothes, and the scabs don't itch as much. My tongue doesn't feel like I pierced it anymore."

"That's good."

"I still look like I got beat up."

"At least you're feeling better."

I listen to Matt inhale and exhale; it makes me shiver.

"Listen, Matt," I begin. "I want to say thank you."

"You're welcome...again," he says with a little laugh.

"I'm serious," I say. "I don't know how I can ever thank you enough. You saved my life. I owe you—"

"Naw," Matt interrupts gently. "We're even."

"For what?" I ask.

"For...you saving me, too," he says.

"What do you mean?"

"I just don't think I'd have gotten through Audrey's death without knowing you were there for me. Even though we didn't talk much, having you in my life...That was enough. It helped. It was huge. I know I'm never going to get over it completely — I wouldn't want to — but now I feel like I can actually deal, and I owe that to you."

We're quiet for a few seconds. I think about how odd it is that after Audrey died, when I didn't hear from Matt, I spent a lot of time wondering if he was slipping away. I didn't know it, but he was holding on for dear life.

"I was about to tell you something right before every-thing happened in Hayes," I say. "Right before you clicked over to the other line."

"What's that?" Matt asks in a low tone.

I take a deep breath and decide to go for it.

"I was going to say that I love you."

I hear a quick exhale on the other end of the line.

"And if you had," Matt says, strong and sexy, "I would have said that I love you, too."

Two weeks and one day after Mason dropped me off, he's back. He says we're flying out the next day, back to Omaha. I bounce with excitement until he slams me back to earth.

"We're being relocated again," he reports.

"But why?" I ask. "God and Cassie are in custody. And I died in Texas. Everyone in Omaha thinks I'm out sick."

"Not everyone," Mason says, looking at me pointedly.

I stare at him, confused.

"The director is aware that Matt was the one who called nine-one-one," Mason continues. "That someone you went to school with in Omaha knows you died."

"But Matt knows I'm alive," I protest. "He knows about the program," I acknowledge aloud.

"I know that, but the director doesn't," Mason says.

"You lied?"

"Of course I lied," Mason says. "I was protecting you."

"But Mason, Revive didn't even bring me back," I say. "I can go back to school and tell everyone that I was miraculously saved by *normal* modern medicine after a bee attack. Everyone will be so impressed."

"That's the director's fear," Mason says.

"What?"

"That this will draw attention to you," he clarifies. "That if you go back and say you were saved from a bee attack, the news will report on you. People will look into your background. There's potential for exposure."

I'm quiet, unsure what to say. Mason looks at me with tired eyes.

"Daisy, I know you don't want to hear this, but it's better this way."

"What way?" I ask, anger rising in me.

"It's better if we go quietly."

"Better for *who*?" I ask, ready to burst. And then, with a few simple words, Mason changes everything.

"Matt," he says. "It's better for Matt."

forty-three

forty-three

forty-three

The house in Omaha already feels foreign; I guess my brain knows when it's time to go. This time, though, my heart wants to stay.

Mason gives me three hours to pack the critical items; the cleanup crew will ship the rest. I spend one hour half-heartedly tossing clothes and books into my suitcase, then I text Matt, asking him to pick me up down the block. I thump my suitcase down the stairs and leave it in the entryway for Mason to carry out to the car.

Mason's in the basement when I leave. Maybe I'll make it back before he surfaces; maybe I won't. Either way, seeing Matt right now isn't optional. I slip out the front door into the crisp afternoon air, then button my jacket, surprised by the wintery chill. I walk two blocks and stop on the corner, only long enough to blow on my hands once before Matt arrives.

The seconds after I climb into his car and shut the door are like the silence between songs on your most emotional playlist. It's a break in the action; the world stops spinning for a few beats. But you know something's coming.

And then it does.

Matt puts his hands on my cheeks, cupping my jaw-bones. His powerful eyes are more intense than I've ever seen them. Captivated, I couldn't look away even if I wanted to. He holds my face for a moment, staring. And then...

"Don't die," he says lowly, his voice cracking a little.

"I won't," I promise, hoping I'm telling the truth.

"I mean it," he says. "I can't take anything happening to you."

"I know," I say, grabbing on to his forearms, holding him holding me.

"Take your damn EpiPen to school," he says.

I laugh, a quick exhale. "I will."

"And stay away from bees," he continues. "In fact, just stay inside."

"Okay," I say, laughing again.

"And..." Matt moves closer; his face is inches from mine. "Stay."

It's like a punch to the chest; tears fill my eyes. Matt's

expression is so raw, so brutally honest, I want to find a reason to look away.

"I can't," I whisper.

"I know," he says.

He wraps his arms around me and pulls me into a tight embrace. I'm leaning sideways over the center console and the gearshift is digging into my hip and still, I'd stay like this for hours if I could. I've never been more comfortable. I've never been warmer. Here in Matt's arms, I'm reminded again:

I've never belonged anywhere but here.

forty-four

forty-four

forty-four

Nomadic as I am, I try hard to see the positives about our new hometown of Alameda, California. A little island between Oakland and San Francisco, Alameda is the sort of homey place that a person could really love...if her heart wasn't stuck somewhere in Middle America.

And yet, I try. Touring the city, I make mental lists of Alameda's pros:

1. The weather.
2. The updated main street, boasting places like hip clothing stores, an indie bookseller, and a vintage ice-cream shop all on the same block.

3. The intimate beach with a clear view of San Francisco's skyline that Matt would love...

It's hard to keep my head in this state. But Mason does his best to help.

When we drive into town two days before I start tenth grade for what I hope is the last time, he pulls into a driveway I mistake for someone else's.

"Are you lost?" I ask, looking at the Victorian that could be a movie set.

"Nope," he says, smiling and craning his neck to see the top of the three-story dwelling.

"Mason, are you messing with me?" I ask, eyeing the wraparound porch skeptically.

"I'm not messing with you," he says, laughing. "It's bigger than we need, but it's a historic home and I like it. Plus, you never know—our family might grow someday."

Before I have time to ask more about that last statement, Mason jumps out and heads up the front steps. He waves at me to follow.

When I walk through the door, I'm awestruck. For what Mason reports is over a century, this home was clearly loved. And why not? There's dark wood trim and paneling along the grand staircase. There are built-in library shelves that make me want to live right in the sitting room. The kitchen is bright and airy, with modern appliances; the living room is massive. And there are five bedrooms. "I get my own bathroom," I say. "And look at this closet!"

"You like it?" Mason asks sheepishly, as if the house is a gift he's giving me. I guess in a way, it is.

"It's awesome," I say before taking a moment to look out each of my three bedroom windows.

"Even though it's not in Omaha?" Mason asks.

I take a deep breath of California air.

"Even though it's not in Omaha."

On the night before school starts, I knock on Mason's bedroom door. He's in pajama pants and a gray T-shirt. He sets aside the novel he's reading and gives me his full attention.

"I was just wondering how things are going with the investigation," I say, lingering in the doorway.

"Oh, Daisy, there's nothing new," he says, rubbing his eyes. "They're still thinking it's going to take months to sort out. Apparently neither of them is being cooperative, and a lot is still unclear."

"So the program's on hold until they figure it out?" I ask.

"Unfortunately so," Mason says. "All the files and lab equipment and the drug itself will remain under tight security until the director can determine whether anyone else was involved."

"What do you think he's going to do after that?" I ask. "Kill the program?"

"I suppose it's possible, but not likely," Mason says. "The director has a science background. My hunch is that he'll take it under his wing and finish off the thirty-year commitment to tracking the bus kids. At that point, though, he might decide to bury it."

"Why?" I ask, surprised. "Wouldn't he want to move forward? Besides God going mental, the program's been a success, at least so far."

Mason swallows hard and looks away.

"Hasn't it?" I ask.

"It has," Mason says. "But you were right."

I think back to what I just said, to what he could possibly be talking about. When I don't say anything, Mason clarifies.

"Daisy, God caused both Nora's death and the original bus crash that started the program. He actually bragged about giving Revive the push it needed. You were right. In fact, it appears from his program files that he was looking for another 'bus.' Another large group of people to be the second test group. He had schematics for places like amusement parks and movie theaters at his office."

"Aquariums," I say, remembering.

"Aquariums," Mason says, realizing that I was probably right about the man under the ocean being God, too.

"How could anyone *do* that?" I ask, not because I'm particularly surprised but because I'm sad for all of us in the program, and for those of us who aren't.

"He'd have to be a sociopath," Mason says. "Which, I guess he is."

"And what about Cassie?" I ask, horrified.

"We always knew she was a genius who graduated early and was recruited out of college," Mason says. "But the truth is that it started much earlier than that."

"What are you talking about?" I ask, confused.

"Daisy, when God called Cassie Jesus that day in Texas, it wasn't much of a stretch," he says. "Cassie is God's daughter."

I gasp, then shake my head. Mason fills in the blanks.

"Her mother left when she was little, and I guess God saw that as an opportunity to mold Cassie into the person he wanted her to be," he says. "When the director figured out their relationship through DNA tests, he went back through Cassie's records more closely. She was rigorously homeschooled and never allowed to have friends. She was trained on weaponry and military tactics as a preteen. She was pushed into early graduation. Basically, she was bred to be an agent." Mason pauses. "With a man like that raising her, she didn't have a chance. She always wanted to please him, and I guess she never grew out of it."

"Why do you think he placed her with us?" I ask.

Mason sighs. I know he feels bad for not sensing that something was very wrong with Cassie.

"I don't think we'll ever know for sure," Mason says. "But my guess is that it was because of you."

"Me?"

"Yes. I think God was a little obsessed with you," Mason says. It sends chills through me. "Back when the bus crashed, he wanted to find you another place to live. He didn't want an agent taking on a child. But I fought for you."

"Why?"

"Did I ever tell you about my wife?" Mason asks.

"No, but I know," I say quietly. I'm not proud of it, but I've snooped in Mason's personnel file. I did it regularly until I found out that he had a wife who died in a skiing accident. After that, I was riddled with guilt and never opened his file again.

"Good," Mason surprises me by saying. "I'm not always the best at talking about personal stuff, but I'm glad you know." He pauses. "You would have liked her. She was really funny. And she was a hell of a cook."

I smile. "I'm sure she was great."

"She always encouraged me," Mason says. "She supported me through med school. Then, when the program first tried to recruit me, I thought I was too inexperienced to take part. I declined at first and she was upset; she said that I was blind to my own potential."

Mason looks distracted for a second, then comes back to earth.

"But she died, as you know. We were on vacation in Colorado. She lost control on her skis and hit a tree. It was immediate." Mason's eyes cloud over. "But what's not in the file is that she was pregnant at the time. It was so early that even she didn't know."

"I'm so sorry," I nearly whisper.

"Thank you," Mason says. "It was awful. But her death brought me to the program. I decided to pursue what she'd wanted me to. And then when you showed up, a child without a home, I saw it as my opportunity. It was as if I could feel Zoe pushing me forward, telling me to do it."

"I'm glad you did," I say.

"Me, too. I just hope that I didn't negatively impact you in some way, like God did to Cassie," Mason says, worried. "I've tried my best, but you've hardly grown up in a typical household."

"But no matter where it's been, it's been a loving one," I say. "That's all that matters. And you're nothing like God. You're a real father. I'll always be thankful for your decision."

Mason holds my stare for a moment and smiles warmly.

"It was the best decision of my life."

When I turn off the light on the day, my conversation with Mason fresh in my mind, a sick thought plagues me: If God was willing to go to such great lengths as purposely killing twenty-two people to start and protect his pet project, what else might he have done?

If, for example, he wanted Mason in the program but Mason wasn't interested, would God give him — or his wife — a little push?

Could he — would he — kill Mason's wife to lure him in?

And what about me and my accident-prone tendencies? Has it really been all about me? Sure, I'm forgetful, and yes, I do silly things. Everyone does. But I was under the thumb of a maniac and his ambitious daughter.

The thought that runs through my head much too late at night is this:

If he killed me once...

Did he do it again?

forty-five

forty-five

forty-five

In Audrey's skinny jeans and a deep purple top, I walk through the doors of Alameda South High School feeling giddy and jittery at the same time. Everyone eyeballs the new girl but, thanks to the tour after registration, I don't have to embarrass myself by asking anyone for directions.

A shorter girl with long blond hair and green eyes not quite as lovely as Mason's smiles at me from her locker, which is next to mine. A pit forms in my stomach as I think of meeting Audrey for the first time. But instead of turning away, I force myself to smile back before going to work on my combination.

"First day?" the girl says, striking up conversation. I look at her.

"Yep," I say. "We just moved here."

"I'm Elsie Phillips," she says, smiling again. "I moved here from Portland in August."

"Nice to meet a fellow transplant," I say. "I moved from Omaha. I miss it, but what can you do?"

"I hear you," Elsie says, tossing her bag in her locker. "I pine for Portland."

I laugh a little and so does she, but then there's an awkward pause in the conversation when it seems like neither of us knows what to say. Again, I think of Audrey. We never struggled. Then again, Megan and I didn't say five words to each other the first time we met.

"Well, I guess I'll head to class," Elsie says. "You know where you're going?"

I screw up my face in concentration and look around a bit. Then I point to the left. "I think I'm headed that way."

"Don't worry, it's an easy layout. The kids are pretty cool. You'll do great."

"Thanks," I say. We turn away from each other, and then I hear her voice call me back.

"Hey, what did you say your name was?" she asks. My stomach rolls. The FDA made me change it, and not just the last name this time, in case they kill the program and this is my permanent home. They claimed Daisy was too distinctive.

This is the first time I'm saying my new name aloud.

"Oh, sorry," I say casually. "I don't think I did. My name is Sophie. Sophie Weller."

Mason had suggested Sophie because it was his mother's first name. And I didn't know until last week, but Weller is his real surname.

"Nice to meet you, Sophie."

Elsie turns and leaves, and I can't help but notice as I walk to first period that I don't mind being Sophie Weller. It doesn't feel like an act. I straighten up and walk a little taller in my brand-new patent flats, hoping that someday soon, the pull of Omaha won't feel so unbearably strong, and that I'll feel like Sophie Weller all the way.

Epilogue

Epilogue

Epilogue

It's late May; my sophomore year is nearly over. In a few short weeks, Matt will arrive in nearby San Francisco for his summer-long music camp. We'll see each other at night and on the weekends, and I'm so excited I can barely contain myself. The thought of feeling his lips on mine again gives me chills; the thought of twirling my fingers through his curls is almost enough to make me skip finals and hop a plane to Nebraska.

Surprisingly easily, Matt and I have managed to stay together with seventeen hundred miles between us. We talk on the phone, text, and email every day; on weekends, when we have more time, we Skype. He told his parents that he was devastated when my dad was abruptly transferred to Alameda; they let him visit over spring break for five whole days. Though distance is often the kiss of death for relationships, somehow with Matt and me, it works. Maybe because both of us know what real loss feels like, physical separation isn't catastrophic.

Even so, Matt's only applying to colleges in northern California.

In and outside of school, I hang out with Elsie, Ella, and Sarah. Ella and Sarah are always trying to get me to ditch Matt and date a guy in our time zone, but Elsie gets it. Even though they broke up when she left, Elsie's still heartbroken over her last boyfriend in Portland. Elsie, Ella, Sarah, and I went to junior prom with Sarah's boyfriend and three of his friends. It was a casual, fun night, but I know that next year, distance be damned, I'm going to my own junior prom on Matt's arm.

The Revive program's still on hold, but Mason thinks it will resume in the fall; apparently the director wants to keep it going. I'm a little surprised to be dreading Mason's return to "agent." I've loved having him close all these months. And it's been just us; when the program starts again, Mason will undoubtedly get a new partner, too.

I'm trying not to think about that part yet.

For now, I'm settled into life in Alameda like I was in Omaha...almost. School and friends and love life on track, there remains a black spot in my heart where a piece of me has gone missing, left in a bedroom with a chalkboard wall; in a sunshiny yellow car; in a locker at Victory; in a beautiful, sparkling laugh.

There's never a day I don't think of Audrey.

There's never a day I don't miss her.

But missing her isn't the same thing as being stuck, like I was in the beginning. I know I'll never be completely whole without her. But I've found a way to be happy as this new version of myself, the version with a missing piece but also a better understanding of the value of friendship.

Of the value of life.

Audrey taught me that.

So instead of crying when I think of her, I talk to her. I make her playlists. I cover my wall with chalkboard paint and write a list of the things that were great about her. I "like" Jake Gyllenhaal on Facebook.

But I embrace my new friends and my new life, too.

Because what I know from the precious time we spent together and from the words in the worn letter I keep close at all times is this: Audrey never wanted to be anyone's heartbreak.

So I'll always remember. . . .

But also, I'll move on.

Acknowledgments

I'm much better when I'm busy.

That's why, in the midst of editing my first novel, *Forgotten*, I started a second. I wrote half, then started a third. Unsure which to finish, I sought advice from my publishing Sherpa, Dan Lazar at Writers House. He told me to go with my gut. I did, and if you enjoyed *Revived*, you have Dan to thank almost as much as I do (which is a lot...the guy is the best agent ever). While I'm at it, I'll also thank the rest of my Writers House network: Stephen Barr, Cecilia de la Campa, Angharad Kowal, Chelsey Heller, and foreign rights agents around the world.

Revived took about a year to write and rewrite and rewrite again. During that time, I leaned on numerous other people to help me get through what I've come to know as Second Book Syndrome. These people helped bring *Revived* to life:

My amazingly wonderful editor at Little, Brown, Elizabeth Bewley. Thank you for your time, patience, and support. Without you, Daisy might be lost in New York and Cassie might still be an Indian man. Also without you, I might never have seen the funniest Internet video ever.

Ali Dougal at Egmont UK, Karri Hedge at Hardie Grant Egmont, and the other editors worldwide who've so enthusiastically helped deliver *Revived* to readers: Thank you.

Nancy Conescu, who bet on *Revived* even before a word was written.

Publicists Jessica Bromberg at Little, Brown; Vicki Berwick at Egmont; and Jen Kean at Hardie Grant Egmont, who just, quite frankly, rock.

Hubby. Thank you for Saturdays with the girls, and for opening the good bottle of wine for every win. For doing less of your hobby so I could do more of mine. For (holy wow by the time this comes out) ten years.

My monkeys. L, thank you for offering to help me draw — instead of write — the line I'm stuck on. C, thank you for suggesting that my next novel should be about "(Uncle) Ryan, a lion, and Barbie." You two are my everything. Just...everything. I love you.

Mom and Dad, thank you for loving me even through my teen years. Thank you for your unwavering support.

My sister, brothers, sister-in-law, brother-in-law, and

nephews. Grandpa and my Cheyenne brood, Teams L.A. and CT. I love you all.

Those who previewed *Revived* and helped me shape Daisy's world. Amy, my dear friend, thank you for being there for me always, and for reading despite Baby E's best efforts. Kristin, my speed-reading Cacee, what would I do without you? Judith, you have both photography and toddler-whispering superpowers. David, I remembered: no bees or pink blouses. Brad and Kim, thank you for being my Omaha experts.

Christopher, my sunshine. Thank you for being the "he" in my he said/she said—not just in the book, but in real life, too. And Arne, just because.

Janine, the smartest person I know. Thanks for explaining what a PCR machine does, and for not laughing out loud when I told you the "science" behind Revive.

Author buddies Jay Asher and Daisy Whitney, thank you for giving up some of your valuable time to offer me advice. My ridiculously supportive network of friends all over the map: Thank you for enjoying the ride with me so far.

And finally:

Sarah, a family friend who inspired the very saddest parts of Audrey's story. I hadn't seen you in many years, and yet, I will always remember your spirit...and your smile.

Lizzie, Ella, and Betsey Best grew up believing
they were identical triplets. But the truth is,
they're even closer than sisters . . . they're clones.

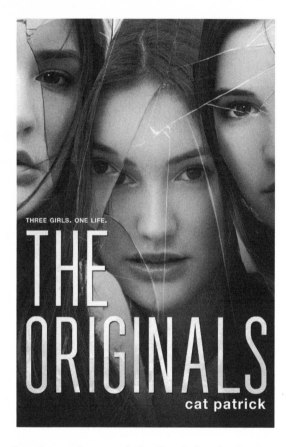

THREE GIRLS. ONE LIFE.

THE
ORIGINALS

cat patrick

Turn the page for an exclusive first look at Cat Patrick's
thrilling new novel, *The Originals*—the story of three teenage girls
who share everything, including a genetic identity.

Coming May 2013.

My part is first half.

I go to student government, chemistry, trigonometry, psychology, and history at school, then do the rest of the day at home. I maintain that Mom was in a mood when she made assignments this year—math and science are definitely not my best subjects. When I reminded her of this, she said, "That's exactly why you're doing first half."

I finish applying lip balm, take a step back from the sink, and frown. I'm used to looking exactly like two other people, but I'll never be used to Ella's fashion sense. I'm actually wearing an argyle cardigan.

"What's up, Ann Taylor Loft?" I mutter to myself, shaking my head.

I lean back and crane my neck so I can see the digital clock on my nightstand: It reads 6:47—thirteen minutes before I need to leave for school. One of Mom's major concerns is us standing out—and therefore being found out. So things like tardiness, bad grades, and attention-grabbing clothes are basically off-limits in the Best household.

I haven't eaten breakfast, but I don't smell bacon, so I decide to grab something from the cafeteria. Instead of sustenance, I opt for straightening. I plug in my flat iron, wait for it to heat up, then quickly but meticulously comb sections and pull the iron along, making the curls disappear. It's got its drawbacks, but at least first half means that I pick the hairstyle for the day.

Expertly moving through the darkened bedroom, I smooth down one last wrinkle at the foot of the bed and throw my pajama bottoms in the hamper. Mom tries to act mellow, but I saw her OCD forehead vein pop out yesterday when she saw the state of my room—she's got enough going on, so I cleaned it up. I gather my books and leave, gently closing the door behind me.

Just as I step from the cushy carpeting to the light hardwood in the hallway, Ella does, too. Her bedroom is across from mine: We face each other head-on. It's like looking at a life-sized picture of me in another outfit: She has the exact same tone of chestnut hair, matching dark brown eyes, the same lips that naturally frown when they're not smiling.

And they're frowning now.

Ella's eyes narrow to slits when she sees my hair. Her posture is pure pissed—underneath her plush robe, she pops a hip and rests her hand there—but more than seeing her anger, I can feel it. She exhales loudly and rolls her eyes.

"Are you done?" I ask. "We're not at auditions for a teen drama, you know. You don't have an audience."

Ella shakes her head at me.

"I mean, you're so selfish it's ridiculous," she says.

"It's just hair," I say, touching it. *Awesome hair,* I don't say. *Hair I'd like to have permanently.*

"It's not just hair," she says. "It's *time*. I'm up early as it is because I didn't finish everything for second half. I have to study before Betsey gets up and then teach her all of the cheers. You know there's a game next Friday! I have so much to do and now I have to flat iron my hair, too?"

"What's going on?" Betsey asks from her door, rubbing her eyes. I feel a little bad for waking her up. Her part is evening, which means that on top of being home-schooled all day, she's the one to juggle our college course, a part-time job, and cheering at night games. She goes to bed at least an hour later than we do.

When Betsey finally focuses on me, her dark eyes widen. "Seriously, Lizzie? Not again," she says with a groan.

"Not you, too," I say, eyebrows raised. She shrugs.

"Yes, her, too," Ella says. "What you do impacts all of us, Lizzie. You should remember that next time. I mean, just, thanks for this. Thanks for ruining my day." She storms downstairs, bare feet slapping gleaming wood floors all the way down.

I stifle a laugh. "Sorry," I say to Bet with a sheepish grin. "But I like it this way."

"It does look good," she says, giving me a small hug. "But I'm still going to kill you."

I stop in the entryway to gather all the stuff I need for school. I put my books in the bag. I unplug the cell phone from its charger and put it in the purse, then shove the purse in the bag, too. I shrug on the light jacket we chose for this fall and then grab the ends of the ball chain necklace and clasp it at the nape of my neck. When I straighten the weighty silver pendant so the vintage-looking pattern is facing out, there's a little twist in my torso. But as I have for the past couple of months, I ignore it.

My mom hears me turn the door handle despite the fact that she's listening to old Bon Jovi on the sound system in the kitchen. Sometimes I think she's part bat.

"Lizzie?" she calls. "Come eat some breakfast."

"I'll eat at school." I pull the door shut behind me, knowing my leaving will probably irritate her but hoping this is one of those days she lets her irritation slide. Otherwise, after school she'll probably force me into a mother/daughter heart-to-heart about the importance of proper nutrition.

Outside, it's a pretty fall day, a little hazy, but the sun's managing to peek through. I inhale the ocean air as I walk across the cobblestone driveway, looking up at the hundred-foot pines that surround the property. With the imposing trees and an iron gate, you'd think a celebrity lived here . . . until you saw our car. Apparently top on the list of "safest cars for teens," the sensible gray sedan is only just slightly better than the bus.

"Stupid old-lady car," I mutter as I climb in and buckle up.

When I turn the key, I'm simultaneously blasted by heat and music; quickly I turn down the blower and flip to the alt rock station. I can't help but laugh at Betsey's taste: She may dress like someone who lives for jam bands, but her real musical love is country. I think back to Florida, when our neighbor Nina babysat us sometimes in the afternoons so Mom could run errands without dragging along three toddlers. We'd sit out by Nina's pool listening to Reba McEntire, sipping sugary drinks we weren't allowed to have at home.

"Now, don't tell your mama, you hear?" Nina would say in her Southern accent. Practically drooling at the sight of juice boxes, we'd nod our little heads and swear on our baby dolls never to tell. Nina would sing along with Reba at the top of her lungs while Bet did backup vocals and silly dances, and I'd laugh to the point of a potty emergency.

Betsey never outgrew her affinity for country music and it's one of the things that I love about her, because it's one of the ways she's different.

Still not used to the driveway—our old house was on

a regular street—I do an Austin Powers maneuver to get the car turned in the right direction. Then I hold my breath as I drive up, hugging the right, since there's a drop-off on the left.

I wait for the gate to inch open, tossing my hair off my shoulders and finally taking a breath. For another morning, I'm safe from death by driveway. Despite my hideous sweater, I have sleek, straight hair. And now, for a few hours at least, I'm out of the house. I smile for no one to see, because these things are worth smiling about.

Two hours later, instinctively, I touch the necklace around my neck. My heart rate is up: I can hear the blood pounding in my ears. I try to calm myself as I picture the alert sounding on my mom's phone, it dragging her from whatever she's doing so she can check the GPS blip and make sure I'm where I'm supposed to be. Back in Florida when we were little, the necklace used to make me feel protected. Now, sitting here in trig, panicking because I don't know the answers, it feels invasive. Not only do I have my own stress to worry about, but I have her stress to worry about, too.

"It's a killer, isn't it?" the guy across the aisle whispers, nodding down at the quiz. He's got unfortunate acne that distracts from an otherwise solid-looking face.

"The worst," I whisper back before our teacher gives us a look and we're forced to focus. But when I do, I realize once again how little I know.

I studied; I really did. Ella is much better at math, and

after the requisite teasing, she helped me the past three nights. But it's too much. Going through the problems, I feel like I'm trying to read Mandarin while blindfolded. Sure, Woodbury is tougher than South was last year, but it's not like I'm an idiot. And yet, we're only a couple weeks into the school year and already, without a doubt, I can honestly say that...

I. Hate. Triangles.

And granted, I'm freaking out right now about a quiz on the first three chapters of the book, so I don't know a lot about it, but it seems to me that triangles are the very essence of trigonometry.

I spend fifty minutes suffering through the most painful academic experience of my life. Even before the bell rings, I am chastising myself for being so stupid. So flawed. Even though my mom's not my DNA donor, I was grown in her womb; her smartness should've rubbed off on me somehow.

How can I just not *get* math?

I jump at the bell, then reluctantly hand in my quiz. I jump again when my phone vibrates in my pocket; I haven't even made it to the classroom door yet. I don't check the caller ID; I know who it is.

"Hi."

"Lizzie, it's Mom," she says, trying to sound calm when I know her well enough to know that she's not.

"I know," I say, weaving around two girls blocking the door. "Hi."

Pause. "Your heart rate just shot up: What happened? You were in math class, right? Is everything okay?" The way her voice sounds right now reminds me of the time in middle school when she forgot there was a museum field trip and the tracker showed me across town during school hours.

"Geez, calm down," I say. "I'm fine. It was just a quiz."

Silence.

"Did you fail?" she asks quietly, saying "fail" like some people say "cancer." I hear her take a breath and hold it on the other end of the line and I can almost see the thoughts running through her brain. Mom places an incredibly high value on doing well in school.

"How should I know?" I say. "I only just handed it in. I won't get—"

"Lizzie, you know."

Pause.

"Yes."

She lets out her breath like a popped tire. "I'm going to come home for a few minutes after Bet's done with night class. We'll have a family meeting to discuss this."

"But, Mom, I—"

"We'll discuss it tonight," she says sharply. "I think we need to—"

Service cuts out and my bars are too low to call her back. I'm left to wonder as I leave the math corridor and head down the main hallway what Mom thinks we *need to* do this time.

After psych and government, I race to my locker, then flip around and rush toward the commons, where I'm blasted by the smell of fried foods. My stomach grumbles—it's been too long since my vending-machine breakfast—but there's no time to stop. I cut through the circular space, weaving my way around tables and kids with trays toward the exit to the student lot. I imagine Ella standing in the entryway of our house with a stopwatch, tapping her toes. The longer it takes me to get there, the less time she has.

"Hey, Elizabeth!"

I look over and see David Something from student government smiling a salesman's smile. "Take a load off," he says, his voice carrying over the lunchtime noise. The other football players at his table look at me curiously as David pats the empty seat next to him.

I smile back and wave politely but keep walking. I stifle a laugh when I hear one of David's friends say, "Burn!" just before I reach the doors.

I make it outside and check my phone for the time: I'm doing okay. Even though lots of kids go off campus for lunch, no one is nearby, so I jog to the car. I throw the bag on the passenger seat and drive home no more than five miles per hour over the posted speed limits. All I need is to get a speeding ticket the same day I fail a trig quiz.

I drive through the gates and down the driveway, then park and turn off the car but leave the keys in the ignition and the bag on the passenger seat. Ella is walking toward me before I've shut the door. With her stick-straight hair and matching cardigan and skirt, I might as well be staring at myself. Most of the time it's just how things are, but today, maybe because I'm already worried about the quiz, it's the bad kind of surreal. The only difference between us at the moment is our posture: Hers is tall and confident, mine is slumped.

"You okay?" she says when she's close enough for me to hear. "I felt it."

I nod, thinking of the sudden sense of unease that comes over me when Ella or Betsey panics about something. "Did Mom totally freak out?"

Ella glances at the front door and then refocuses on me. "A little," she admits. "I think she's just disappointed."

"Ugh," I say. "She said she's coming home for a family meeting tonight. She never comes home at night!"

When we were born, our mom gave up her real passion of being a scientist so she could work nights and be home during the day with us. Instead of doing the genetics research she loves, she's using her *other* degree to be an ER doctor, somehow functioning on three hours of sleep a night.

"I know. It's weird," Ella says, stepping forward to give me a quick hug. "But it'll be okay," she says into my hair. "We'll figure it out." Dramatic as she is, in a real crisis, Ella's always there. We pull apart and smile at each other: Mine's forced, because she's trying to lift my spirits.

"Anything I need to know?" she asks.

I shrug again. "Other than the trig debacle...no," I say. "Oh, wait, that guy David from student government tried to wave me over at lunch." Ella doesn't have a class with David, but she nods anyway.

"What'd he want?"

I shrug. "I don't know. I just waved back and kept going. I didn't want to make you late."

"Thanks," she says with another small smile.

"No problem. Good luck."

Ella laughs. "I've got the easy part," she says wistfully, like she misses the challenge, even though she has cheer practice, which she loves. "I think I can handle Spanish and dance."

"Don't forget creative writing," I say, the wistful one now.

"Oh, right," she says as she reaches out to unclasp the necklace from my neck. She puts it on, then hugs me goodbye and goes to the car. I walk across the cobblestones and, from the front porch, turn back to watch Ella go. It's like I'm having an out-of-body experience—like I'm watching myself. Except that Ella drives straight up the middle of the driveway, fearless.

And I love her for it.

The rest of the day is like clockwork. I spend three hours at homeschool with Betsey and my all-business mother (who through pursed lips refuses to acknowledge what happened in trig whatsoever during "school time").

We trudge through the same subjects that Ella's studying at Woodbury, just like Ella and Betsey did with my morning schedule. When Mom leaves for work at 3:30, I crank the music in our home gym for the same treadmill session that Bet and Ella did earlier, while Bet catches up on chemistry. Ella returns after cheer practice, and shortly after that, Bet leaves for night class. Ella and I eat dinner and do homework, comparing notes and chatting casually until Bet comes home again.

Then I get nervous.

"She'll be here anytime now," I whisper, seconds before the door opens downstairs.

"You're totally psychic," Betsey says with a laugh, but I'm not in the mood. Instead, I try to judge my mother's level of pissed-ness by the way she kicks off her shoes and rushes up the stairs.

"Oh, good, you're all here," she says when she rounds the corner to the rec room. Her hair is pulled back at her neck and she's wearing ill-fitting but remarkably clean scrubs with a cardigan over them.

"Hi, Mom," I say as she hurries into the room and sits down on the couch next to Ella. She pats Ella's knee, smiles at Betsey, then frowns when her eyes meet mine.

"Hi, Lizzie," she says before sighing like I'm the absolute worst there is for not knowing about stupid freaking triangles. "I don't have a lot of time, so let's get right to it."

"You should have just told us whatever you wanted to

say when you saw us earlier," Ella says. "Don't you have patients?"

"I wanted to talk to all three of you at once," Mom says, making me feel sick. That doesn't sound good at all. "And besides, earlier I was still figuring out what to do." She pauses for breath, glancing at the clock on the wall.

"What do you mean, 'figuring out what to do'?" Ella asks, looking suddenly concerned.

Mom faces her. "I've decided we're going to make a change in light of Lizzie's . . . challenge," she says. I can feel Ella glance at me, but I keep my eyes on Mom. No one else speaks, so she continues.

"First, I want to say that we're lucky that it's taken this long for noticeable differences to crop up," she says. "I was fearful every day through puberty, and yet thankfully, that wasn't an issue." I don't have to look at the others to know they're blushing, too. Nobody wants to hear their mother say the word *puberty*.

Mom goes on.

"But now, it's grown obvious to me that Lizzie is developing more right-brain tendencies," she says, looking into my eyes. "I'm sorry, Lizzie, I thought that by allowing you to be the one in those classes at school, you'd grasp them more easily. I thought maybe I was doing a poor job of teaching them. But it seems that math and science just aren't your forte." Mom gives me a sympathetic smile that's completely annoying.

"But if today is any indication, our current setup isn't working," she continues. "We're not even three weeks in and already it's clear that to remain on this path could draw attention to us, and therefore threaten everything. Because of this," Mom says, shifting like she's bracing for a triple teen outburst, "I am switching junior year assignments."

I feel myself stiffen; Ella sucks in her breath.

"Are you serious?" Betsey asks. Mom nods.

"Ella will take first half," she says authoritatively, but not meeting Ella's eyes, probably because she knows how disappointed Ella's going to be to miss out on cheer practice. "Lizzie will take second half. Betsey, you'll stay with evenings." Betsey visibly relaxes in her chair.

"But we have the schedule down," Ella says in protest. "This isn't fair."

"I know," Mom says. "But you've made straight A's your whole life. You just transferred—and Principal Cowell specifically commented on your high marks. If suddenly you start getting C's in math, it'll attract attention. And beyond that, it's time to start thinking of college. Of your future."

Start thinking of college? I feel like she's been thinking of college since we were two days old. The funny thing is that none of us knows how we'll even handle college logistically, so we've all just put our heads in the sand about it. I blow out my breath, but everyone ignores me.

"So, it's settled then," Mom says, checking the clock again as she stands up. "I've got to get back to the hospital."

"How soon?" I ask, knowing that I need to brush up on the cheers Ella's learned so far. My stomach lurches at the thought of manufacturing pep.

"I called the school and told them that you had a migraine today," Mom says. "I talked them into letting you retake the quiz."

Nerves rage in my insides—I can feel mine, and the others', too. She can't be saying what I think she's saying. "How soon, Mom?" I ask again.

She looks at the clock one more time, then looks back at me.

"Tomorrow."